The Secret of High Eldersham

The Secret of High Eldersham

Miles Burton

With an Introduction
by Martin Edwards

Poisoned Pen Press

Copyright © 2016 The Estate of Cecil Street 2016
Originally published in 1930 by Collins
Introduction copyright © 2016 Martin Edwards

Published by Poisoned Pen Press in association with the
British Library

First Edition 2016
First US Trade Paperback Edition

10 9 8 7 6 5 4 3 2 1

Library of Congress Catalog Card Number: 2015949435
ISBN: 9781464205835   Trade Paperback

Poisoned Pen Press
6962 E. First Ave., Ste. 103
Scottsdale, AZ 85251
www.poisonedpenpress.com
info@poisonedpenpress.com

Printed in the United States of America

To
A. H. and P. R.
my godmothers

Introduction

The Secret of High Eldersham, the second novel by Miles Burton, was originally published in 1930, at the height of the Golden Age of Murder between the two world wars. This book introduced Desmond Merrion, who became a popular character; by the time his career reached an end in 1960, he had appeared in almost sixty novels. If Burton's early readers were impressed by the crisp professionalism of his story-telling, the explanation is that Miles Burton, like High Eldersham, had a secret. The name concealed the identity of a writer who, under another pseudonym, was already a well-regarded author of detective novels. But the book contained no biographical information, and the fact that the two authors were one and the same man did not become widely known for four decades.

The opening part of the first chapter amounts to a prologue, telling a tale of two pubs, the thriving Tower of London in the East Anglian town of Gippingford, and the struggling Rose and Crown in the remote village of High Eldersham. When the Rose and Crown's landlord moves in search of better trade, the vacancy arising is filled by a former policeman, Samuel Whitehead. Four and a half years later, the village constable calls at the Rose and Crown late one night, only to discover that the landlord has been stabbed to death.

The Chief Constable promptly calls for help from Scotland Yard, but on his arrival in High Eldersham, Detective Inspector Young finds that the village is a mysterious place, "saturated with local legend", where strangers encounter an inexplicable hostility. Although an obvious suspect soon comes into view, he is able to produce a convincing alibi. Level-headed as he is, Young finds himself "surrounded by impalpable forces beyond his power to combat", and decides to seek help from his friend Desmond Merrion.

Brilliant and brave, wealthy yet charming, possessing luxurious rooms in Mayfair and a devoted sidekick called Newport, Desmond Merrion typifies the Great Detective beloved of so many Golden Age authors and their readers. After being badly wounded during the war, he transferred to the intelligence branch of the Admiralty, and became "a living encyclopaedia upon all manner of obscure subjects which the ordinary person knew nothing about". Merrion turns up while the inquest is taking place, only to encounter a war-time acquaintance, a maverick called Laurence Hollesley. Hollesley is intent on marrying the attractive daughter of his neighbour, Sir William Owerton, and Merrion too falls for Mavis Owerton. But do Sir William and the young woman know more about the strange and secretive goings-on in High Eldersham than they are willing to admit?

The story combines the action, pace and atmosphere of a thriller with a detective sub-plot, and the book enjoyed considerable success. Decades later, its qualities were extolled by Jacques Barzun, the legendary French-born American cultural historian, and the scientist Wendell Hertig Taylor, two friends whose erudition, and deep knowledge of classic detective fiction, shine through the pages of their voluminous and highly opinionated compendium *A Catalogue of Crime*. When a publisher asked the pair to select for republication fifty definitive crime novels from the first half of the twentieth century, their choices included this book. Although they admired much of the author's work, and acknowledged that many of his other novels boasted more elaborate puzzles, they concluded that: "a primary function of the mystery story is to entertain in a variety of ways, and on this score *The Secret of High Eldersham*…has no superior." High praise indeed from two men writing at a time when Golden Age crime fiction had fallen far from fashion. One likes to think that they would have relished the popularity of the British Library's series of Crime Classics, and the revival of interest in authors such as Miles Burton.

So who was the mysterious Mr Burton? Despite the popularity of his work, it was not until after his death that the secret of his identity was revealed to the reading public; indeed, for years the puzzle was complicated by a red herring suggesting that he had been born twenty years later than in fact was the case. Further to muddy the waters, he wrote two different books under two different names—one of them as Burton—but both with the same title: *Up the Garden Path*. The truth finally came out thanks to literary detective work on the part of critic Francis M. Nevins, and further research by Barzun.

Burton's real name was Cecil John Charles Street. He was born in 1884 in Gibraltar, where his father was serving in the British Army. Street too joined up, and returned to the army at the start of the First World War after a spell working as chief engineer in an electric company. Wounded three times in battle, and awarded the Military Cross, he moved to Military Intelligence when his injuries rendered him unfit for service in the front line. His CV did, therefore, bear at least some resemblance to Merrion's.

Street began to establish himself as a writer, initially with non-fiction, before publishing a couple of thrillers under the rather thinly disguised pen-name of John Rhode. Once he created Dr Lancelot Priestley, a learned but somewhat grumpy armchair detective, there was no stopping him. Books poured from his pen, and before long a reviewer bestowed on him the title "Public Brain-Tester No.1".

Street was so astonishingly productive (he published almost 150 crime novels *after* reaching the age of forty) that the John Rhode books risked flooding the market. His solution was to create the *alter ego* of Miles Burton; he also wrote four novels as Cecil Waye, another pseudonym that was not penetrated for many years. The first Burton novel, *The Hardway Diamonds Mystery*, was a stand-alone thriller, but the introduction of Merrion demonstrated his recognition of the powerful appeal of a series character. Merrion is much more of a heroic action man than Priestley, but his later cases often gave him the chance to display his skills in deductive reasoning; an example is *Death in the Tunnel*, also republished as a British Library Crime Classic.

Scarce first editions of books by Rhode, Burton and Waye have been eagerly sought by collectors for many years, and some titles change hands for eye-watering sums. It is a pleasure to introduce this author, and Desmond Merrion, to a much wider readership.

Martin Edwards
www.martinedwardsbooks.com

Chapter I

Nobody knew better than Mr. George Thorold, the senior partner of Thorold and Son, the well-known Gippingford brewers, that in these days of highly-taxed beer it would not be an easy matter to find a tenant for the Rose and Crown. Consequently, when Hugh Dunsford called to see him and announced his intention of giving up the house, Mr. Thorold listened to him with a slight frown upon his handsome features.

"It's like this, you see, sir," explained Dunsford, an elderly man, short of stature, and with that curious furtive, half-mistrustful air not uncommon among the natives of East Anglia. "There's not a decent living to be made at the Rose and Crown, and that's a fact. I'm not saying that the place wasn't a little gold-mine before the war, but those times are gone. A chap can't afford his couple of pints of an evening with beer at the price it is, leastways the chaps about High Eldersham can't. I might hold on if I was a single man, sir, but you see there's the missus and the family to think of."

"Yes, I know how difficult things are for the tenants of the smaller houses," replied Mr. Thorold. "You know that we would do everything we could to keep you. What do you think of doing when you give up the Rose and Crown?"

Dunsford coughed awkwardly. "Well, sir, I did hear that old Hawkins, of the Tower of London in this town, was going to retire. And I was going to make so bold as to ask you, seeing that it's one of your houses, if you'd consider me in his place. There's a fine trade to be done there, and I could manage it proper, with my boy Dick and the missus to help me."

Mr. Thorold picked up a pencil that was lying on his desk, and began to trace a series of complicated geometrical figures on a piece of paper that lay before him. It was true that Hawkins intended to retire in the following September, and it was certain that Dunsford, whose father before him had been a tenant of the brewery, would make an excellent landlord for the Tower of London. But the problem of the Rose and Crown presented itself with all its manifold difficulties. It stood in an isolated spot, and customers were few and far between. There was nothing about the house to tempt a man who wanted to earn money by the trade. And besides, it would take a stranger—a foreigner, as High Eldersham dubbed any one not born in the immediate neighbourhood—months, perhaps years, to establish that confidence so essential between a landlord and his local customers.

"Well, Dunsford," said Mr. Thorold after a long pause, "you and your parents have been friends of the brewery far too long for me to stand in your way, even if I wanted to. Of course you can have the Tower of London if you want the house, and I shall be very glad to know that it is in such good hands, and to have you here in Gippingford. But I'm sure I don't know who I shall get to take your place at the Rose and Crown. You don't happen to know of anybody out your way who would like it, do you?"

Dunsford shook his head, "No, sir, that I don't," he replied. "'Tisn't as if the place had a bit o' land with it, so as a chap could pick up a bit with a few cows or something o' that. There isn't nobody round High Eldersham way as could do any good with the Rose and Crown, trade being what it is. Why, as I tell you, sir, I can't myself."

"Then I'm sure nobody else could," remarked Mr. Thorold, with a smile. "Well, I shall have to see what can be done, that's all. Since you are here, we may as well go into the matter of your tenancy of the Tower of London."

When Dunsford had gone, Mr. Thorold sat for some time elaborating the design he had commenced, and thinking of the Rose and Crown. That it had long ceased to be profitable he knew well enough, and his only surprise was that Dunsford had not come to the same conclusion earlier than this. The house was unfortunately placed. It was about twenty miles from Gippingford, the county town, and stood upon the old coach road running northwards. At one time it had been a favourite spot for changing horses, but with the advent of the car its popularity had departed, since it was neither imposing or romantic enough to attract the attention of the passing motorist. Further, within recent years a new main road had been built, absorbing the through traffic and reducing the old coach road to little more than a country lane. The result was that few strangers entered the portal of the Rose and Crown.

It had to depend, therefore, for its trade upon the inhabitants of High Eldersham, a straggling village upon the banks of the River Elder. But here again the Rose and Crown was unfortunate. The population of High Eldersham was in any case very small, not more than two or three hundred in all. And the more substantial people, farmers and so forth, were almost without exception "chapel folk," who would have lost caste among their neighbours had they been seen entering so disreputable a place as a public house. The purchase, on market days in Gippingford, of whisky by the case, for consumption behind drawn blinds, they regarded, however, as a perfectly natural and respectable proceeding. Besides these, the population of High Eldersham consisted mainly of labourers, and they, as Dunsford had said, could not afford more than an occasional visit to the Rose and Crown. Finally, still further to add to the disadvantages of the house, it was situated some little distance from the village itself, which lay a mile or more away, at the end of a side turning branching off from the coach road opposite the Rose and Crown.

But, as Mr. Thorold was well aware, it was not the material drawbacks that presented the most serious problem. There is always a comparatively large number of people whose highest ambition is to become the tenant of an inn, and from among these there would be no difficulty in choosing a landlord for the Rose and Crown. But Mr. Thorold had a long experience of strangers as tenants in East Anglia. However hardworking and conscientious they might be, however keen to promote trade, the receipts of their houses had a way of falling off until they were perforce compelled to relinquish their tenancy. And this curious distrust of strangers, common throughout East Anglia, was particularly active in remote villages like High Eldersham. Yet Dunsford had said that no local man would take the Rose and Crown, and he knew every soul in the village and for miles around. There was nothing for it but to advertise.

Mr. Thorold devoted considerable pains to drawing up the advertisement. As an afterthought, he added the words, "the house would suit a pensioner," and smiled grimly as he did so. It was no use accepting a tenant who had not some source of income independent of the takings of the house. The man would either give notice after his first quarter or go bankrupt. The advertisement was inserted in the *Gippingford Herald*, and for the next few days Mr. Thorold was inundated with replies, most of which, from the obvious unsuitability of the applicant, he consigned to the waste-paper basket.

Among the replies which he laid aside for consideration was one that especially appealed to him. The applicant described himself with refreshing brevity. Whitehead, Samuel Edward, aged 55, late sergeant Metropolitan Police, retired on pension, widower, no children. Would like to take the house if it had half an acre or so of garden.

Now, as it happened, the Rose and Crown had a very good garden, which Dunsford, an enthusiastic gardener himself, had always kept in very good order. Further, a police pensioner would make a very desirable tenant, there would be little fear of any irregularities taking place which might endanger the licence. After considering the matter carefully, Mr. Thorold wrote to the address in Hammersmith given by Whitehead, and asked him to come to Gippingford for an interview.

Whitehead came, exactly at the appointed hour, and Mr. Thorold was very favourably impressed. Whitehead, in spite of his height and girth, which were well beyond the ordinary, even for a policeman, looked active and alert. He was respectful and eminently self-possessed, and his cheerful face positively radiated good nature. Just the man for the place, thought Mr. Thorold. If anybody could get on with those queer High Eldersham folk, he could. It seemed almost a pity to exile such an excellent man to a place like the Rose and Crown.

"I ought to warn you, Mr. Whitehead, that the Rose and Crown does not do a very extensive trade," said Mr. Thorold. "You may find at first that the profits do not quite come up to your expectations."

"That won't worry me, sir," replied Whitehead. "My pension is more than enough to keep me, and I'm anxious to get out of London and amuse myself growing a few flowers.

I thought of taking a cottage somewhere till I saw your advertisement. Then I thought that a pub would be more cheerful, seeing that there would be somebody to talk to."

The interview ended by Whitehead signing the lease of the Rose and Crown.

This had happened five years ago. Whitehead had entered into possession of the Rose and Crown in September, when Dunsford and his family had moved to the Tower of London, in Gippingford. And there he had remained, apparently perfectly contented with his lot. Rather to Mr. Thorold's astonishment, the beer consumption at the Rose and Crown, after showing a decline for the first few weeks of the new tenant's occupancy, had gradually risen to the average figure it had shown in Dunsford's time. And Mr. Thorold's traveller, whose business it was to visit all the houses belonging to the brewery, reported that "that new chap Whitehead seemed to be getting on very well."

Almost exactly four and a half years after Whitehead's first day as landlord of the Rose and Crown, on the evening of March 31st, Constable Viney, the High Eldersham village policeman, was cycling back home at the conclusion of his round. His way led him past the Rose and Crown and he had intended to go in and have a word with Whitehead, with whom he was on very good terms. However, his duties had taken him longer than he expected, and it was after eleven o'clock when he reached the door of the inn. Whitehead, as he knew, was in the habit of going to bed soon after closing time, ten o'clock, and the constable decided that it was too late to knock on the door.

He was about to pass on when he caught sight of a flicker of light in the window of the bar. Perhaps Mr. Whitehead had not gone to bed after all. Viney approached the window and looked in. The curtains were drawn, but did not meet by half an inch or so. Through this narrow aperture Viney could see that the lamp was out but that the fire was still burning. This was the light which he had seen.

Viney was on the point of turning away when a flame leapt up from the dying fire, illuminating the room with its flickering light. A massive wooden arm-chair was drawn up in front of the fire, and in this was the motionless figure of Mr. Whitehead, in an attitude of complete relaxation, his head fallen forward upon his breast. Viney smiled. He had known Mr. Whitehead doze off in his chair after a hard day's work, before this. He rapped smartly upon the window, but Mr. Whitehead did not stir. Viney almost fancied he could hear him snoring.

Had it not been that the constable felt an urgent desire for a drink, he would have gone on home, and left Mr. Whitehead undisturbed. As it was, he knocked again, seeming in the still night to make enough noise to rouse the whole neighbourhood. But Mr. Whitehead made no sign of having heard him, and suddenly something in his attitude sent a thrill of apprehension running down the constable's spine. No man could sleep through a noise such as he had just made, nor could he rest quietly in such a position. Filled with the conviction that Mr. Whitehead must be ill and in need of assistance, Viney hesitated no longer. He tried the door, but it was locked. There was nothing for it but more desperate measures; if Mr. Whitehead objected, he would pay for the damage himself.

He returned to the window, and put his elbow through a pane of glass. Then he reached for the catch, and opened the window. After a short struggle, he wormed his way through, and stood on the floor of the bar. Mr. Whitehead showed no signs of being aroused by these proceedings. The flame had died down by now, and the room was illuminated only by the dull glow of the fire. Viney put his hand on Mr. White-head's shoulder, only to withdraw it with a startled cry. At his touch Mr. Whitehead slid from his chair and collapsed in a heap in front of the fireplace. But Viney hardly heeded him. He fumbled for his torch, and cast its rays upon the hand which had rested for an instant on Mr. Whitehead's shoulder. He had not been mistaken. The horrible stickiness which covered it was blood.

Chapter II

Constable Viney, in spite of the uniform he wore, stood appalled and trembling in the face of his gruesome discovery. During the years in which he had been stationed at High Eldersham his police duties had been confined to a more or less benevolent supervision of the villagers, punctuated by occasional stern warnings to farmers guilty of the offence of allowing their cattle to stray upon the highway. In the whole of his experience he had known nothing like this. For several seconds he stood rooted to the floor of the bar, a mere ordinary mortal, utterly thrown off his balance by the sudden presentment of tragedy and horror.

It was with a violent effort that he pulled himself together and turned his torch upon the body of Mr. Whitehead. That it was a body and not a living man he knew by instinct. His soul recoiled from the idea of touching it again in the vain hope that any spark of life yet remained. His senses registered the simple facts, that Mr. Whitehead was dead, that his clothes were soaked in blood, that a pool of the same sinister fluid had spread beneath the chair and over the hearth. And then it occurred to him with sudden urgency that he must take steps, at once, without delay.

The thought was welcome, beyond anything else that he could imagine. It meant that he must leave this little low room in which he felt the numbing atmosphere of fear, and hurry to the village for help. He walked swiftly to the door and tried the handle. It was locked, as he might have known. Mr. Whitehead, law-abiding publican as he was, invariably locked the door of the bar at closing time, ten o'clock. But the key was not in the lock. For an instant Viney hesitated. In all probability it was in Mr. Whitehead's pocket. But in his present state he could not bring himself to seek it there. He climbed out of the window as he had entered, shut it carefully behind him, and pedalled frantically along the road that led to the village. The sharp night air braced his strained nerves like a tonic.

He made straight for the house of Doctor Padfield, and rang the bell. To his relief the doctor himself answered the door, a tall spare figure, whose hand, holding an uplifted candlestick, trembled slightly. He regarded the constable with a puzzled stare, as though unable to account for his sudden appearance. It was not until after an appreciable pause that he spoke. "Well, Viney, what is it?" he asked in a curiously deadened voice. "Come in, don't stand in the doorway like that."

Viney stepped into the hall, in darkness but for the candle in the doctor's hand, and closed the door behind him.

"It's Mr. Whitehead, up at the Rose and Crown, sir," he replied in a low tone, in which his excitement was still audible. "He's dead, sir, covered with blood, looks to me as if he had been murdered."

If he had expected Doctor Padfield to display any excitement at this news he was disappointed.

"Dead, is he?" said the doctor discontentedly. "What's the good of coming to me, then? I can't bring dead men back to life!"

Viney stared at the doctor, completely taken aback by his nonchalance. "Well, sir," he replied, "even if you can't do that, at least you can tell what killed him. My instructions are always to call a doctor in when a man's found dead. But, of course, sir, if you won't come—"

"Oh, I'll come," interrupted Doctor Padfield carelessly. "The Rose and Crown, you say? That's barely a mile away. It will be as quick to walk there as to waste time getting out the car, especially as it is a fine night. Wait a minute while I get my bag."

"May I use your telephone, sir, while you are getting ready?" asked Viney.

"Certainly, if it amuses you," replied the doctor. "There you are, in that corner."

He left the hall abruptly, taking the candle with him. Viney, left in the dark, had recourse to his torch, and with its assistance found the telephone instrument. He put a call through to the officer on duty at Gippingford Police Station and reported. "I'm all alone here, sir, as you know," he concluded. "If you could send some one to take charge, I'd be grateful."

The answer must have been satisfactory, for Viney replaced the receiver with an air of relief. At that moment Doctor Padfield returned and the two set out on the road towards the Rose and Crown, Viney leading his bicycle. Doctor Padfield seemed irritable and morose, and after one or two attempts to engage him in conversation Viney desisted from the attempt. They pursued their way in silence until they reached the inn.

"If you'll wait a moment, sir, I'll open the back door," remarked Viney, as he prepared to scramble once more through the window. "The front door is locked, and I haven't found the key yet."

He entered the bar and cast a hasty glance at the body. It was lying in the same position as he had last seen it, and he hastened out through the back to admit Doctor Padfield. The key of the back door was in the lock and he turned it. The door opened, and Doctor Padfield strode in, apparently without taking the slightest notice of his surroundings.

"Better stay where you are till I get a lamp lit, sir," remarked Viney. "I saw one in the back kitchen as I came through." He fumbled with a box of matches, and appeared carrying an ordinary paraffin lamp, which threw curious and grotesque shadows on the bare walls. Followed by Doctor Padfield, he led the way into the bar, and held the lamp so that its light fell on the huddled figure of Mr. Whitehead. "There you are, sir!" he exclaimed in an awed voice.

"Put that damned lamp down on the table!" commanded Doctor Padfield sharply. "Can't you see that it's shining right in my eyes? That's better. Now then, bear a hand and help me to get the man's coat off. Ah, that's the trouble, is it?"

They had taken Mr. Whitehead's coat from his shoulders, exposing the back of his waistcoat. The fabric showed a cut, about an inch and a half long, and round this was soaked in blood. It was evident, even to Viney's inexperienced eye, that the dead man had been stabbed with a broad-bladed knife, apparently driven into his left shoulder from behind.

For the first time that evening Doctor Padfield showed some symptoms of interest. "A very neat stroke," he commented. "Very neat indeed. The man who struck that blow knew his job. It must have been almost immediately fatal. Who was it, Viney?"

"I don't know, sir," replied the constable, startled by the directness of the question. "I found him like this, and then came straight along to fetch you, sir."

Doctor Padfield shrugged his shoulders. "Well, it's your job to find out who killed him, not mine," he said. "I can't do anything, as I told you before. I'm going home to bed. You'll find me in my house till ten o'clock in the morning, if you want me." And with that he strode out of the room, without bestowing another glance at the dead man. Viney, left alone, could hear his footsteps on the road until the sound of them was swallowed up in the distance.

He glanced at his watch. It was barely midnight, and he knew that he could not expect his colleagues from Gipping-ford for some time yet. It was his obvious duty to remain with the body, that was certain. But not necessarily in the same room. He could not face the prospect of a prolonged vigil in that ghastly bar. He wandered out into the back passage, where his eye fell upon a barrel of beer, ready tapped. After a moment's hesitation, he picked up a pint pot, filled it, and drank the contents off at a draught. This done, he laid the pot down with a sigh of content. He felt distinctly better.

His wits, so rudely scattered by his tragic discovery, began to return to him. Suddenly it occurred to him that here was his chance to distinguish himself. A murder had been committed, of that there could be no possible doubt. Knives did not get driven into people's backs by accident, he reasoned. Nor could it be a case of suicide. He took out his truncheon, and, holding it as a knife, tried to stab himself with it in the back of his left shoulder. Well, it could be done, though it would be very awkward. But then, if Mr. Whitehead had done it himself, the knife would have been left in the wound, or, at all events, would have fallen on the floor somewhere near the body. No, it was a case of murder, right enough.

The thought that he was actually concerned in a real murder case thrilled him. He tried to remember, from his perusal of the sensational Sunday newspapers, how those super men, the chiefs of Scotland Yard, acted in similar circumstances. So far as he could make out, they interrogated a number of people until they found a clue. But here, in this lonely house, there was nobody to interrogate, and he felt himself at a loss. He took out his note-book and entered a few brief particulars in rather a shaky hand. Then, finding inaction impossible, he began to wander about the house, seeking rather aimlessly for traces of the murderer. At last a bright idea struck him. Motive! That was it, that was what all great detectives established immediately a crime was discovered. The till was in the corner of the bar, he knew. He had often seen Mr. Whitehead counting his takings in the evening, after closing time. He approached it eagerly, and found it locked, but with the key in place. Opening it, he found two or three notes, and a number of silver and copper coins. Definitely disappointed, he was forced to the conclusion that robbery had not been the motive for the murder.

Dawn broke at last, and the rising sun sent a pale shaft of light into the bar, shaming the feeble glow of the lamp, and revealing the pool of blood as a dark and ominous patch upon the scrubbed flagstones. In the growing light the body of Mr. Whitehead lost much of its terror and took on an aspect pitiful, almost ridiculous. Viney, in no wise enlightened by his investigations, regarded it wonderingly. Who in the world could have committed this seemingly purposeless crime?

And while he stood there, he heard the sound of an approaching car, which slowed up as it neared the Rose and Crown. Viney ran out of the house, in time to meet the car, which contained the Superintendent from Gippingford, accompanied by a military-looking man, whom Viney recognised as the Chief Constable of the county.

Viney led them into the bar, and told his story. "Stabbed in the back, eh?" commented Colonel Bateman, the Chief Constable. "That's a bad business. The poor chap can't have had a chance to defend himself. You say that the till hasn't been touched? What do you make of all this, Bass?"

"It's difficult to say, sir, at present," replied Superintendent Bass cautiously. "What sort of a man was this fellow Whitehead, constable? Was he popular in the district? Did anybody have a grudge against him?"

"I think he was well enough liked, sir," replied Viney. "He didn't make any friends that I know of. Being a Londoner, it would take these village folk a long time to chum up with him. They're terrible mistrustful of strangers, in these parts. But from what I saw of things, there was plenty of the chaps that would come up here of an evening for a drink, and he seemed to get on well enough with most of them."

"I dare say he wasn't above serving some of them during prohibited hours, eh, Viney?" suggested Colonel Bateman.

Viney shook his head. "No, sir, he'd never do that," he replied. "Mr. Whitehead was very strict; you see, sir, he had been a policeman himself. He wouldn't serve a drink a minute after closing time, and he wouldn't have anybody on the premises who'd had a drop too much. He's been known to turn several of the chaps out, before now."

"Were there many people in here last night?" asked the Superintendent.

"I can't say, sir," replied Viney. "I didn't pass this way during opening hours. But, being Friday night, I expect that there was a good few. The men mostly gets paid on Fridays, sir."

"I see," remarked Colonel Bateman. "Now, look here, Viney. There will be plenty for you to do for the next few days. You've been up all night, you say. Cut off home, and have a few hours' rest. The man who drove us out can take charge here till this afternoon. Off you go, and keep your mouth shut for the present."

As soon as they were alone, Colonel Bateman turned to the Superintendent. "I don't know what you think, Bass, but in my opinion this is a case for Scotland Yard," he said.

The Superintendent frowned slightly. "I don't know, sir," he replied. "It looks to me a simple enough murder. I have no doubt that a few inquiries round about would soon make it pretty clear who did it."

"I don't think so," said the Chief Constable slowly. "That fellow, Viney, who seems to possess at least average intelligence, has obviously no idea of the criminal, and he knows the people about here pretty well, I suppose. Of course, we might track the fellow down for ourselves, I don't deny that. But on the other hand, we mightn't, and then we should be forced to call in the Yard when the scent was cold. You see that, don't you, Bass?"

"Yes, I see that, sir," replied Bass reluctantly. "It's for you to decide, sir."

"Very well, then. Will you stay here with the driver, and tidy the place up a bit? I'll go back to Gippingford, and get on to the Yard on the 'phone. They'll send a man down at once, you may be sure. Then I'll see the Coroner, to arrange about an inquest, and I'll look in on Thorold, and find out what he knows about this man Whitehead. I'll be back in the afternoon, as soon as I can. And, by the way, Bass, I think I'd leave the body pretty much as it is, until the man from the Yard has seen it."

Colonel Bateman gave the necessary instructions to the driver of the car, who relinquished his seat to him. As he drove back to Gippingford, he wondered whether at last the veil that seemed to divide High Eldersham from the outside world was about to be lifted.

Chapter III

Colonel Bateman returned to the Rose and Crown early that afternoon, accompanied by the police surgeon and a stranger whom he introduced to Bass as Detective-Inspector Young. The latter was a stoutish man of about forty, clean-shaven, and with a humorous expression. There was nothing in any way striking about him, and it was evident from the first that the Superintendent was not at all favourably impressed.

"Mr. Young has very kindly come down from Scotland Yard to help us," announced the Chief Constable cheerily. "I've told him the story, so far as I know it. You would probably like to look at the body before Dr. Barrett makes his examination, wouldn't you, Inspector?"

"I think you said that the body had already been moved by the constable who discovered it, sir," replied Young. "If that is the case, it seems unnecessary for me to see it at present."

"Very well, then," said Colonel Bateman. "We'll have a chat in the back kitchen while Dr. Barrett does his job. Ah, you've got back, I see, Viney. Come along with us, and you can tell your story to the Inspector at first hand."

Viney repeated his story, and then the Chief Constable turned to Bass. "Have you made any further discoveries since I saw you this morning, Superintendent?" he asked.

"Since the case was to be put in the hands of Scotland Yard, I have confined myself to keeping guard over the house, sir," replied the Superintendent icily. "Three or four customers came here between the hours of half-past ten and half-past two, when the house should have been opened for the sale of intoxicating liquors. I informed them that the place was closed. They were apparently unaware of the death of the landlord."

"Well, that's all to the good," commented Colonel Bateman. "I saw the Coroner, and he will arrange to hold the inquest here on Monday. I then saw Mr. Thorold, who could tell me very little about Whitehead, beyond the fact that he was an ex-policeman, and an excellent tenant in every way. By the way, he is sending a man out to-morrow to take charge of this place temporarily until he can find a new tenant. Then I met Inspector Young's train and drove him straight out here. That's all I have to report. Ah, here is Dr. Barrett. Well, doctor, what do you make of it?"

"The man was stabbed from behind with a broad-bladed weapon, such as a butcher's knife," replied Dr. Barrett. "The blow must have been delivered with considerable force, and by a man who had some knowledge of anatomy. The main artery is severed, and death must have been practically instantaneous. There are no marks on any other part of the body, no signs of a struggle or anything like that. In my opinion the blow was delivered before the victim was aware of the presence of his assailant."

"I'm much obliged to you, doctor. That settles that point, at any rate. Now, Inspector, we are in your hands. Is there any assistance that we can render you in your investigation?"

"I think not, thank you, sir," replied Young. "I shall remain here, of course, with Constable Viney. I dare say that there is a spare bed in the house, or, if not, I can find one in the village. I shall naturally report any progress I may make to you."

"Very well. If you have no further questions to ask, we will get back to Gippingford. There is a telephone in the village, should you wish to communicate with us. In any case, I shall run over here sometime to-morrow morning. Come along, Superintendent. Doctor Barrett has an appointment and is anxious to get back, I know. Good-bye, Inspector, and good luck to you."

The car having driven off, Inspector Young returned to the bar, where Viney was awaiting him. "Now we can get to work," he said cheerfully. "Sit down, constable; I want to have a chat with you. I'm a stranger here, and I've never been in this part of England before. You've been here some years, I understand, and I expect by this time you know all about the place and the people who live in it. I got the impression from the Chief Constable that there was something queer about the place, but what it was, exactly, I couldn't quite make out."

"Well, it is a queer place, sir," replied Viney. "I'm from East Anglia myself, and I know that our folk are always a bit shy with strangers, but I never knew it so bad as it is here. I think it's because all the people have married among themselves for so long that they're all sort of related like. They settle things among themselves, you'll never hear of one of them going to law with another, or anything like that. And they don't like outsiders coming in and interfering with their affairs. And, you can take it from me, sir, strangers don't never prosper in High Eldersham."

"You mean that they are frozen out, that people won't trade with them, and that sort of thing?"

"Not only that, sir. They don't seem to have any luck, as you might say. Soon after I came here, one of the biggest farms in the parish was for sale, and it was bought by a gentleman from the other side of the country. He brought his men with him, and a very good farmer he was, by all accounts. But nothing went right with him. Two of his horses died within a month of his coming here, to begin with. Then his carter fell sick, and Doctor Padfield didn't seem able to do anything for him. At last his wife, who was as good a farmer as he was, and had never had a day's illness in her life, got that run down she couldn't do her day's work. Doctor Padfield told her straight out that the place didn't suit her. She stuck it as long as she could, but in the end they sold the farm and went away. It was bought, pretty cheap, I believe, by a brother of the man who owned the next farm."

Inspector Young smiled. "Well, that was a chapter of accidents, certainly," he remarked. "But, after all, that's only an isolated case, which might have happened to anybody anywhere. Nobody could help the place not agreeing with the farmer's wife, could they? And this isn't the only place where horses die and carters go sick, you know."

"Ah, but that wasn't the only case, sir," replied Viney. "It's not more than a year or so since another stranger took a lease of the very next farm to this, the first house on the left as you go down towards the village. He had the finest herd of Jerseys as ever I see, and he used to send his milk into Gippingford, all done up special in them glass bottles. Fetched a very high price, they used to say. Well, after a bit there was an epidemic of sorts broke out in the town, and they traced it to this chap's milk. It seems they found some germ or other in it. Well, naturally, people wouldn't buy his milk after that, and he went broke. Cleared off in the night, he did, leaving his cows behind him. So that was another stranger as couldn't get on in High Eldersham."

"Yes, I can see how the place acquired a peculiar reputation," said Young. "But, after all, this has nothing to do with the case of this man, Whitehead. The natives do not seem to have had anything to do with the misfortunes of these strangers, which were obviously due to circumstances. I'm not going to believe that somebody in the village stuck a knife into Whitehead just because he did not happen to be a native. Now, tell me something about the village, and the people who live in it."

"They say that years ago the village used to be a fair sized port, before the mouth of the river got silted up, sir. Now you can't get anything bigger than a barge up, and that only at certain tides. You see them lying sometimes at the old quay, loading corn or beet, but that isn't often. There'll be a round dozen farmers in the parish, and a couple of decent sized houses. Sir William Owerton lives in the Hall, he's an oldish gentleman, a bit of a scholar, with a son in India and a daughter that lives with him. About a mile away is Elder House, belonging to Mr. Hollesley. Fine sportsman is Mr. Hollesley, shoots, keeps a beautiful little yacht, and all that. Lives there with his mother, who's pretty nigh bed-ridden, when he isn't in London. They do say that he's sweet on Sir William's daughter."

"Oh, they do, do they? What about the village itself? Who lives there?"

"There aren't any gentlefolk, bar the parson and Doctor Padfield. Parson's an old man who was born in the next parish, and Doctor Padfield's father was a big farmer somewhere hereabouts. They're natives, so to speak, both of them. Then there's the village shop, and the rest is all cottages, what the farm hands and such live in. There's not much to be seen in High Eldersham, that I can promise you, sir."

"It doesn't sound a very lively place, certainly," agreed Inspector Young. "Now then, Viney, you know these folk pretty well. Do you think it likely that any of them would have deliberately murdered Whitehead?"

"No, sir, that I don't. They're a queer stand-offish lot, but this I will say for them. I've never found what you might call a real bad character among them, and that's more than you can say for a lot of villages. There's one or two of them like Ned Portch, who get a bit noisy like if they has a drop too much liquor, but that's all. And, since Mr. Whitehead's been here, none of them have had a chance of taking too much. He wouldn't serve them if he thought they'd had enough already. Why, it's not more than a month ago that he turned Ned Portch out of this very bar, and told him to keep away from the place."

"I see. Well, now that I know something about the people here, I can have a look round for myself," said Inspector Young, after a meditative pause. "It seems to me, Viney, that the first thing to be done is to find out who was up here last night, and if possible, who last saw Whitehead alive. Will you take a stroll round the village, and see what you can learn? I want to stop here and examine the house."

Viney accordingly set out along the road that led to the village. He had not gone far before he overtook an old man walking in the same direction, with a sheep dog by his side.

"Good-afternoon, Mr. Hammond," said Viney pleasantly. "You've finished work early to-day, then?"

"Finished? Who says I be finished?" replied the old man. "I've got they sheep to hurdle up over by the hanging ground afore I knocks off. I be coming from the big flock over by the marshes. Been out there all the morning, I have."

The marshes were some little distance from the village. If old Hammond had been there all day, it was unlikely that he had heard anything of the tragedy of Mr. Whitehead. But Viney knew from experience that it was hopeless to try to extract information from any of the High Eldersham people by direct questioning.

"I didn't see you up at the Rose and Crown last night, Mr. Hammond," he remarked casually.

"Then you didn't look far," replied the old man. "I was a-sitting up there in the corner, along of Bob Marsham and the rest."

"Oh, I didn't look in, I only glanced through the window as I was passing. Cold outside it was, too. Reckon you didn't turn out till closing time, Mr. Hammond."

"Ah, but I did that, I was back in the village come nine o'clock. And there wasn't many left up there when I came away. Only Ned Portch and one or two others, that I mind."

A few yards further on Mr. Hammond parted from the constable, turning off through a gate into the fields. But Viney had learnt something from his conversation. An hour or so before closing time the only customers at the Rose and Crown had been Ned Portch and one or two others. It was rather curious that Portch should have been there. Since he had been shown the door by Mr. Whitehead he had frequently declared, with considerable heat, that he would not enter the place again, even if he had to walk to the Black Dog in the next parish for his beer. He must have thought better of it, obviously. Anyhow, Ned Portch was a possible source of information. It might be worth making inquiries in his direction.

Viney continued on his way towards the village, until he reached one of the scattered cottages of which it consisted. He knocked on the door, which, after a while, was opened by a middle-aged woman in an apron. It seemed to Viney that she suddenly went deadly pale at the sight of him, and made a movement as though to slam the door in his face. As it was, she thought better of it, and, planting herself squarely in the doorway, surveyed the constable with an obviously forced smile.

"Good-afternoon, Mrs. Portch," said Viney politely. "Your husband isn't back from work yet, I suppose?"

"No, that he isn't, Mr. Viney," she replied. "Were you wanting to see him?"

The anxious note in her voice could not be mistaken. "I just wanted a word with him, that's all, Mrs. Portch," said

Viney. "As a matter of fact, I wanted to know what time he left the Rose and Crown last night. It has been reported to me that there were some gipsies about yesterday evening, and I wondered if he had seen them on his way home."

"I—I don't think he came straight home last night, Mr. Viney," replied Mrs. Portch hesitatingly. "It was past eleven when he came in, and then he went straight to bed. But I'll ask him about those gipsies when he comes in, if you like. Maybe he saw them up by the coach road."

"Oh, don't bother, Mrs. Portch, I'm sure to run across him later in the evening." And, to Mrs. Portch's intense relief, Viney turned away. But he did not pursue his inquiries elsewhere. An idea had come to him, an idea pregnant with such grave possibilities that he hastened back to unfold it to Inspector Young.

Chapter IV

Inspector Young had despatched Viney on his errand as much to be left alone as in the hope that the constable would secure any useful information. He realised that he was thrown entirely upon his own resources, and rather gloried in the fact. He recognised in Colonel Bateman a chief constable who, while anxious to help in every possible way, had no knowledge of police work other than routine. Bass, he gathered, was bitterly jealous of the affront put upon the local force by the summoning of the man from Scotland Yard, and it was pretty certain that he would not be sorry to see the failure of the investigation. And Viney—well, he was just the usual village constable, nothing more and nothing less.

The Inspector smiled as he considered Viney and his queer stories. It was perfectly plain to him that the man, an ordinary countryman with a veneer of police training, had been so long in High Eldersham that he had become saturated with local legend. In his own interests, thought Young, he ought to be transferred to a town where he would have a chance of coming into contact with the realities of life. But, for the present, he could be useful, if only as a means of introducing Young to the local worthies.

Now, as to the crime itself. It seemed quite obvious from the position of the body as first seen by Viney, and also from Dr. Barrett's examination, that Whitehead had been taken unawares. The probability was that he was dozing in his chair over the fire, and that his assailant had crept up from behind without being heard. The Inspector had already examined the bar very carefully, and had found no signs of blood in any other part of the room. This disposed of the possibility of the body having been moved after the blow was struck.

The next point of interest was the state of the doors and windows upon Viney's arrival. There were only two doors to the house. The front door, which was the one used by the customers, opened directly into the bar. This had been locked, but the key had not been in place. The back door, opening into the kitchen, had also been locked, and Viney had found the key on the inside. All the windows had been closed and fastened.

Where was the key of the front door? If Whitehead had been alive at ten o'clock, when the bar closed, he would, according to his usual habit, have locked the front door. He might either have left the key in the lock, or have put it in his pocket. Had the latter been the case, any one possessing a duplicate key could have opened the front door from outside and entered the bar.

Young approached the body, which had by now been laid out upon a table, and with deft fingers searched the pockets. He found several trifles of no importance, among which was a bunch of keys, all obviously too small to fit the door. This was interesting. The front door would not have been locked till ten o'clock. Suppose that Whitehead's customers had retired early, say about half-past nine. Whitehead might well have seated himself in his chair by the fire, leaving the door unlocked in case some belated customer would present himself before ten o'clock, and then dozed off. If any one had been awaiting the opportunity to murder Whitehead, he could have crept in silently, committed the crime and departed, locking the door behind him and taking the key with him. This would have been a perfectly natural procedure on his part, in order to ensure that no one should enter the house and discover the crime. He would have also taken the precaution of putting out the lamps. This theory placed the time at which the crime had been committed between the moment when the last customer left the house and ten o'clock.

The Inspector had reached this stage in his analysis when Viney returned, in an obvious state of suppressed excitement. He closed the door carefully behind him, and walked down the room to where the Inspector sat. "I've found out something I'd like to tell you about, sir," he said impressively.

"Very well, Viney, fire away!" replied Young cheerfully.

"It's like this, sir. You remember me telling you about Ned Portch, him that Mr. Whitehead turned out and refused to serve? Well, sir, Portch was up here last night, and didn't get home till eleven o'clock."

"That sounds curious. Are you quite sure of your facts, Viney?"

"Quite sure, sir, Mrs. Portch told me herself. Now this is the way I look at it, sir. Portch was no friend of Mr. Whitehead's, as anybody in the village can tell you. He would have jumped at the chance of doing him an injury, to get his own back for being turned out of the house. And there's more in it than that, sir. Mrs. Portch went all of a dither as soon as she saw me. She'd got something on her mind, I could see that at once. She didn't ask me into the house, and she wasn't going to tell me any more than she could help. She knows something about the business, I'll warrant, sir."

"That certainly sounds interesting, Viney," remarked the Inspector. "You didn't see Portch himself, I suppose?"

"No, sir, he wasn't back from work. He's one of Farmer Gulliford's men, and has worked for him since he was a boy. Quiet sort of chap, except when he's got a drop of liquor in him, when he's apt to fly into a temper for nothing."

"I see. And what time does Portch usually get home in the evening?"

"Depends upon the season of the year, sir. I reckon he ought to be back between six and seven this evening, sir."

"I think that I will go down to the village about seven, and interview this man Portch, leaving you up here in charge. Now, tell me exactly what passed between you and Mrs. Portch, what you said to her and what she said to you."

Viney complied with this demand, and, when he had finished, the Inspector lighted a pipe and smoked for some minutes in silence. Portch, it appeared, had remained among the last of the customers at the Rose and Crown the previous evening. He might well have left the house before closing time, and waited about outside until Whitehead was alone. Then, when the coast was clear, he could have peeped in through the window as Viney had done later. The lamps would have been alight, and he could have seen clearly the interior of the room. Then, when he was satisfied that Whitehead was dozing, he could have entered once more and committed the crime.

The deed accomplished, his natural instinct would have been to get rid of the weapon and the key. He had probably carried them to some remote place, possibly an unfrequented spot on the bank of the river. Having disposed of them, he would have returned home, all of which would have taken some time, and would account for his not having reached his cottage before eleven.

This was no more than a possible theory which fitted in with the circumstances. But to the Inspector it seemed not improbable. He knew from experience that brutal murders, inspired by some entirely inadequate motive, were not uncommon. They were nearly always due to the workings of an unbalanced mind, brooding over some fancied grievance, until the lust of blood was awakened. Then the hitherto harmless and peaceful individual became a criminal, endowed with the cunning and ruthlessness of a savage. He would await his opportunity and deliver the blow. And, the deed once perpetrated, he would return to normal sanity. It was not unlikely that the murder of Whitehead was due to such causes.

At a few minutes to seven, the Inspector left the Rose and Crown and walked down towards the village. He had obtained from Viney an exact description of Portch's cottage, and had no difficulty in identifying it. It stood surrounded by a well-kept garden, at the end of which was a fowl-house and a pigsty. Young glanced round him as he walked up the path, and then knocked sharply at the door.

Mrs. Portch answered his summons, and Young saw at once that Viney was correct in his statement that she had something on her mind. Her face dropped at the sight of this stranger standing on her doorstep, and she remained for a few seconds wild-eyed, incapable of speech or motion.

The Inspector took advantage of her bewilderment to advance into the doorway. "Mrs. Portch, I believe?" he said. "I am Detective-Inspector Young from Scotland Yard, and I should like a few words with you and your husband."

She recoiled a step with a pitiful, half-strangled cry. Young closed the door behind him and continued. "I should like to see your husband first, Mrs. Portch. He is back from work by this time, I expect?"

At last Mrs. Portch found her voice. "Yes, sir, he's been home, but he's gone out again, and I don't know when he'll be back."

"That is rather unfortunate, as I wanted to speak to him," said Young. "Never mind, perhaps you will be able to help me, Mrs. Portch. I am looking for a man who is believed to be hiding in this part of the country. He is believed to be with a party of gipsies. Constable Viney tells me that your husband was out late last night, and I thought that possibly he might have seen a stranger about."

Mrs. Portch's face lost something of its terror at this explanation. "Yes, sir, Portch was out the whole evening," she replied eagerly. "He was only in here for a mouthful of tea about seven, and then he went straight up to the Rose and Crown. I didn't see him again till nigh on eleven o'clock, and then he came straight to bed. But he didn't say nothing to me about seeing no strangers, sir."

During this conversation the Inspector had gradually advanced into the kitchen, Mrs. Portch retiring before him and giving ground slowly. It was plain that she wished to get him out of the house, and was at her wits' end how to do so without arousing his suspicions. That there was some secret hidden within the walls of the cottage, the Inspector was certain. Perhaps it was that Portch was actually in one of the rooms.

Without waiting for an invitation, the Inspector seated himself, and began to search in his pockets. His every sense was on the alert; from where he sat he could see both the front and the back doors, and he listened intently for any sound which would reveal the presence of a third person in the house. At last he produced a bundle of official looking papers, of which he selected one. "That is a description of the wanted man, Mrs. Portch," he said deliberately. "I will read it to you. Height about five feet eight, slightly built, swarthy complexion, black eyes and hair. Has a mole on the right side of his chin and a thick, dark moustache. When last seen was wearing breeches, a long coat and a cloth cap. You haven't seen anybody answering to that description about the village lately, have you, Mrs. Portch?"

"No, sir, that I haven't," replied Mrs. Portch positively. "Nor Portch either, or he'd sure to have mentioned it. 'Tisn't often we get strangers in High Eldersham, sir, and a man like that would never pass without being noticed."

This reply scarcely astonished the Inspector, who had invented the description as he went along. He was merely endeavouring to gain time, in which to examine every inch of the room in which he sat. His penetrating glance was already absorbing every detail. One side of the room was occupied by the fireplace, with a cupboard on either side of it. Against the opposite wall stood a massive dresser, reaching from the floor to the ceiling, the shelves of which were crowded with miscellaneous objects. It was clear that Mrs. Portch had recourse to these shelves when she was at a loss where to put anything. Besides the household china, displayed in all the glory of its garish pattern, there were stockings awaiting darning, useless ornaments bearing the legend "A present from Clacton," or some other popular seaside town. It seemed as though the shelves themselves did not suffice to hold all the objects that Mrs. Portch consigned to the dresser. Hooks had been screwed at the sides, and upon these hung things like toasting forks and tea cosies. Among them was a crudely moulded wax doll, apparently used as a pin-cushion, since into it was stuck a darning needle, with a piece of tape threaded through the eye.

All these trifles Young noticed, while he sought for some means of driving Mrs. Portch from the room for a moment. At last an idea came to him, and he acted upon it without any great hopes that he would achieve his end. "Well, I am very sorry to have troubled you, Mrs. Portch," he said pleasantly. "I am sorry your husband was not in, I shall have to ask him if he saw any strangers last night, if only to satisfy my own mind. Perhaps I shall meet him in the village somewhere. By the way, how shall I recognise him if I do? I suppose you haven't got a photograph of him you could show me?"

Mrs. Portch hesitated, and for the moment Young thought he had failed. Then, apparently, she decided that there was no harm in complying with the request. "If you'll wait a minute, sir, I'll get you one," she said. "It is in the front room."

She had scarcely passed through the door when Young sprang from his chair with the swiftness and silence of a cat. He opened the drawer of the dresser, peered into it eagerly and, with a sudden smile of triumph drew from it something that flashed for an instant before he thrust it between his waistcoat and his shirt. By the time that Mrs. Portch returned, he was seated once more in his chair, his coat buttoned as though for departure.

Mrs. Portch handed him the photograph. "That's my husband, sir," she said, with a strange tremor in her voice.

Young studied it for a moment. "Thank you, Mrs. Portch," he said as he returned it. "I shall recognise him now if I meet him." He rose to his feet and turned towards the door. "By the way, Mrs. Portch, have you any children?" he asked, as he stood on the threshold.

"Two girls, sir," replied Mrs. Portch. "But they're grown up and in service in Gippingford."

"It must be lonely for you without them, Mrs. Portch. Good-evening, I hope I have not troubled you."

Young walked swiftly back to the Rose and Crown. Viney had pulled the curtains and lighted the lamp in his absence. The Inspector passed into the kitchen, beckoning to Viney to follow him. There he withdrew the object which he had hidden under his waistcoat and laid it on the table. It was a butcher's knife, bright and recently sharpened.

"Well, Viney, what do you think of that?" he asked in a tone of satisfaction.

Chapter V

Constable Viney stared at the knife as if fascinated. "Why, sir, wherever did you find that?" he inquired.

"In Portch's cottage," replied the Inspector. "I'm beginning to think that your suspicions are justified, Viney. This isn't an ordinary knife, like you would expect to find in any kitchen. It is the sort of knife used only by butchers and, from the look of it, it is quite new. It was only by luck that I found it, but I thought it was worth while looking among Mrs. Portch's knives and forks, and my curiosity was rewarded."

"Well, that pretty well settles it, sir!" exclaimed Viney excitedly. "You'll apply for a warrant for the arrest of Ned Portch, I suppose, sir? Sir William Owerton, up at the Hall, is a magistrate."

The Inspector shook his head tolerantly. "No, we can't go ahead quite so fast as that," he replied. "We haven't got any evidence against Portch yet, you know. All we can say is that we have reason to believe that he was up in this direction at the time the crime was committed, and that a knife, which might have been the weapon employed, was found in his cottage. It's a good beginning, certainly, but it isn't conclusive. Before we go any further, I should very much like a few words with Portch. Mrs. Portch says that he is about the village somewhere. I want you to go down there and find him. Tell him that I want to see him—don't frighten him, of course—and try to bring him back here with you."

Viney set out at once. In the village he noticed groups of men and women standing about in eager discussion. They became silent and eyed him furtively as he paused. It was evident that the news of the tragedy at the Rose and Crown had spread at last. Viney glanced at each group as he passed, looking for Ned Portch. And then, as he turned the corner by the church, he saw Portch himself, accompanied by a neighbour of his, Walter Hosier, walking swiftly towards him.

He was about to accost them, when Portch came up to him. "Good-evening, Mr. Viney," he said eagerly. "I heard as how you and a gentleman from Scotland Yard has been asking about my doings last night. There's been a mistake, the missus—"

"Yes, Inspector Young is anxious to see you," interrupted Viney. "He wants to ask you a question or two. He's up at the Rose and Crown now, and I'd like you to come up there with me."

"I'll come, right enough," replied Portch. "And, if you've no objection, I'll bring Walter here along with me. He can bear out what I have to say. Terrible thing about poor Mr. Whitehead! It's right that he was found murdered, isn't it?"

"Yes, it's right enough," replied Viney shortly.

"I shouldn't doubt it was them gipsies as you was telling the missus about," continued Portch, who seemed consumed with nervousness and unable to stop talking. "You never can trust them, no further than you can see them."

Viney made no reply, and the three men made their way up the road, followed by the inquisitive stares of the villagers. As they passed, an eager whispering could be heard, like the sound of the wind among the rushes.

Arrived at the Rose and Crown, Viney led them through the back way into the kitchen, where they found Inspector Young awaiting them. Viney introduced the two men to him, and Young bade them sit down.

"Now, Portch, I want to ask you a few questions," he said sternly. "You needn't answer them unless you like, but I think it will be better for you if you do. I know that you were up here last night. What time did you leave the bar?"

"About half-past nine, sir, or maybe five and twenty minutes to ten," replied Portch. "Walter here came out with me, didn't you, Walt? And Mr. Whitehead walked to the door with us when we left."

"I see, the two of you left together at about half-past nine. Were there any other customers in the bar when you came away?"

"No, sir, we was the last to leave. There had been a dozen or so of the chaps up here earlier in the evening."

"If you left at half-past nine, it seems rather queer that you didn't get home till eleven, doesn't it, Portch? What were you doing between the time you left here and the time you got home?"

Portch had obviously been waiting for this question, but, all the same, he changed colour visibly as it was put to him. "I didn't hang about up here, sir," he replied. "Poor Mr. Whitehead was as hale as any man when I last saw him, that I'll swear. And we didn't see that gipsy fellow you was asking the missus about, did we, Walt? You see, sir, it was like this, I wouldn't tell you an untruth, not to save my soul. Walt and I went straight back to his place, and there sits down and plays a game of nap for an hour. That's right, isn't it, Walt?"

"Aye, that's right," mumbled Walter Hosier, with his eyes fixed on the table in front of him.

For several seconds Inspector Young looked sternly at the two men, without speaking. It was perfectly plain from their manner that they were lying, that they had concocted the story of the game of nap between them. If it were true, why had Mrs. Portch betrayed such obvious uneasiness on being questioned?

The Inspector decided upon a dramatic stroke. With a sudden movement he opened the table drawer, withdrew from it the knife, and flung it on the table.

"This is the weapon with which Mr. Whitehead was killed!" he thundered. "How do you account for it having been found in your cottage this evening, Portch?"

Portch uttered an exclamation of horror and then, leaning over the table, stared at the knife as though fascinated. The blood ebbed from his face, and then suddenly returned, suffusing it with a guilty flush.

"Well, Portch, I'm waiting for your explanation," said Inspector Young impatiently.

"That's not the knife with which Mr. Whitehead was killed," said Portch at last slowly. "I can swear to that, for I used that very knife myself last night, about ten o'clock."

"You did? And what did you use it for?" demanded Young sharply.

Portch glanced at Hosier, who nodded gloomily. "Best tell him, mate," he muttered.

"Well, sir, there's nothing for it but to make a clean breast of it," said Portch with an air of resignation.

"If I owns up, perhaps the magistrates won't rub it in too hard. Fact is, sir, while Walter and me was up here last evening, the missus had the copper on, boiling up the water. We waits till there wasn't anybody about in the village, and then Walter and I goes back to my place, fetches a young porker out of the sty, and cuts his throat. Then we scalds him and cuts him up. When Mr. Viney comes along this afternoon, the missus was in a terrible state in case he should come in and see the offal and that. As soon as I comes home from work, she tells me about it, and I goes straight out again and sells the joints to the chaps I'd promised them to. And that's the truth, sir. Walter and the missus will bear me out. I bought this here knife in Gippingford last market day, for to do the job with."

In spite of Inspector Young's annoyance, he could not escape the conviction that Portch was telling the truth at last. This clandestine killing of the pig would explain the guilty consciences of Portch and his wife. It is an offence, punishable by heavy fines, to kill any beast whose carcase is intended for sale anywhere but in a licensed slaughter house, and Portch had rendered himself liable to a fine which he might well find some difficulty in paying. On the other hand, if his story could be verified, his alibi was established, and he could not be the murderer of Whitehead.

"You would have saved yourself a good deal of trouble if you had told the truth at first, and not made up that tissue of lies about playing a game of nap," said Young severely. "Constable Viney will make inquiries, and if it is found that you did actually kill this pig and sell pork you will certainly be summoned. As it is, you are very lucky not to have been arrested on a charge of murder. That would have taught you and Mrs. Portch not to tell lies to the police. In any case, you can tell your wife that she may find herself in serious trouble for showing me a photograph of somebody else when I asked her for one of you. Now, clear out, and remember that I shall keep a pretty tight watch on both of you for the future."

Portch and Hosier took themselves off, and Young turned to Viney. "You'd better make it your business to find out about that wretched pig," he said. "If Portch was telling the truth, we've got to look elsewhere for the murderer. But there's one thing. He and his friend were the last people, so far as we know at present, to see Whitehead alive. The

Coroner will want to see them, I expect. Now, you get back to the village. The news seems to be out now, and you may pick up some useful gossip. You needn't come back till the morning. I see that there's plenty of food in the larder, and later on I shall lie down on Whitehead's bed. But I want to do a bit of quiet thinking first."

Left to himself, Inspector Young made himself comfortable with a pipe. This case, which had seemed so simple when it had first been described to him, seemed now in his imagination to be wrapped in sinister mystery. The Inspector was peculiarly sensitive to his environment, and here, in this remote spot, he felt himself surrounded by impalpable forces beyond his power to combat. It was as though the atmosphere of High Eldersham, so inimical to strangers, had already begun to influence him. There was undoubtedly something queer about the place, upon this everybody seemed to be agreed. But the theory he had for a moment formed to account for this queerness was so impossible, so utterly fanciful, that to entertain it was to doubt his own sanity.

Young was normally an extremely self-reliant person. In his most difficult cases he had always relied upon his own powers of reasoning, and so far they had rarely failed him. But, confronted with the murder of Whitehead, he felt the urgent need of discussing the circumstances with some kindred spirit, whose incisive brain might solve the riddles with which he felt himself surrounded. Such a person existed, if only he could be induced to take an interest in the case. During the war, Inspector Young had been in constant communication with the intelligence branch of the Admiralty, and in the course of his duties had contracted a friendship with a very brilliant individual of his own age, then serving on that staff.

Desmond Merrion was a bachelor of independent and very considerable means. At the outbreak of war he had secured a commission in the Royal Naval Volunteer Reserve, and in that capacity had been very badly wounded when the vessel in which he was serving had been blown up off the Belgian coast. Upon his partial recovery, he had been transferred to the Admiralty, where Young had met him, and found him a living encyclopaedia upon all manner of obscure subjects which the ordinary person knew nothing about. The two men had continued their friendship after the war, and Young frequently visited Merrion's luxurious rooms in Mayfair, seeking advice upon some knotty point. Merrion was just the man he wanted, if he could persuade him to visit High Eldersham.

Young took a writing pad from his suit-case, and sat down to write the following letter:—

My dear Merrion,—Take out the sheet of the Ordnance Survey of East Anglia, and look along the coast till you find the River Elder. About six miles from its mouth is a little village called High Eldersham. A mile west of the village is the old road from Gippingford northwards. On this road, where a side road runs off into High Eldersham, you will find the word 'Inn.' The name of the inn is the Rose and Crown, and that is where I am at present.

The landlord of this inn was murdered yesterday evening (March 31st) in a particularly brutal manner. The local police communicated with the Yard, and I was sent down to investigate. I arrived shortly before three o'clock this afternoon (Saturday). The inquest is to take place here at eleven o'clock on Monday, and, if you can possibly manage to be present, I will see that a seat is reserved for you.

You will ask why in heaven's name you should take the trouble to attend an inquest in such a remote spot upon a man you never heard of. Well, frankly, I can't tell you. All that I can say definitely is that I believe that the identification of the murderer is not going to be as easy as it sounds. My own efforts, so far, have not been crowned with any conspicuous success. I have employed my time following up a most promising clue, which has certainly led me to the discovery of a murder, but of a pig, not a man.

Seriously, my dear fellow, if you can possibly spare the time, I should be very much relieved to have you here and to consult you. It is not exactly the murder itself which worries me, but the surrounding conditions. There is something mysterious about the whole of this countryside, something which I cannot possibly fathom, but which seems to me is more or less in your line, and may possibly interest you. I can't get away from a wild and insane idea which I dare not even hint to you, lest you should think I had gone clean off my head. If there is anything in it, which, to a reasonable man, seems utterly unthinkable, High Eldersham holds one of the most remarkable secrets of recent years.

I'm not going to say any more, hoping that what I have said will be enough to arouse your curiosity. I repeat, if you possibly can, drive down on Monday, and we will have a chat after the inquest.

Yours,
Robert Young

Chapter VI

Inspector Young was busily engaged in cooking himself some breakfast on the following morning, when a knock upon the door announced the arrival of Viney.

"Come in, Viney!" said the Inspector cheerfully. "Had your breakfast? You have? All right, you can sit down and watch me eat mine. That's right. Now, what have you got to report?"

"There's no doubt that Portch's story about the pig is right, sir," replied the constable. "I made inquiries round the village after I left you last night, sir, and I've traced most of the pork. And I've found a couple of chaps who saw Portch and Hosier in Portch's back yard about ten o'clock that night."

"Well, that seems to settle the matter, and we'll have to start afresh," remarked the Inspector. "Now, there's one thing I should like to be clear about. Portch had a grievance against Whitehead, on account of his having been turned out of here on one occasion. I gather that he threatened—or, if he didn't actually threaten, he abused—Whitehead in consequence. Do you know of anybody else in the neighbourhood who had any grievance against the dead man?"

"No, sir, I don't. As I told you at first, Mr. Whitehead was a man who was generally liked in the village. And, as you will understand, sir, that was very exceptional for a stranger."

The Inspector smiled, but said nothing for several seconds. His mind was obviously pursuing a train of thought from which an effort was needed to recall it.

"Well, look here, Viney," he said at last. "Even though Portch's alibi is established, we haven't done with him. He and Hosier, if they left here together, were the last people who saw Whitehead alive. We shall have to get some sort of statement from them. I didn't question them last night, for I don't think Portch was capable of giving a coherent answer. But I would like to see them this morning, before the Chief Constable comes. Slip down and fetch them up for me."

Viney departed, and duly returned with the men in question. But if Young had expected to extract any information of value from them, he was disappointed. All he could learn, in spite of the most adroit questioning, was that they had left the inn together between half-past nine and twenty-five minutes to ten, and walked straight down the road to Portch's cottage. There had been no other customers in the house when they left, Whitehead had gone so far as to compliment Portch on his behaviour, and had told him that as long as he conducted himself properly, as he had that evening, there was no objection to his frequenting the bar of the Rose and Crown, or words to that effect. The three had been sitting round the fire, Whitehead in the chair in which his body was found, and when Portch and Hosier rose to leave, Whitehead got up and followed them to the door. The last they saw of him as they went down the road was his figure standing in the doorway. It was also established that Portch had not the knife with him when he visited the Rose and Crown. His first action on reaching home had been to take it out of the drawer of the dresser and sharpen it in preparation for the slaughter of the pig.

The Inspector had hardly dismissed the pair when Colonel Bateman arrived in his car. He was, as Young observed with relief, alone. He walked into the kitchen, and took up his position, with legs wide apart, in front of the fire which the Inspector had lighted. "Well, and how are you getting on?" he asked genially.

"Not very fast, so far, sir," replied Young. "It didn't take us long to pick up a scent, but it proved to be a false one." The Inspector gave an account of Portch's actions and their detection, at which Colonel Bateman laughed heartily.

"Well, Inspector, you've already ferreted out a crime that probably would not have been discovered without you," he said. "You say that you're satisfied that these men Portch and Hosier had nothing to do with the murder. But I suppose, in spite of the apparent absence of motive, that you are satisfied that somebody in the village did it?"

"I'm not sure, sir," replied the Inspector. "We must not forget that this house stands on a through road, although it does not appear to be much used. Since I have been here, I have seen about a dozen cars drive past, to say nothing of carts and bicycles. What I mean, sir, is that people pass here without having any business with High Eldersham, or going down into the village. It is quite possible that sombody passed along the road soon after the departure of Portch and Hosier. If Whitehead had left the door open and returned to his chair, that person might have seen him."

"Then crept in through the open door and murdered him with a knife which he happened to have handy," said the Chief Constable. "It is possible, of course. But, frankly, you don't think it's likely, do you, Inspector?"

"No, sir. I don't believe it was a stranger who committed the murder. I believe that the motive is to be found locally, and I believe that I can guess what it was. But as to the ownership of the hand which struck the blow I am at present completely in the dark."

Rather a puzzled look came into Colonel Bateman's face at this somewhat cryptic statement. "Well, Inspector, the case is in your hands, and I'm not going to butt in with injudicious questions," he remarked. "By the way, I have seen the Coroner again, and had a chat with him. He has decided, in view of the fact that the crime almost certainly involves some person or persons in the village, that it will be better not to summon a local jury. He will therefore sit without a jury. You will have your witnesses ready, I suppose. Now, unless I can be of any further use to you, I will get back to Gippingford."

"There's one thing I will ask you to do, sir," replied Young. "I am very anxious that this letter should be delivered in London by the first post to-morrow morning. If you would be good enough to hand it in at Gippingford Station for postage at Liverpool Street, I should be very grateful."

"Of course, I'll willingly do that for you," said Colonel Bateman. "You're quite sure that there's nothing else you want? All right, then, I'll be off."

But the Inspector was destined to have other visitors that Sunday. Less than an hour after the Chief Constable's departure a hired car drove up to the Rose and Crown, from which descended an individual with a couple of large suit-cases. The Inspector admitted him, and the two stood for a moment regarding one another, the newcomer with an expression of veiled mistrust.

"Are you the chap what's in charge of the case of this poor chap, Whitehead?" he asked after a pause.

"Yes, I am Detective-Inspector Young. You are the new tenant of the Rose and Crown, I suppose?"

"Well, I wouldn't go so far as to say that. You might say, in a manner of speaking, that I'm the old tenant. 'Tis like this, you see. Mr. George Thorold, he comes to me yesterday in a terrible stew. I keeps the Tower of London in Gippingford, you must understand. 'Dunsford,' he says to me, 'if you'll do something to oblige me, I'll see that you're not a loser by it.' Well, Mr. George has always been very good to me. 'If I can do anything to oblige you, sir, you know I'll do it,' I says. 'Well,' says he, 'a terrible thing has happened. Poor Whitehead out at the Rose and Crown at High Eldersham has been murdered, and there's no one to look after the house. Could you go over there and keep it open for me for a few days? Mrs. Dunsford and Dick can look after the Tower of London while you're away, and if they want help I'll pay for it. I'll find a tenant for the Rose and Crown as soon as I can, I promise you.'

"I thinks to myself that it'll be a bit awkward, for trade's pretty brisk at the Tower of London, and the missus isn't as spry as she used to be. But Dick's a good lad, and knows his way about. Besides, I'd go a long way to do a good turn to Mr. George, and there's nobody knows more about the Rose and Crown than me, seeing as I kept it for twenty years or thereabouts, and my dad before me. So I tells Mr. George I'd be over this morning, and here I am."

The Inspector listened to Dunsford's explanation with interest. It occurred to him that this man's presence might prove very useful. His long residence in the place must have rendered him more thoroughly acquainted with the village and its inhabitants even than Viney. And, now that he had deserted it in favour of Gippingford, he would probably have lost the parochial instincts which might have hindered him from imparting information to a stranger.

"I'm very glad you've come, Mr. Dunsford," he said heartily. "I slept in Whitehead's room last night, but, of course, I'll give that up to you now. You won't mind if I fix myself up in one of the other rooms, will you?"

It seemed to the Inspector that Dunsford hesitated for an instant before he replied. But, when he did so, his voice was cordial enough. "That'll be all right," he said. "We'll get along well enough together, I dare say. Are you likely to be here long?"

"I can't say. It depends on the progress I make with the case. But there's nothing to prevent you carrying on exactly as if I wasn't here."

That afternoon, while Dunsford was busy settling in and taking stock, the Inspector, leaving Viney at the Rose and Crown, set out upon a tour of exploration. He walked through the village, unobtrusively observing the inhabitants as they stood about discussing the tragedy. He then went further afield, and, with the help of a map which the Chief Constable had given him, identified the principal features of the surrounding country. It was not until he had made himself thoroughly familiar with the lie of the land that he returned, in time to share the excellent supper provided by Dunsford. He spent the rest of the evening talking to his host, who displayed the greatest readiness to gossip about the inhabitants of the parish. When he went to bed he felt that his knowledge of High Eldersham and its population was already extensive. But he had learnt nothing which tended to throw any light upon the identity of Whitehead's murderer.

On the following morning the Inspector and Viney were kept busy arranging for the inquest. It was to be held in a large room above the old stables of the Rose and Crown, used occasionally as a club room. Long before eleven o'clock the road outside the inn was thronged by a crowd of the curious, waiting for admission. Colonel Bateman arrived in his car, bringing with him Superintendent Bass, Dr. Barrett, and the Coroner. A short consultation ensued between them and the Inspector, and then Viney was instructed to open the doors of the club room to the public.

The Inspector stood beside him as the audience filed in, listening to his whispered identifications. "That's Mr.

Hollesley, sir, him what lives at Elder House," said Viney, as a tall, dark man of about thirty-five came in. "The chap he's talking to is old Fairbairn, who rents the home farm from him. I heard he was going up to London to-day, but I expect he's stopped to see the proceedings. Ah, and here's Sir William, with his daughter, Miss Mavis. If you'll excuse me, sir, I'll find them a couple of chairs. They won't like to sit on these hard benches."

Young nodded, and Viney made his way across the room. Sir William Owerton was an elderly man with white hair and the rather absent-minded look of the student. But it was his daughter who attracted the Inspector's attention. Mavis Owerton would have been noticeable anywhere, with her fair hair and blue eyes, which are generally accepted as the type of English beauty. In this bare prosaic room, surrounded by the rather stolid countenances of the East Anglians, she seemed like some goddess descended among mortals, even the unsusceptible Inspector was moved to admiration. "By Jove!" he muttered. "That's one of the prettiest girls I've ever seen!"

It was immediately apparent that his admiration was shared by Mr. Hollesley. That gentleman, whose eyes had never left the door of the room, abruptly broke off his conversation with Fairbairn at the entrance of the Owertons, and made his way through the crowd to meet them. He escorted them to the chairs which Viney had placed for them and sat down on a bench just behind Mavis. She nodded to him, rather offhandedly, Young thought, and then leant across to speak to an old man in the next row. Sir William, however, turned round in his chair and engaged Laurence Hollesley in earnest conversation, to which the latter appeared to listen with ill-concealed impatience.

The significance of the incident was not lost upon the Inspector, in spite of the fact that his attention was divided between it and the faces of the people still filing in through the door. "Looks as though she wasn't as keen on him as he is on her," he said to himself. "He's a good-looking fellow enough, but I dare say a girl like that has more than one string to her bow, even though she lives in an outlandish place like this. But I wonder what's happened to Merrion? He's pretty sure to come along, if he got my letter. I wonder if the old boy remembered to take it to the station?"

His attention was diverted by a sharp rapping of the table, and he glided to the door and posted himself at it. Silence having been obtained, the Coroner opened the proceedings. He explained that he was sitting to inquire into the circumstances surrounding the death of Samuel Whitehead. He had viewed the body, and would proceed to call witnesses. The first was Constable Viney, of the local police force.

Viney was about to take the oath, when the door at the back of the room opened. The audience turned as one man at the sound, and saw Inspector Young escort a stranger to a vacant seat at the back. The newcomer was short but powerfully built, with an expression which seemed to denote complete boredom. He winked at the Inspector, and took his seat with an air of comical resignation, as though accepting some unwelcome penance.

The proceedings, thus momentarily interrupted, were resumed. Viney gave his evidence, and was followed by Doctor Padfield, Doctor Barrett, Portch, Hosier and the Inspector himself, each shepherded into place by Superintendent Bass. Nothing fresh transpired, in spite of the persistent questioning of the Coroner, a little man with a self-important manner. He finally summed up in a rather pompous speech, and delivered his verdict. "Wilful murder by some person or persons unknown."

The verdict was hardly out of his mouth when Laurence Hollesley slipped from his seat and made his way rapidly to the back of the room. The stranger rose to meet him, and the two men shook hands. "Why, good lord, Merrion, I couldn't believe my eyes when I saw you come in!" exclaimed Hollesley. "What the devil are you doing here?"

"I might ask you the same question," replied Merrion. "When I last saw you you were commanding a M.L. in the Dover Patrol. I certainly never expected to see you attending an inquest in a village pub somewhere beyond the end of the world."

"My dear chap, I live here," said Hollesley. "Didn't you know? Look here, I've got to dash up to town this afternoon, but there's just time for you to come to my place and have lunch. Then you can tell me all about it."

"Well, that's very good of you," replied Merrion. "I was just wondering if this local pub of yours ran to bread and cheese. If you don't mind waiting a minute, I'll run my car into the yard."

"I'll come with you, my car's in the yard too," agreed Hollesley. The two left the room together, Merrion without bestowing as much as a glance upon the Inspector.

The latter watched their departure, an expression of bewilderment upon his face. "Well, I'm damned!" he exclaimed softly.

Chapter VII

It was nearly three o'clock before Inspector Young, waiting uneasily at the Rose and Crown, saw a car stop outside the inn, and Merrion descend from it. He observed that Hollesley was driving the car, and when it had moved on, he went out and joined his friend.

"You're a nice chap!" he said indignantly. "I ask you to come down here because I want to talk to you, and the first thing you do is to clear off and lunch with somebody else. Perhaps you can spare me a few minutes of your valuable time now?"

Merrion laughed cheerfully. "Sorry, old man, but I had to act on my own, you know. Your letter wasn't very explicit. You hinted that there was something queer about this place and, when I found, unexpectedly, that I knew one of the natives, it struck me that lunching with him would be a heaven-sent opportunity for getting the hang of things. I'm quite ready to exchange notes with you now. But where? Not in this pub, I suppose."

"You put your car into the yard, didn't you? Well, get it out, and we'll drive along the road till we find a quiet spot where we can't be overheard."

Merrion agreed to this. Three or four miles from the Rose and Crown they found a spot where the car could be drawn up on the grass by the side of the road. There, seated in the car, they discussed the matter that had urged the Inspector to summon Merrion to his aid.

"You'd better let me tell my story first," said Merrion, as he lighted a large pipe. "I gathered the bones of your trouble from the evidence at the inquest, but you don't know the link between me and Hollesley. I met him first during the war, when he was commanding a motor launch. We all thought him rather a queer chap in those days, but it's difficult to explain exactly why. He was quite good at his job, brave, daring, resourceful, all the rest of it, but there were times when he seemed to be unable to control his actions. It wasn't drink, I'm pretty certain of that, for nobody ever saw him touch more than a couple of whiskies in a day. His conduct at lunch just now bears that out. He drank nothing more than one glass of Burgundy.

"I'll give you an instance of what I mean. One night his craft was sent out of Dover on some work or other, I don't remember what it was. It was a beautiful night, full moon, almost as bright as day. Hollesley, as I was told afterwards, was in a curiously exalted state, do or die, and all that sort of thing. Somewhere in midchannel he swore that he had sighted a German submarine, and worked himself up to a fearful state of excitement. He took the wheel, and went full speed for this blessed submarine of his. The rest of the ship's company very soon saw what it was; one of the buoys connected with the barrage. But Hollesley wouldn't listen to them and kept on straight for it, swearing he was going to ram it. At the very last moment his petty officer or somebody snatched the wheel from him and put it hard over. Lucky thing for Hollesley, for if he'd hit the buoy he'd have crumpled up his M.L. like a box of matches.

"Hollesley flew into a terrible rage, and put the man under arrest. When they got back to Dover, there was a deuce of a row, as you might suppose. However, it was smoothed over in some way, and a little time later Hollesley was sent to another station. I never saw or heard of him again until this morning."

"I see," remarked Young. "And what did you make of him this time?"

"Oh, he seemed pretty normal," replied Merrion. "We spent a good part of our time chatting about old times, but at last I managed to switch him on to the present. Naturally, he wanted to know what I was doing at that infernal inquest of yours. I made up a yarn for his benefit; told him that I was on my way from Hunstanton to Gippingford, and had chosen this way so as to avoid the traffic on the main road. I had been looking out for somewhere to stop and have a drink, and seeing half a dozen cars outside the Rose and Crown, stopped there, thinking it was probably a suitable place. Hearing that an inquest was going on, I looked in out of sheer curiosity. That's why I tried to look as if I didn't know you when Hollesley and I left the room."

"You succeeded, all right. Did you happen to learn anything about the people hereabouts?"

"Quite a lot, but I don't know whether any of it will interest you. Elder House is not a very big place, but distinctly comfortable and very efficiently run. The family consists of Hollesley and his mother, who is an invalid and did not appear. There must be a very capable cook, judging by the lunch, but the only one of the servants I saw was the butler, big chap, middle-aged, with a perfect butler's manner. Hollesley happened to mention that he hadn't been with him long.

"I gathered that the nearest neighbours were Sir William Owerton and his daughter. I had noticed them at the inquest, and it struck me then that Miss Owerton wasn't the sort of girl that one expects to find in a place like this. Owerton, it seems, spends most of his time in his library, which, according to Hollesley, is full of rare books. Miss Owerton spends most of her time out of doors. She's fond of every kind of sport, and keeps a sailing dinghy in the river. She's expecting one of those speed-boat things every day, Hollesley said. By the way, once he had got on to the subject of Mavis Owerton, it was pretty difficult to ride him off it again. I fancy that he has every intention of persuading her to abandon the Hall in favour of Elder House."

"That certainly seems to be the opinion locally. Hollesley didn't mention Doctor Padfield by any chance, did he?"

"The village medico, who gave evidence at the inquest? Yes, he told me that he was attending his mother, and that he had great faith in him. A very capable man, he said, who might have done great things if he had consented to leave his native village. But it seems that he isn't ambitious, and has enough to live comfortably, apart from his practice. The village people like him well enough, though he is apt to be a bit off-hand in his manner. I noticed that for myself when he was giving his evidence."

"Off-hand is rather a mild word, judging by what Viney told me of his behaviour on Friday night. Did Hollesley say anything else about the village or its inhabitants?"

"Nothing very definite. I gathered that they were all a happy family, and got on very well without bothering much about the rest of the world. My perceptions may be a bit insensitive, but I didn't detect any trace of that mystery at which your letter hinted."

"You wouldn't, at Elder House. It's in the village itself that it exists, if it exists at all outside my own imagination. I've thought, since I wrote that letter, that I should find it impossible to explain, even when I saw you. But I'll try, confining myself to bare facts and leaving you to draw the inferences. In the first place, there is no doubt that High

Eldersham doesn't favour strangers. I know that very few English villages do, especially in this part of the country. But the antipathy to strangers is more highly developed here than anywhere else that I have heard of. I don't mean that the inhabitants throw stones through their windows, or manifest their hostility in any way. They don't, you'll find them as polite and well behaved as you could want. But strangers, as Viney, the local cop, puts it, just don't prosper in High Eldersham. He told me a couple of very curious incidents, which I will repeat to you later, both of which occurred under his own eyes. Of course, Viney's intelligence isn't of the highest order, and I confess that I was inclined to smile at his stories when I first heard them. It is only since something utterly bizarre came under my own observation that I have wondered whether there could not possibly be some queer influence acting against strangers in this place. And yet it seems so utterly fantastic—"

"Upon my word, Young, you've found the secret of arousing my curiosity. You haven't been going in for spiritualism lately, have you? You're talking more like a member of the Society for Psychical Research than a mere flat-footed tec. Can't you be a little more explicit? What was it that came under your own observation and started you off in this fanciful vein?"

"That I'm not going to tell you. I want you to approach this problem with an absolutely open mind. A little later on you shall have the chance of seeing what I saw. If you see nothing out of the ordinary in it, I am willing to confess I am suffering from hallucinations, and you shall go back to London. On the other hand, if it seems to you as remarkable as it does to me, you shall stay in the neighbourhood. You'll have to put up at Gippingford. For one thing, there's no decent accommodation any nearer, and for another I don't want you to be seen hanging about here too much. Strangers about here are too rare to escape notice. Is that a bargain?"

"Well, I suppose so. If this mystery you hint at appeals to me with half the force that it appeals to you, I shan't want to leave it till we've got to the bottom of it. When is the trial of my observation to be made?"

"Very shortly. But first of all I want to give you an idea of what I'm driving at. It very soon became clear to me that there is a pretty general impression in this part of the world that there is something queer about High Eldersham. What it is, what the queerness consists of, nobody can tell me. It just isn't definable. Even the Chief Constable, a retired soldier and a very decent old stick, hinted at it ten minutes after I first met him. I got the impression that he wouldn't be surprised at anything that might happen at High Eldersham. It also struck me that he lost no time in calling in the aid of the Yard, as though he knew that the murder of Whitehead would provide a problem quite beyond the power of his own people to deal with."

"That reminds me that this murder, which is presumably the only reason for your presence here, is the one thing we have not yet discussed."

"I know. The reason why I haven't told you more about the murder is because I believe the problem can only be approached through a study of the peculiarities of High Eldersham."

"Oh, dash it all, man! Your conversation has been pretty obscure, you'll admit, but, if I understand you right, this is what you are trying to make me believe. You suspect some mysterious influence in this village inimical to strangers, and it is your theory that this influence, or some manifestation of it, drove a butcher's knife into the vitals of an unfortunate and inoffensive publican. And that sort of thing is really outside the realm of ordinary terrestrial detection."

Young smiled at his friend's bantering tone. "Go on," he said. "This is just what I expected. I am a lunatic, I know,

wholly unfitted for the duties which I am expected to perform. Never mind, bear with me as patiently as you can.
I want to tell you Viney's stories about the experiences of
other strangers in this village."

Merrion listened attentively. "Curious!" was his comment
when Young had finished. "But I think that the psychology
of the situation is fairly easy to analyse. Here are two cases
where strangers settling here have failed to succeed in their
businesses, owing to circumstances beyond human control.
The locals, constitutionally antagonistic to strangers, persuade themselves that what happened in two cases must be
instances of the operation of a universal law. Hence the origin
of the legend that disaster must always overtake strangers in
High Eldersham. Isn't that the rational way of looking at it?"

"I don't know. I thought so at first, myself. Now, that's
all I've got to tell you. There's nothing in the actual murder
but what you heard at the inquest. The story of the sleuth
whose brilliant researches led to the discovery of the brutal
assassination of the pig I'll tell you as we go back. You'll find
it amusing, I suppose. If you'll start up this perambulating
hen-coop of yours and drive me back to the pub, I'll take
you for a little walk down the village. I needn't warn you, if
you see anything that astonishes you, don't let your expression betray you."

They drove back to the Rose and Crown, and Merrion put
his car into the yard once more. The Inspector went into the
house and after a few words with Viney, joined Merrion outside. The two walked slowly down towards the village, which
had resumed its normal aspect. They had got as far as Portch's
cottage when the Inspector stopped. "I've got to go in here
for a minute," he said. "You may as well come in with me."

They knocked at the door, and Mrs. Portch appeared. She
had evidently resigned herself to the inevitable, and made no
difficulty about admitting them. The Inspector cast a swift

glance round the kitchen, and saw with inward satisfaction that nothing in it had been moved since his last visit.

"I've brought you back your knife, Mrs. Portch," he said. "I hope this incident will be a warning to you to tell the truth to the police in future. Your husband had a very narrow escape from being arrested on suspicion of being concerned in the murder of Mr. Whitehead. I do not know what view the magistrates will take of the offence of slaughtering a pig in an unlicensed place, I am sure. Perhaps, if you were to show me where the pig was killed, I could put in a word."

"It's a sight cleaner than some of they slaughter houses there are about, sir," replied Mrs. Portch indignantly. "I scrubbed it out myself, top and bottom, that very afternoon. If you care to come through to the back, sir, you can see for yourself."

She led the way out of the back door, and the Inspector followed her, leaving Merrion alone in the kitchen.

A few minutes later the Inspector returned, and the two men left the cottage together. They pursued their way in silence until they reached the river, a sluggish stream about fifty yards wide, running between banks of mud. The village street ended in a miniature quay, which at this time of day was completely deserted.

Merrion strode to the edge of the quay, and stood for many minutes staring down at the water beneath him. Then suddenly he turned, almost petulantly, and faced the Inspector. "You're quite right, Young," he said. "The thing's absurd, incredible, impossible, anything that you like to call it. But still, it's there, and I'm damned if I know how on earth to tackle it. Did you happen to notice the moon last night?"

"No, I can't say that I did," replied the Inspector gravely. "Although lunatics are supposed to, I believe."

"We could tell if we knew the tidal establishment of the place. It seems to be dead low water now. Failing that, we'll have to borrow a calendar from somewhere."

"I've got one in my pocket. What do you want to know?"

"I want to know the date of the next full moon."

The Inspector took out a pocket diary and turned over the pages. "April 8th. That's Saturday next," he said.

Merrion nodded, but said nothing. They turned away, and walked back in silence towards the Rose and Crown. It was not until they had nearly reached the inn that either spoke. Then Merrion broke the silence abruptly. "You guessed what was written on that piece of tape, I suppose?"

The Inspector shook his head. "I haven't dared," he replied. "This business is dark enough without any guessing."

"Well, it was 'Sam Whitehead,' if you care to know," said Merrion.

Chapter VIII

By a common impulse Merrion and the Inspector turned away from the Rose and Crown when they reached the old coach road, and walked slowly on. "There are too many people about the inn to make it possible to talk quietly there," said Young. "The open road is much safer. Well, old man, what am I to do now?"

"I can't advise you, yet," replied Merrion slowly. "I shall have to go back to London for a couple of days and study the subject. I'm familiar enough with the general lines, but I'm a bit rusty as to detail, and if we're to trace this thing to its source, we shall have to have every detail at our finger ends. That's as much as I can say at present."

"I gather from your attitude that you are satisfied that there can be no mistake?"

"Absolutely. You gave me no hint as to what I was to look for, and I spotted the doll right away. Mommet is the correct word, I believe. From what I could see in my very hasty examination, the traditional ritual had been very closely followed. The doll had been moulded in wax, the sort of wax that is used for church candles, I should say. Pretty roughly moulded too, obviously by some one not exactly an expert in the plastic arts. Again, the needle had been driven into the figure, about where the heart would be, when it was hot. There were traces of the wax having been melted round it, and the needle itself was black where it had been in the flame. Finally, there was the piece of tape—certainly an improvement on the traditional paper—with the victim's name written on it and threaded through the eye. No, there's no room for doubt. It certainly is one of the most amazing things I ever came across. But what puzzles me, if you don't mind my saying so, is how you guessed the significance of this doll."

"Give me credit for a few scattered crumbs of general knowledge," replied Young, with a smile. "I've read my *Ingoldsby Legends*, for one thing. And, for another, cases of dolls being baptised with the name of a destined victim are not unheard of, even in these degenerate days. There was a case near Langport, in Somerset, in 1929."

"Yes, very possibly. These cases do crop up from time to time, especially where tradition has lingered in remote country places. But I have never before heard of an authenticated instance where the baptism of the doll was followed by the death by violence of the victim. I say, Young, it gives one furiously to think. Does the witch-cult still survive in High Eldersham? Were the misfortunes which overtook those two strangers you told me about consequent upon unholy incantations? And, if so, what on earth or in hell are we up against?"

"Nothing that a mere policeman can be expected to unravel. That's why I asked you to come down. Mind you, I'm not suggesting that Whitehead's death was due to occult forces, that he was stabbed by some supernatural hand, or anything like that. But I do believe that his murder is in some way connected with the existence of that doll. I believe the doll to be the clue, not only to this murder, but to all the queer and inexplicable happenings in High Eldersham."

"I think you are very probably right. The best way that I can help you, as I say, is to go back home for a couple of days and spend every minute of my time reading up every available book on the subject. Meanwhile, you must say or do nothing that could possibly reveal your suspicions. If I'm not mistaken, that doll still has a part to play, and if the people concerned are not alarmed, we may learn a good deal by waiting. In any case, I don't think anything is likely to happen before Saturday night."

The Inspector agreed to this course, and within half an hour Merrion was on his way back to London. The Inspector spent the evening in the kitchen of the Rose and Crown, studying the customers who thronged the place. Never before had the inn done such a profitable trade. It seemed to Young that nearly all the male population of High Eldersham must have visited the place, partly out of curiosity to see the very spot where Whitehead was murdered, partly to see Hugh Dunsford once more. From where he sat Young could overhear the conversation in the bar. Dunsford was overwhelmed with inquiries as to his family, as to how he was getting on in Gippingford. There were a few awed inquiries "Be this the chair as Whitehead was sitting in when he was killed?" But the details of the murder were hardly alluded to, and certainly never discussed. It seemed to Young that the very mention of Whitehead's name imposed an instant hush upon the assembly. The subject would be immediately changed, to Ned Portch's misfortune in being detected in the illegal slaughter of the pig, and speculation of what it would cost him, or to some other topic of local interest.

This was contrary to all the Inspector's experience. Normally a murder, especially a murder of which the perpetrator was still at large, caused a tremendous sensation. The whole countryside talked of nothing else for weeks, and the centre of such conversation would naturally be the local inn. He could not avoid the impression that there was some sinister significance in the avoidance of the subject of the inhabitants of High Eldersham. It seemed to him, in the light of what he had already learnt, that everybody about him knew more about the matter than he did. Perhaps they were not aware of the identity of the actual murderer, but it would bring bad luck, perhaps even swift disaster, to refer to the subject at all. One more stranger had been removed from High Eldersham. The cause of his removal was better left unsought.

Young slept very little that night. For a long time he tossed and turned upon the narrow bed which had been assigned to him, and finally, in desperation, he dressed and crept quietly out of the house. The moon was just setting, casting a pale and uncertain light upon the flat country, over which a low steamy mist was creeping slowly from the sea. Above the mist stood out the tall tops of the trees, and below him, in the village, the summit of the church tower. All else was hidden, wrapped in mystery and silence.

The Inspector set out at a brisk pace along the old road, hoping that by tiring his muscles sufficiently he might induce the sleep which so craftily eluded him. But his brain refused to be lulled by the exercise, and persisted in turning over and over the amazing problem which confronted him. He, Inspector Young, notoriously the least imaginative and most practically minded man in Scotland Yard, had accepted as a fact the existence of witchcraft in High Eldersham, and was prepared to base his investigation into the murder of Whitehead upon this fantastic circumstance.

Stated thus, his position was ridiculous. What was witchcraft, anyhow? Witchcraft, he supposed, was one of the manifestations of the dominance of a superior intelligence over a backward community. Curious and inexplicable things happened among primitive peoples, so much was generally accepted. Various so-called explanations of these happenings had been put forward. They were due to hypnotism, to telepathy, to the operation of superior will-power. But no one had ever contended that the high priests of these mysteries, witchcraft, voodoo, black magic, call them what you like, had power to stab a man in the back without the intervention of human agency. From the bottom of his heart Young wished that he had never seen that confounded doll in Portch's cottage. It had obscured his vision, introduced a baffling subtlety into the problem. What did it indicate, after all? Nothing except possibly that Portch had a grudge against Whitehead, and had chosen this childish way in which to express it. Even so, there was nothing new in this, the existence of the grudge was common knowledge. Young told himself bitterly that he had allowed himself to be influenced by the atmosphere of High Eldersham, had fallen a victim to the ridiculous but generally held superstition that the place was in some undefined way queer. This being the case, he had been on the look out for something bizarre and unusual, and had persuaded himself that he had found it. Would it not be better to ask for permission to abandon the case, in order that it might be placed in the hands of some one with a less fervid imagination?

He must have covered a good five miles before he returned to the Rose and Crown. The dawn was breaking when at last he fell asleep.

The funeral of Mr. Whitehead took place on the following day at one o'clock. Young attended it, in common with most of the inhabitants of the village who were not at work. When it was over, he walked slowly back to the Rose and Crown. He noticed, as soon as he turned the corner, that a Rolls-Royce limousine, bearing a London registration number, and driven by a uniformed chauffeur, was standing outside the inn.

Young frowned. The car, he felt sure, must belong to some sensation monger, anxious to explore the scene of a crime which had already gained some notoriety in the newspapers. He was not in a mood to be asked questions, and he was on the point of turning back and waiting till the car should have driven on. It occurred to him, however, that he could enter the house by way of the yard and the back door, and so reach the kitchen without whoever was in the bar being aware of his presence. He crept in furtively, taking care that the sounds of his footsteps should not be heard.

The door between the kitchen and the bar was shut, but the panelling was thin, and through it Young could hear the sound of voices. One of them he recognised as Dunsford's, the other, he noticed with considerable surprise, was that of a woman. An argument of some kind was evidently in progress, and Young, inspired by curiosity, moved up closer to the door. Although he could not catch the woman's actual words, there was an unmistakable note of pleading in her tone. And when Dunsford answered her, it was in a low voice, in which the Inspector could detect more than a little uneasiness.

"It's no use, madam," he said. "As I've told you already, I can do nothing for you while I'm here. I can't think why you came all this way to see me. It's most imprudent."

"They told me at the Tower of London that you were here, and I told the chauffeur to find out the way and drive me here." The woman's voice trailed off into a whisper, and the Inspector could not hear the rest of her speech. But the words he had heard were in an educated voice, speaking with an urgency that aroused his utmost curiosity.

"No, madam, it's impossible. I haven't got it with me. You must wait until I get back to the Tower of London in a week or so. You had no business to run the risk of coming here. You might have given the whole game away. Why, there's a detective from Scotland Yard actually staying in this house. Fortunately, he's out just now, but he might come back at any moment. I must ask you to go away at once, before anybody sees you."

Dunsford's warning was evidently sufficient. Young heard a low cry of horror, and the sound of rapid footsteps. He slid rapidly out through the back door and into the yard. He was too late to catch sight of the woman, she had already entered the car and the chauffeur had started the engine. But, as the car drove away in the direction of Gippingford he read the number and made a note of it. He waited where he was for a few minutes, wondering who the visitor could have been, and trying to guess the purport of her conversation with Dunsford. Then emerging from his place of concealment, he walked into the house through the front door.

Dunsford started visibly at his entrance, but the Inspector hastened to lull his suspicions. "Hallo!" he exclaimed, with a glance round the empty bar. "You don't seem to be doing much business. Everybody is at the funeral, I suppose. I've just come up from there myself."

"Yes, things is pretty quiet," replied Dunsford, his face assuming an expression of obvious relief. "I haven't had a soul in here the whole morning."

After a hasty lunch, Young hired the village Ford, and drove to Gippingford. He went straight to the police station, and learnt to his relief that Superintendent Bass was not on the premises. He found, however, a most obliging sergeant on duty, who, at his request, placed the telephone at his disposal. Young put a trunk call through to London, and, as a result of his inquiries, discovered that the car of which he had noted the number was registered in the name of Mrs. Fowler, of Park Street. A colleague at Scotland Yard promised to make inquiries as to this lady, and let him know the result. This matter having been disposed of, Young engaged the sergeant in conversation.

"What do you know about the Tower of London, sergeant?" he asked.

"The Tower of London, sir?" replied the sergeant, with a puzzled expression. "Oh, you mean the pub in Water Street, sir—Dunsford's place. It's quite a respectable house, sir, and very well conducted. We never have any trouble with it, any more than we do with any of Thorold's houses. They're very particular about their tenants, sir. But the Tower of London isn't an ordinary pub, by any means. Dunsford has raised the tone of the place a lot since he has been there. He gets a very good class of people, visitors passing through the town use the place a great deal. The smoking room is more like an hotel lounge than anything else, although the house is not an hotel. That's to say there are no rooms for people to sleep in, sir."

As he drove back to High Eldersham, the Inspector tried to find some hypothesis which would explain the words he had overheard that morning. This Mrs. Fowler, assuming that she had been the occupant of the car, was obviously acquainted with the Tower of London, and had called there to ask Dunsford for something. Not finding him there, she had proceeded to the Rose and Crown, where her request was refused on the grounds that Dunsford "had not got it with him." What was this mysterious "it" and why should Mrs. Fowler's presence at the Rose and Crown "give the game away," presumably to the police? What game, in heaven's name? Could the incident have any connection with the murder of Whitehead? It seemed impossible, but perhaps some light would be thrown on the matter when he received some information regarding Mrs. Fowler.

There was nothing to be done but wait, and to this Young resigned himself with such patience as he could summon.

Wednesday passed without any further developments, and he was contemplating yet another night of inactivity when a car drove up to the Rose and Crown, and Merrion descended from it, looking pale and very weary.

Young greeted him warmly. "Well, old chap, have you found out anything bearing on the case?" he asked. "I haven't got much further, but a queer thing happened here yesterday that I'd like to tell you about."

"Don't tell me now, there's a good fellow," replied Merrion. "My brain isn't in a fit state to absorb anything fresh. I haven't been to bed since I saw you last, I've been reading steadily all the time. I only just come over to let you know I was back. I'm going to Gippingford now, to put up at an hotel and go to bed. I'll start for here again at nine o'clock to-morrow morning. You'd better start at the same time on foot and meet me on the road. It's safer than talking here."

"All right," agreed the Inspector reluctantly. "But can't you give me a hint before you go?"

"Well, I don't mind warning you that you're not likely to get much sleep on Saturday night," replied Merrion, as he started up the car and drove away.

Chapter IX

Before Inspector Young set out to keep his appointment on the following morning, he received a letter in reply to his inquiries as to Mrs. Fowler. That lady, it appeared, was an elderly and wealthy widow, who lived in considerable state, and spent a great part of her time attending meetings of the committees of the various charities with which she was connected. She was reputed to be of a very generous disposition, and had many friends in consequence. Beyond this, nothing of any interest was known about her.

Young frowned as he perused this letter. Although he had not actually seen the woman who had called at the Rose and Crown, he had heard her voice, which, as he remembered it, seemed to him more that of a young woman than of an elderly widow. Had Mrs. Fowler a companion, he wondered? The situation was baffling like everything else at High Eldersham. All he had learnt from the conversation he had overheard was that Dunsford had been apprehensive lest the unknown woman's visit should betray some secret to the police. There were two ways of approaching the secret, through the woman or through Dunsford. And neither of these methods of approach were devoid of difficulty.

It would be comparatively easy for Young to keep an eye on Dunsford, so long as he remained at the Rose and Crown. But he would shortly be returning to the Tower of London in Gippingford, and to watch him there would involve invoking the aid of the local police. Superintendent Bass might be efficient enough, but it would be too much to expect him to enter with enthusiasm into an investigation founded upon such a vague clue. On the other hand, if the unknown woman were made the point of departure, the matter could be kept in the hands of Scotland Yard. Her identity could no doubt be discovered by discreet questioning of Mrs. Fowler's chauffeur. And then, perhaps, if her movements were watched, some clue could be found to the mysterious business which had driven her to seek an interview with Dunsford.

Having resolved to communicate with his colleagues at the Yard, and meanwhile to say nothing locally, the Inspector set out to walk toward Gippingford. He met Merrion a couple of miles or so from the Rose and Crown, and, as before, the car was driven to a secluded spot by the roadside.

"Well, I suppose you want to hear the results of my researches into the subject of witchcraft," said Merrion, as soon as the car came to rest. "Of course, you realise that it isn't a subject like trigonometry, for instance. You can't swot it up from textbooks, I mean. They don't exist. One has to search through old records, and read the books of the modern investigators into those records like the excellent work of Miss Margaret Murray, for example. There are, of course, no contemporary records, since the witch-cult, in this country at any rate, is supposed to have ceased centuries ago.

"I'm not going to worry you with a lecture on the subject. All that I need tell you at the moment are a few points which seem to bear on the present case. In the first place, it is rather an interesting fact that witchcraft seems at one time to have flourished in this part of the world. There are records of witch-trials all over East Anglia. The tradition may have persisted in High Eldersham, handed down from father to son, so to speak. But as to that, I have my own private opinion, which is of no particular interest at present."

"Your private opinions are usually worth listening to, all the same," remarked the Inspector. "But, before you go any further, I want to have rather a clearer idea of what it all means. What was the object of witchcraft, anyhow, and how was it worked? We've all heard of people being bewitched, but nobody has ever defined what that means exactly."

Merrion smiled. "Not an easy question to answer, my friend," he replied. "It seems pretty generally agreed now that the witch-cult was—or is, if you prefer it—a survival of the worship of some pre-Christian deity. Originally, it was not necessary malignant, in the sense that it was not directed against those who did not practise it. But, in its decadent days, there is no doubt that the followers of the cult, the witches, in fact, took every opportunity of revenging them-selves against those who persecuted them. The records are full of instances of the enemies of the witches having suffered for their activities, either in person or property.

"The exact means by which the witches carried out these acts of revenge are impossible to determine. The records of the witch trials are so hopelessly unscientific that they afford no clue. You get condemnations of witches of having 'overlooked' their neighbours, or their neighbour's cattle, with dire results. In the majority of cases it seems probable that the misfortunes ascribed to evil influences were due to natural causes, and that the unfortunate witch, so-called, was innocent of any share in the matter. But now and then it seems evident that the accused person had actually produced the ill effects complained of.

"How the effect was produced seems never to have been investigated. Judges, witnesses, and the public appeared to be quite satisfied that it was due to the operation of some occult power, and never troubled to look any further. The witch had sold herself to the devil and, in return, had received the power of doing harm. The queer thing is that the witches themselves believed this to be the case. They frequently confessed that they had met the devil, usually in the shape of 'a black man,' who had promised them this mysterious power if they would worship him.

"In this more sceptical age we are inclined to believe that the occult power thus bestowed was insufficient, and that material means must have been employed to aid it. Now, if witches had been individuals, working on their own, so to speak, it might be difficult to imagine what these means were. But the witches were not solitary individuals, they were members of a community or coven, meeting periodically under the presidency of the devil. The grievances of the individual witch thus became the concern of the whole coven, with the result that a more or less extensive conspiracy was set on foot against the object of a witch's vengeance. What the witch could not effect alone several persons, working in secret for the same object, might easily accomplish. Do you get what I'm driving at?"

"Yes, I think so," replied the Inspector. "But there's just one point. A conspiracy of witches, who, I take it, were quite uneducated people, would have to be organised by some one if it hoped to succeed."

"Exactly. There is plenty of evidence that these conspiracies were so organised, and that by the devil. I don't mean by his Satanic Majesty himself, though the witches probably believed that their director was Satan in person. Each assembly of witches had a president, usually a man, who represented himself as the devil, and was known as such. It was he who directed the meetings of the covens, and determined upon the actions to be taken by the witches. The usual course for a witch who wished to take personal vengeance upon an enemy was to make a clay or waxen image, and to take it to the assembly. Here the devil received the image, and baptised it with the name of the intended victim, at the same time holding a needle in a candle and then plunging it into the heart of the image. I've been using the word witch, by the way, as a generic term to include both sexes. But witchcraft was not confined to the female sex. The male equivalent to the witches, the wizards, are frequently mentioned as members of the covens.

"There is an old saying that the devil looks after his own. This arose from the fact that the local devil took care, by issuing instructions to the members of the coven, or by taking action himself, that the intended victim suffered in the way promised to the witch. To the ignorant witches, the effect seemed supernatural, and the devil's prestige was correspondingly increased.

"The identity of the devil was always concealed behind a veil of elaborate and frequently most unedifying ritual, designed for the purpose of accentuating his supernatural character. Some of the more enlightened members of the coven may have suspected him to be mortal, but he was careful not to afford them any clue as to who he was. He always appeared in disguise, for instance. Actually, no doubt, he was some cunning individual who found it convenient to have at his disposal a band of followers devoted to his service. It is also probable that in most cases he was a man of superior education, a person of some standing in the parish, whose more highly-developed intelligence was capable of discovering means to injure the objects of the witches' dislike."

"Are you suggesting that there is such a person in High Eldersham at this moment?" interrupted the Inspector incredulously.

"At present I am only telling you the result of my researches," replied Merrion. "There may be such a person, or there may not, nor, if he exists, is it not necessary that he should reside in High Eldersham. His presence would be required only at the meetings of the coven—assuming that the doll, the only piece of evidence we have to go on, points to the existence of a coven. We have as yet no evidence of this supposititious person's identity, nor that he has any connection with the murder of Whitehead. In fact this, as I see it, is how we stand. We know that in Portch's cottage is, or was, a wax doll, evidently made by an amateur, pierced with a needle, in the eye of which is a tape bearing the name of Samuel Whitehead. We know that Portch had expressed a grievance against Whitehead. We are satisfied with Portch's alibi, and are convinced that he did not commit the murder. It's for you, not for me, to make deductions from these facts."

"It would have been simple enough three centuries ago," remarked the Inspector. "From what you have told me, we should deduce that Portch had effected the death of Whitehead by witchcraft. We should arrest him, adducing the doll in evidence, and he would promptly have been condemned. But I don't see myself convincing a jury on these lines to-day."

"No, we have to prove method as well as motive. All the same, ridiculous as it appears, I can't help thinking that witchcraft is at the bottom of this business. It can't be a coincidence that the doll was found in Portch's house. I mean that he can't have made it and stuck the pin into it as a gesture of spite, evolved out of his own brain, and without any knowledge of the significance ascribed at one time to such an act. He must have known of that significance, and believed in the efficacy of his act. How? Either because witchcraft is practised in High Eldersham, or because he has studied the subject. The second of these alternatives I refuse to contemplate. From what you tell me of Portch, he does not strike me as the kind of man who would go in for abstruse reading."

"Good lord, man, you don't seriously mean to suggest that this medieval superstition still persists here, do you?" exclaimed Young.

"I thought I'd made it clear that there was a good deal more than superstition in it," replied Merrion patiently. "Now look here, let me propound a theory which, however extraordinary, is independent of the influence of the occult. We will suppose, and it is by no means a far-fetched assumption, as any one familiar with the English countryside would tell you, that some vague memory of witchcraft actually persists here. I dare say that, within the memory of people still living, individuals were openly pointed out as witches, and credited with the evil eye, and other unpleasant attributes. Suppose again that somebody who had made a study of the subject became aware of the persistence of this tradition, and resolved to revive the actual cult to his own advantage.

"It would not be impossible for him to establish a coven, with himself as the leader or devil. I won't stretch the analogy between the past and the present too far. I won't suggest that his followers imagine him to be actually a supernatural being. But I do say that it would not be difficult to persuade them that he was a person endowed with powers beyond their understanding, behind whose disguise it would be inadvisable to pry. A few scientific conjuring tricks would be sufficient to impress the ignorant. And, if it were proved to them that this mysterious person had the power of annoying their enemies, his position would be established.

"I admit that this is a long way from the murder of Whitehead, or even from the misfortunes that befell the two strangers that you told me about the other day. But it is within the bounds of possibility that before these misfortunes occurred their images had been moulded and presented to the devil for baptism at the assembly of the coven. A fantastic idea, if you like. But then, the murder itself appears to me fantastic and motiveless."

"There may be something in what you say," remarked Inspector Young, after a long pause. "But, if there is, I don't see how on earth we are to verify it. If, as you suggest, the village is banded together in what is, in effect, a secret society, antagonistic to strangers, direct inquiry into the murder is not likely to help us, in spite of the fact that it may be common knowledge who perpetrated it. On the other hand, if we take up the clue of the mommet and pursue inquiries in that direction, we show our hand at once, and the coven, or whatever you call it, would merely suspend operations till the affair blew over. I'm blest if I know what to do, and that's a fact."

"You forget that the moon is full on Saturday," replied Merrion quietly.

"You keep on harping upon Saturday, and hinting that something will happen then," exclaimed Young irritably. "What about Saturday, and what the devil has the moon got to do with all this?"

"In the old days, the covens assembled on the night of the full moon. And, if there's any meeting of that kind in High Eldersham on Saturday, I'm going to do my best to be present."

Chapter X

Saturday turned out to be a bright, cold day, with a fresh breeze from the north-westward. Towards the evening, however, the wind backed to the south-west and the weather grew considerably milder. At the same time, fleecy masses of cloud began to float slowly across the hitherto clear sky.

Inspector Young spent the evening at the Rose and Crown, in a mood of bitter despondency. He had by now spent an entire week upon the investigation of what had seemed at first a comparatively simple murder, and he could not disguise from himself that he was no nearer the solution of the problem than he had been on the day of his arrival. Only that morning Colonel Bateman had called at the inn, ostensibly on his way elsewhere, and had asked him how he was getting on. His manner had been perfectly friendly, but the slight air of disappointment with which he heard Young's reply betrayed the fact that his faith in the efficacy of Scotland Yard was on the wane.

It was only at the urgent request of Merrion that Young had refrained from making routine inquiries throughout the village, and he wondered whether his action had been wise. After all, the clue that he was following was so intangible that it could scarcely be held to justify any delay in the investigation. But Merrion had pleaded so hard, had even declared that if nothing transpired on this very night he would be the first to abandon his fantastic hypothesis, that Young had consented to the plan they had worked out between them.

At last, unable to endure his own companionship any longer, the Inspector left the kitchen, which had been tacitly assigned to his use, and entered the bar. Although it was barely nine o'clock, the place was deserted. Dunsford seemed restless and ill at ease. He glanced up sharply as the Inspector came in, then resumed his task of polishing the glasses on the counter. This accomplished, he busied himself with various details in the room, stirring the fire, putting benches in their places against the wall, and so forth. The Inspector noticed his restlessness, so much at variance with the usual placidity of his nature, and wondered what could be the cause of it.

He made no remark, however, until the hands of the clock pointed to a few minutes to ten. "You don't look like getting any more customers to-night, Dunsford," he remarked. "Rather quiet for a Saturday evening, even in a place like this, isn't it? I expect things are different at the Tower of London?"

"Ah, you're right there," replied Dunsford. "I reckon the missus and Dick has got their work cut out about now. But it was always like this, here, even in my time. 'Tis too far from the village for the chaps to come, like."

"I should have thought that they would have enjoyed a short walk on an evening like this," remarked Young idly. "I shall certainly go out and take a turn for a few minutes before I go to bed."

It seemed to the Inspector that Dunsford started slightly. "Shouldn't do that, if I was you," he replied, after an instant's hesitation. "The wind's gone round, and like enough it'll rain before very long. I shouldn't wonder if that's what's kept the chaps away this evening."

"Oh, I'll chance the weather," said Young lightly. "A few drops of rain won't hurt me, and I shan't sleep if I don't get a bit of air."

"Well, perhaps you're right," agreed Dunsford rather unexpectedly. "If you think of going towards the village, I'll come with you. I've been meaning to look up some of the folk what I used to be friendly with when I lived here."

"I wasn't thinking of going towards the village," said the Inspector. "It isn't much of a walk, and I prefer the high road."

He rose as he spoke, opened the front door, and walked out. At that moment the full moon was shining brightly through a gap in the clouds, and the road was brightly illuminated. He set off at a smart pace in the direction of Gippingford, and, having walked fifty yards or so, looked suddenly over his shoulder, just in time to see Dunsford's head withdrawn rapidly from the doorway.

There could no longer be any doubt about it. Dunsford intended to keep a watch upon his movements, for some mysterious purpose of his own. He had tried to dissuade him from going out at all, and had then wished to accompany him towards the village. Now that he had set out in the opposite direction, Dunsford's anxiety appeared to be allayed. The Inspector kept on his way steadily, until he judged that his footsteps would be inaudible from the inn. Then, as an advancing cloud covered the moon, he stepped on to the grass by the side of the road, and began to make his way slowly back, under cover of the hedge. He would turn the tables on Dunsford and try to discover the secrets of that baffling publican.

Young reflected that he had at least an hour to spare before it was time for him to carry out the arrangement he had made with Merrion. He crept silently back, until he had reached a spot from which he could see both entrances to the inn. He had scarcely taken up his position, when he saw Dunsford emerge and, after a furtive look round, set off rapidly in the direction of the village.

Merrion, meanwhile, had not been idle. About ten o'clock he left his hotel at Gippingford, carrying a suit-case, and took out his car. He drove to a point, already reconnoitred, some two miles from the Rose and Crown, where the car could be run under the shelter of some trees, and would not be likely to be noticed by casual passers by. Here he stopped, and having extinguished his lamps, undressed and changed into the clothes he had brought with him in the suit-case. When he stepped out of the car, he was clad in breeches and an old shooting coat, with heavy boots and leggings.

It was quite plain that he had studied the country. Although the moon was momentarily hidden, and it was barely possible to see twenty yards ahead, he left the road and made straight for the gate of a field, which he vaulted easily. From there he set a course across country, with the object of approaching the village from the back. He was within a few hundred yards of an outlying farm, when the moon appeared from behind the clouds, flooding the open fields in front of him with its pale light.

He glanced up at the sky as he crouched beneath the nearest hedge. Another bank of clouds was driving slowly up, but it would be several minutes before it obscured the moon once more. There was nothing for it but to stay where he was; he would run too great a risk of being seen if he ventured into the open, and the hedge in which he lay hidden was the only cover for some distance round. He listened intently as he waited. The only sound that came to his ears was the barking of a dog, somewhere in the distance.

Then at last when the clouds had almost reached the moon, a figure came into sight from under the shadow of the farm. It was that of a woman, muffled in a cloak, with apparently a shawl covering her head. With infinite caution Merrion crept towards her, keeping the hedge between them. To his astonishment, she set off at a queer gait, half-running, half-walking, not towards the village, as he had expected, but in a direction which he knew would lead her to the river, a mile or so above the quay. Then, while he was still wondering whether to follow her or to keep on his original course, the moon disappeared, and he was left in darkness once more.

It was too late to follow the woman, even had he wished to. Her form was swallowed up in the gloom, and he was not sure enough of his bearings to strike off in the direction in which she had vanished. He decided to keep on towards the village and, giving the farm a wide berth, he took to the fields once more. At length he reached the point for which he had aimed, where a path led through a tangled thicket, close to the confines of the village.

He judged that it must by now be past eleven o'clock. Everything was very still about him, and he was wondering whether it would be possible to venture along the path into the village itself, when his keen ear caught the sound of hurrying footsteps advancing towards him. He shrank back into the undergrowth and waited. The footsteps drew nearer until they were abreast of him. Then, very faintly, he could discern a figure, clad as the first had been, in a skirt and cloak, with its head hidden in the depths of a hood. But this was no woman. By the shape of the figure and the length of its stride he knew it to be that of a man.

A thrill of excitement ran through Merrion as the figure passed. His conjectures had been right, down to the last detail. An assembly, following the old tradition in every respect, was to be held. But, in the midst of his exultation, he cursed himself for his own lack of precaution. Too late he remembered that those who attended the Witches'

Sabbath did so "clad in female garb, cloaked and hooded, men and women alike." Dressed as he was, he could never hope to make his way into the Assembly. The utmost he could do would be to lie in wait and learn what he could from a distance.

The footsteps drew away from him and died out. But, after an interval, others followed them. Securely hidden in the thick bracken, Merrion witnessed the passing of a strange shadowy procession of hooded figures, hurrying silently, singly and in pairs, along the path before him. Not one of these figures spoke or turned their faces aside. They pressed onward through the darkness, apparently oblivious of everything save the necessity of reaching their destination. They moved as figures in a dream, hurrying onward, seeming to glide rather than walk. They gave the impression of floating through the air, of touching the ground scarcely with their toes; their cloaks, caught now and then by the breath of the south-west breeze, floated round them like dark and ominous wings. Merrion, in spite of his robust nerves, felt a sudden thrill of supernatural terror, as though the cold hand of evil had reached out and clutched him. It was only with a powerful effort that he restrained himself from turning aside and fleeing from a spot which he felt to be accursed.

But he held his ground, and the passing of the figures grew less frequent until it ceased altogether. When the last of the footsteps had died away in the distance, Merrion emerged cautiously from his hiding place and prepared to follow them. But, even as he did so, he heard a sound behind him, and shrunk back again into cover. The sound advanced swiftly; it was evidently that of some last straggler, hurrying to overtake those who had gone before.

At that moment, to Merrion's horror, the moon burst through the clouds once more, and the path was flooded with the ghostly radiance that penetrated through the leafless branches above it. He dared not move, although he was within a yard of the path and could scarcely fail to be seen by any one who looked in his direction. The cloaked and hooded figure advanced, the moon shining full upon it as it crossed the patches of light. Merrion stood rigid, holding his breath, ready to run for it if he should be discovered. This time the figure was unmistakably that of a woman, and Merrion calculated that he could make his escape before he could be recognised.

But the figure looked neither to the right nor to the left. It came towards him with that queer floating gait, which was neither walking nor running, swaying slightly from side to side. Its cloak spread out on either side, brushing the twigs as it passed. But the deep hood hid the face, of which at last Merrion could see the eyes glowing in the shadow like points of flame. And then Merrion knew that he was safe. Those eyes, fixed rigidly on some unseen point, never wavered for an instant in their set intensity. And then, with a shock of horror, the truth dawned upon him. The woman was in a trance, a trance which made her oblivious of everything save some fixed and mysterious purpose.

She passed him so close that by stretching out his hand he could have touched her. For an instant the moon shone into the depths of her hood, and Merrion's heart leapt. It was Mrs. Portch and she was carrying the doll, still with that sinister needle driven through its heart.

This time he waited until fully five minutes had elapsed since her passing. No further sound came to him, no further figures came hurrying from the direction of the village. Merrion stepped on to the path, and strode along it rapidly in the direction in which the procession had disappeared. It emerged from a thicket and wound through the fields, ever tending slightly down hill, towards the banks of the river. A high hedge ran along one side of it, and Merrion was careful to keep in the shadow of this. Beyond the shadow the country was brightly illuminated. He could see the line of the river, and, some distance ahead, a tall dark patch, which he made out to be a group of trees.

At length the hedge came to an end, and Merrion paused irresolute. He looked up at the sky, and shook his head despondently. The moon was sailing in a clear vault, surrounded by stars, and there was not a cloud upon the horizon. He could not reckon upon the friendly cover of darkness, at least for some time to come. A wide band of silver stretched before him; it was high tide, and the river filled its channel from bank to bank. A couple of hundred yards from where he stood, it forked into several branches, probably muddy ditches at low water, but now deep and unfordable. Two of these branches enclosed what he took at first to be an island, and in the centre of this stood the clump of trees which he had already seen in the distance. Looking more closely, he saw that they stood on what was not strictly an island. A narrow causeway connected it to the mainland, and at the end of this causeway stood two cloaked figures, rigid and motionless as sentries.

Everything was clear to him now. The meeting-place of the coven was in the heart of the grove of trees, secure from observation. It was obviously impossible to cross the causeway under the eyes of the sentries. Merrion had for a moment the idea of trying to swim across one of the branches of the river, but in order to do that it would be necessary for him to leave the shadow of the hedge and come out into the open, courting certain discovery by those motionless figures.

As he stood there, baffled and hesitating, a pin-point of light appeared between the trunks of the trees. It was followed by others, until he could count a dozen or more feeble and flickering glimmers. The mysterious meeting had opened.

Chapter XI

About the same time that Merrion saw the points of light appearing among the trees, Inspector Young, who had been watching in the vicinity of the Rose and Crown for Dunsford's return, walked down the side road towards High Eldersham. He noticed that the village street was deserted, and that no lights were visible in the cottage windows, but this was not unusual at half-past eleven at night. He made straight for Doctor Padfield's door, and rang the bell. Somewhere in the depths of the house he could hear it pealing loudly.

For a while there was no reply. Then a flickering light appeared in the fan-light above the door, which gradually grew brighter. Footsteps sounded within the hall, and the door was unlocked. At length it opened, revealing the form of Doctor Padfield, clad in a dressing-gown, with a candlestick in his hand. "What do you want?" he inquired.

Until now, the Inspector had been standing in the shadow, but at Doctor Padfield's words he stepped into the doorway. The doctor stared at him for a moment, a variety of emotions, among which the most prominent was astonishment, struggling for expression in his eyes. "Inspector Young!" he exclaimed at last. "I did not expect to see you at this time of night. Don't stand there. Come in, and tell me what I can do for you."

The Inspector entered the hall, and the doctor closed the door behind him. "I was on the point of going to bed when I heard your ring," continued the latter. "I keep early hours, you see. I never know when I may be called out to a confinement or some other urgent case. Come into my study; I think there is the remains of a fire there."

He led the way, and Young followed him into a small room, plainly furnished, and lined with cases containing medical books. Here the doctor lighted a lamp and poked up the fire. This done, he scanned the Inspector's face anxiously. "Well, tell me what I can do for you," he said.

"I'm sorry to put you to all this trouble," replied Young cheerfully. "The fact is, doctor, I've a nasty twinge of rheumatism in my shoulder. I've had it for a couple of days now, and I can't rest properly at night. I was wondering whether you could give me anything to ease it a bit."

Doctor Padfield sank into a chair, as though suddenly overcome by fatigue. "Rheumatism?" he said. "There's a fortune waiting for the man who finds a cure for that. I can give you something that will relieve it, I dare say. A few grains of sodium salicylate will do that. I'll give you some in a minute or two. But you're not in any hurry, I suppose?"

"I'm in no particular hurry," replied Young. "But I don't want to keep you out of bed, doctor."

"Oh, you needn't worry about that," said Doctor Padfield hastily, rising and going to a cupboard in the corner of the room, from which he took a decanter and a couple of glasses. "I was only going to bed because there was nothing in particular to stay up for. I'm a lonely man, Inspector. Marriage has never appealed to me, and I've lived in this house for twenty years with nobody but my old housekeeper to talk to. You can imagine that when anybody fresh comes in to see me, I'm not anxious for them to go away. Try some of this whisky. It's pre-war, and I'm sorry to say there isn't much of it left."

"I can quite believe that you find life in High Eldersham a bit dull, doctor," replied Young. "The people here can hardly be congenial company for you."

Doctor Padfield smiled a curiously one-sided smile. "The people here are all right when you understand them," he said. "I'm one of them myself, as I dare say you know already. We're queer folk, Inspector, with a rooted mistrust of strangers, which I suppose makes them mistrust us. But, as a matter of fact, we're simple enough at heart when we're allowed to go our own way. I don't want to touch on forbidden subjects, but I'm willing to bet that it wasn't a native of High Eldersham who killed that poor chap Whitehead."

"Maybe not," replied Young. "But I've learnt even in the short time that I've been here that the people of High Eldersham don't altogether relish the presence of the police in their midst."

Doctor Padfield raised his glass and looked at it thoughtfully, as though to find inspiration in the amber fluid it contained. "Now, I wonder what exactly you mean by that remark," he murmured.

"I was thinking of Dunsford," replied the Inspector. "It's quite obvious to me that he would be immensely relieved if I were to take up my quarters anywhere but at the Rose and Crown."

Again Doctor Padfield smiled. "I can quite believe it," he said. "And I think you'd find the same mistrust anywhere else in this village. You can't expect us to regard the law quite in the same way as you do, you know. Laws are made, and it is your business to enforce them. But we, in common with most country folk, regard a good many laws as unnecessary and ridiculous, and we do our best to evade them. You've already had an instance of it in the case of Ned Portch and his pig. What harm could it possibly do anybody if he did slaughter it in his own back yard? None, as you know well enough. Yet, in the eyes of the law, though certainly not in the eyes of anybody in this village, it is an offence, and he will be fined for it.

"It's probably the same with Dunsford. Morally speaking, why shouldn't he serve a customer out of hours, or commit any other of a thousand technical offences? I dare say he does quite a nice little business selling pheasants and hares, even in the close season, and without a licence to sell game. Keepers have to shoot them sometimes, you know, and it would be a pity to waste them. And all the time you're up there the wretched man is on tenterhooks, in case you should find him out. I don't wonder he wishes you at the bottom of the sea sometimes."

The conversation lasted for some time longer, Young finding the doctor a most entertaining companion. It was not until nearly half-past one that the Inspector rose and took his leave. As he walked through the village he noticed that lights showed in more than one cottage window. This was certainly significant, and he hastened his steps accordingly. When he reached the corner he glanced at the Rose and Crown, and saw that a light was burning in the room occupied by Dunsford.

But he did not enter the inn. He walked swiftly past, taking care that his footsteps made no sound. Once safely past he continued along the road until he reached the spot where Merrion's car stood drawn up under the trees.

There was no sign of life, and Young supposed for the moment that Merrion had not yet returned. He opened the door prepared to sit and wait for him, but as he did so a figure huddled in the corner yawned and stretched itself, and he heard Merrion's voice in sleepy protest. "Hallo, where the dickens have you been all this time? I've been waiting for you half an hour or more."

"I've been sitting talking to Doctor Padfield and drinking his whisky," replied Young. "And a very interesting chap I found him."

"Oh, you have, have you," said Merrion. "Enjoying the good things of life while I've been doing your job for you. Well, I've had a most interesting evening too. I'll tell you all about it, if you'll sit still and not interrupt. I've been transported back through the centuries, and to-morrow I shall find it difficult to believe that what I saw was real and not a particularly vivid dream."

Merrion proceeded to give an account of his adventures, up to the moment when he saw the lights appearing among the trees. "As I told you," he continued, "it was quite impossible for me to get any closer without my being discovered, and that was the last thing I wanted to risk. So I just stayed where I was and waited. Of course, I hadn't the slightest doubt by this time that an assembly of the coven, a Witch's Sabbath, as it was called in the old days, was taking place on the island. Everything was exactly in accordance with the descriptions preserved in the old records. The men and women dressed alike, cloaked and hooded, the curious trance-like gait and fixity of expression. And then the incident of Mrs. Portch carrying the doll. I tell you, whoever runs this show has taken great care to follow tradition in every detail."

"It's the most extraordinary story I've ever heard," commented Young. "But I don't understand this trance-like state. All these people can't have been hypnotised before they started, can they?"

"No, I don't think they were hypnotised. The witches who confessed to attending Sabbaths always spoke of being conveyed to and from the scene by some mysterious means. They usually spoke of flying, which gave rise to the popular conception of witches flying on broomsticks. The explanation seems to have been a comparatively simple one. They were given a preparation which they rubbed into their skin, which produced a temporary trance or delirium. While under the influence of this preparation, they were unconscious of everything except their immediate object. Later, they would not remember having walked to the assembly. They just knew that they had got there, and supposed they had been transported miraculously. Elizabeth Style, one of the witches whose confessions are preserved, stated that 'before they are carried to their meetings, they anoint their foreheads and hand-wrists with an oyle the Spirit brings them, and they are carried in a very short time.' Elsewhere recipes have been found for the preparation of this 'oyle' or ointment. The basis consisted of the fat of babies, bat's blood, and all sorts of other horrible ingredients. But with these were incorporated aconite and belladonna, which were the active principles. Modern medical authorities have stated that such a composition might well produce trance or delirium, and give the sensation of flying through the air. And I don't doubt that the people I saw to-night had been using some modern equivalent of this ointment."

"The preparation of which would imply some knowledge of medicine," remarked the Inspector, after a long pause. "I understand now why you asked me to call on Doctor Padfield this evening. You fancied he might be the devil, the high priest of these mysteries. He's ruled out, anyhow, since he was at home while the assembly was proceeding. But how would Dunsford strike you as a possible candidate? He's been behaving rather oddly to-night."

Merrion listened to Young's account of Dunsford's behaviour. "It's possible that Dunsford is the devil," he said thoughtfully. "I didn't know. I couldn't get the slightest clue to the president of the assembly. But I'll wager that Doctor

Padfield knew that it was being held. I can't help thinking that his hospitality was exerted to keep you safely indoors while the members of the coven returned home. However, I may be misjudging him.

"Anyhow, you had better hear the rest of my adventures. I stayed under that hedge for about half an hour or so, waiting. Nothing much happened, only those lights kept on flickering among the trees. They were candles held by the members of the assembly, I fancy. That was part of the rite. You've heard of holding a candle to the devil, haven't you? And the candles were not merely of ritual significance. The devil would want some sort of light to see what he was doing by. It must have been pretty dark under those trees, in spite of the moon.

"After a bit, I saw rather a stronger glow, as if a fire had been lighted. This puzzled me a bit, until I remembered something I had come across the other day. It seems that when anybody died as the result of the machinations of the witches, the mommet representing that person was taken to the next assembly and there solemnly burnt. The person's soul was dedicated to the devil, who had brought about the death. The burning of the mommet was symbolic of the consigning of the soul to hell, the devil's kingdom. That's why Mrs. Portch took the doll representing Whitehead to the assembly with her.

"In a few minutes the fire died down, and then the candles were extinguished, one by one. I knew that marked the close of the meeting, and that it was high time for me to clear out. I was right on the path by which the people must come back to the village. So I made my way back to the thicket, and chose a place where I could see those who passed without any danger of being seen myself. I hadn't been there long before they began to troop back again in that curious trance-like state. Then, when I was sure they had all passed, I left my hiding-place and struck across country towards the car. I had an idea of going back to the island and exploring it. But I reflected that it was a bit risky, and that the exploration could wait till daylight.

"I was about half-way here, when I heard what I thought at first was a car on the road. I stopped and listened, and then I made out that it was a motor boat on the river. It was going upstream, away from the island and therefore away from the village. I was much too far from the river to be able to see the boat, much as I should have liked to. For it was at least possible that this motor boat contained the devil, who had waited for the dispersal of his worshippers before departing in this prosaic manner."

"Somehow, the idea of the devil in a motor boat sounds too utterly fantastic," remarked the Inspector.

"The whole business is fantastic, and, to me at least, utterly incomprehensible!" exclaimed Merrion. "What is the object of this elaborate mumbo-jumbo, and who is the organiser at the bottom of it? It wasn't got up for the purpose of disposing of the unfortunate Whitehead, of that I'm perfectly certain. Of course, that murder has enormously increased the prestige of the devil, whoever he is. One of his worshippers has a grudge against the man, a mommet is baptised, and the man dies. It is an extraordinary and rather alarming manifestation of his power. But there's more in it than that. The whole business has been got up for some obscure purpose, you mark my words. And to that purpose we haven't as yet got the slightest clue."

"Well, in spite of your confirmation of the fact that witch-craft, or at least a colourable imitation of it, is practised in High Eldersham, we don't seem to have got much further," remarked the Inspector despondently.

"There's time yet. The business isn't finished, by a long way. There's one thing I haven't told you. As I said, I watched the members of the coven as they returned from the assembly.

I was too far away to recognise them, even if their faces hadn't been hidden by their hoods. But one thing I noticed, without any fear of being mistaken. One of them, a man this time, was carrying a doll. It wasn't the one Mrs. Portch had taken with her, of that I'm certain. It's a pretty safe assumption that that doll was made and baptised during the meeting."

"By jove! I'd give a good deal to know the name that was given to it!" exclaimed the Inspector.

"So would I," agreed Merrion sombrely.

Chapter XII

As the result of a consultation in the car, which lasted until the grey light of dawn began to appear in the eastern sky, Inspector Young and Merrion decided to approach the problem from different directions.

"You'll never get any forrader, even if you cross-examine every soul within ten miles of this place," said Merrion positively. "Even if it's common knowledge who killed Whitehead, which I am very much inclined to doubt, these people won't give anything away. You say you have a suspicion that Dunsford is engaged in some illegal activity, which may possibly be connected with Whitehead's death. If I were you, I would follow up any clue you may have in that direction. For my own part, I'm going to try to get to the bottom of this witchcraft business. If I'm successful, we ought to see our way a bit clearer. I know how to get in touch with you if I want you. Of course, I'll report progress—if I make any, that is."

With that he drove off to Gippingford and his belated rest.

He spent the greater part of Sunday in bed. On Monday, shortly before noon, he paid his hotel bill, and drove away from Gippingford along the London road. A few miles outside the town he turned off to the right, and, after a circuitous journey, found himself at a point some ten miles north of High Eldersham. It was then between half-past two and three. He drove on towards the village, and turned up the drive which led to Elder House.

Here he rang the bell, which was answered by a parlour-maid. On inquiring for Mr. Hollesley, he was informed that that gentleman was just finishing a late lunch, having only just returned from London. He was shown into the study, where in a few minutes Hollesley joined him.

"Hallo, Merrion!" exclaimed the latter as he shook hands. "It's very good of you to look me up like this. I didn't expect to see you in this part of the world again so soon. As a matter of fact, I've only just come back myself. I've been in London ever since I saw you last."

"I'm on my way to Hunstanton again for a few days, to play golf," replied Merrion. "Since I had practically to pass your door, I thought I might just as well look in and see if you were at home."

"Capital!" said Hollesley heartily. "Look here, your time's pretty much your own, I suppose? Why don't you stop here for the night, and go on to-morrow? We could have a quiet yarn this evening."

After some demur, Merrion agreed. The necessary arrangements having been made, Hollesley turned once more to his visitor. "I want to go over to the Hall and see the Owertons," he said. "You know who they are, you saw them at the inquest the other day, and I told you about them at lunch afterwards. You'd better come too; they're jolly nice people, and I'm sure they'll be glad to meet you. You'll find the old boy well worth talking to."

They set out together through the grounds of Elder House, until they reached a gate which gave access to the park surrounding the hall. Both estates were bordered by the river, which, after passing by the village, followed a tortuous course towards the sea. It swept in a wide curve round the park, and then bounded the fields belonging to Elder House, finally approaching within a couple of hundred yards of the house. Three miles or so further on, it joined the sea through a gap in the long line of sand-dunes which fringed the coast.

"We're next door neighbours, you see," said Hollesley, as he opened the gate. "There's the house, you can see it through the trees. It's not a very big place, but parts of it are very old. I think you'll agree it's well worth seeing."

They were admitted by an old servant, who, it struck Merrion, did not appear any too pleased to see them. "Sir William is in the library, sir," he replied, in answer to Hollesley's inquiry. "Miss Mavis is not at home. I believe she is down by the river."

He led the way, almost reluctantly, to the library, and ushered in the visitors. It was a very beautiful room, fully panelled, with a magnificently painted ceiling. It was so full of books that little room remained for furniture. Bookcases stood out at right angles to the walls, leaving narrow passages between them to enable their contents to be reached. Only in front of the fireplace, a magnificent example of ancient ironwork, was there anything like a clear space. And here, in an arm-chair to which a reading-table was affixed, sat Sir William Owerton.

He rose, as Hollesley and Merrion entered the room, with surprising agility, considering his years. He was certainly a distinguished looking old gentleman, thought Merrion, seeing him thus close at hand. "Ah, so you are back again, Laurence?" he said. "It is very good of you to come over so soon after your return. How did you find your mother when you came back?"

"Very much as usual," replied Hollesley. "She seems more cheerful, though, now that the spring is coming on. Let me introduce Mr. Merrion. We were together in the war, but curiously enough never met again until we ran into one another the other day. He happened to be passing when the inquest on that poor chap Whitehead was taking place, and dropped in out of curiosity. I saw him at the back of the room, and that's why I ran away so suddenly."

"I am very glad to meet any friend of Laurence's," replied Sir William courteously. "Are you staying in this secluded district of ours for any length of time, Mr. Merrion?"

"Only until to-morrow, sir," replied Merrion. "Hollesley has very kindly invited me to spend the night at Elder House. I was greatly interested in that inquest, although I only attended out of curiosity. The verdict was one of murder, I remember. I have kept my eye on the paper for further news, but the case does not appear to have been mentioned. Has any clue been found to the murderer?"

"I believe not," replied Sir William. "I do not go out very much, but most of the gossip of the village comes to my ears, one way or another. I am told that there is a detective-inspector from Scotland Yard staying at the Rose and Crown. What progress he has made in the matter, I cannot say."

"Staying at the Rose and Crown, is he?" remarked Hollesley. "I wonder how he gets on with old Dunsford, who has come back to take charge of the place temporarily! In my opinion, he's wasting his time. I'd bet any money that the murderer won't be found in High Eldersham. They're primitive folk in these parts, in many ways, but there's not a man in the place who would commit a brutal murder like that."

"I am inclined to agree with you," said Sir William. "I am of the opinion that the murder was committed by some one passing along the road. Crimes of violence appear to be on the increase, I regret to say."

The conversation was interrupted by the entrance of Mavis Owerton. Hollesley rose swiftly and advanced to greet her, but she merely nodded at him and went up to her father. "I'm so sorry," she said. "I didn't know until Christy told me just now that he was keeping tea waiting till I came in. I told him to be as quick as he could."

"Never mind, my dear, a few minutes more or less do not matter. This is Mr. Merrion, a friend whom Laurence has brought over to see us."

"I think I saw you at the inquest the other day, Mr. Merrion," said Mavis, rather distantly, Merrion thought. His quick wits were at work trying to discover the relations between these people. But at present he was baffled. Sir William was evidently a scholar at heart, with few interests outside his library. Mavis—well, Mavis he could not analyse. She was many-sided as a diamond, her interests covered everything, from the antiquities of the house to the speed-boat which she had just purchased. With one exception, Merrion noticed. In spite of Hollesley's efforts, he seemed unable to interest her in anything that he had seen or heard in London during the past week. In fact, she barely listened to him, and devoted the greater part of her attention to Merrion. Before very long the two of them were involved in a lively discussion upon boats and their behaviour.

"You must come down and see this new toy of mine, Mr. Merrion," she said, as soon as tea was over. "You needn't worry about leaving father, Laurence can stay and talk to him. It's quite close, only down at the bottom of the park."

"I don't see why I shouldn't see it too, Mavis!" exclaimed Hollesley. "Why shouldn't we all go, Sir William?"

"I have already inspected this new toy," replied Sir William. "I cannot say that it holds any great attraction for me."

"Father won't even come for a run in her," Mavis put in. "You can see her for yourself at any time, Laurence. I want Mr. Merrion to look at her. He's got ideas about boats. Come on, Mr. Merrion."

In spite of the annoyance visible in Hollesley's face, Merrion rose and followed the girl from the room. She led the way out of the house by a side door, and they were soon walking side by side across the closely cropped turf of the park, Mavis talking animatedly about the boat. It was not for some time that Merrion found the opportunity of making a remark. Then, abruptly he voiced what was in his mind. "I say, Miss Owerton, I don't think Hollesley was best pleased at being left behind."

"Really, Mr. Merrion, you're a most observant person," she replied mockingly. "For my part I am quite sure he wasn't. Laurence isn't in the habit of hiding his feelings when he's thwarted. How well do you know him, Mr. Merrion?"

"Well, I used to know him fairly well once," replied Merrion, rather taken aback by the question. "That was when we were together during the war. But I lost sight of him after that, and we never met again till the other day."

"When, I suppose, he asked you to come and stay with him as soon as he got back from London?"

"Well, no. As a matter of fact he did not ask me to stay until I looked in to see him just now, and then only for the night."

"Oh, that's all right!" exclaimed Mavis, with obvious relief. "I was afraid you were some part of his plan. I couldn't quite make out what part you were to play. That's why I asked you to come down and see the boat."

Merrion laughed heartily. "I assure you, Miss Owerton, that I'm not conspiring with Hollesley in any way. I don't even know anything about this nefarious plot of his. Has he got one?"

"I should have thought that it was fairly obvious to any one of your powers of observation," she replied. "Laurence is determined to marry me, and I'm equally determined not to marry him. I get quite a lot of amusement out of watching him trying to get round father, who would, I'm sure, like to see the young people happy. Between you and me, Mr. Merrion, I think Laurence's game was to land you with father this afternoon, leaving him free to dance attendance on me. As it is, we've managed to get to windward of him. Well, there she is. What do you think of her?"

They had reached the shores of the river. Moored in the stream, a few paces from the bank, was a squat-looking speed-boat, brightly varnished, with a tiny cockpit just big enough to hold two people. Merrion looked at her appreciatively. His trained eye scanned her lines and the possibilities of speed which they indicated. "Looks as if she could travel," he remarked.

"She can!" exclaimed Mavis enthusiastically. "Come on, we'll go for a run in her. There's just time before it gets dark. Help me launch the dinghy. That's right!"

Almost in spite of himself, Merrion became infected with her enthusiasm. They pushed the dinghy, a frail little prahm, off the mud, and boarded the speed-boat. "I'll take the helm," declared Mavis. "I know the river, and you'd probably run her on the mud. We shall have to go downstream, the tide's running out fast, and there won't be enough water to get far above the quay at High Eldersham. When the tide's in, you can go for miles beyond that, up to Elderminster, in fact. It's a pity you aren't staying longer, or I would take you up there to-morrow. All right, let go!"

Merrion cast off the moorings, and with the engine purring softly, the boat shot out into midstream. Mavis steadied her, and then, as she opened the throttle, they tore down the river at full speed in a cloud of spray.

"I told you she could move!" shouted Mavis, above the now almost deafening roar of the engine. "Look, there's Elder House already. That five-tonner moored under the bank is Laurence's. Not a bad craft, but she doesn't carry enough sail for me. That little sailing dinghy of mine can make rings round her in a breeze."

They shot by Hollesley's little yacht in a flash, and entered a long and comparatively straight reach. The line of the dunes came in sight, and they neared them rapidly, until the entrance of the river opened before them. A slight swell was rolling in over the bar, but the speed-boat rode it like a duck. Within a very few minutes of their departure they were out on the grey waters of the North Sea.

"Hold on!" cried Mavis. As Merrion clutched the coaming in front of him she turned the wheel over, and the boat swung in a sharp circle, nearly flinging them from their seats. At the same tremendous speed as before they shot in through the entrance and between the muddy banks that bordered the channel, the boat making light of the ebb tide that sluiced out against her. Mavis brought her up to her moorings and switched off the engine. "Now!" she said triumphantly, in the sudden silence. "Isn't she topping?"

Merrion gazed at the face of the girl beside him, lighted up with the excitement of the run. "She is!" he replied fervently. But he was thinking rather of the girl than of the boat.

Mavis turned her head aside quickly. "Get the dinghy alongside, will you, Mr. Merrion?" she said coldly. "We must be getting back; Laurence will wonder what has become of us."

They landed and walked up towards the house in a slightly awkward silence. It was not until they had reached the door that Mavis spoke. "I wish you were staying longer, Mr. Merrion," she said. "We could have gone for a run up the coast."

"I should have enjoyed nothing more, Miss Owerton," replied Merrion meekly.

They entered the library together, Merrion with a slightly guilty feeling. Hollesley rose as they came in. "It's time we were getting back, Merrion," he said curtly. "I have one or two letters to write before dinner."

He said good-bye to Sir William, but contented himself with a nod in Mavis's direction. The two walked back to

Elder House, Hollesley curiously unresponsive to Merrion's attempts at conversation. The former led his guest to the study. "You'll be all right here, won't you?" he said. "I'll send Thorburn in with the whisky. Dinner's at eight, by the way."

And with that he left the room. Merrion could hear him dragging his feet heavily up the staircase, as though a great weariness had suddenly overtaken him.

Chapter XIII

Hollesley's manner did not presage a very cheerful evening. But, greatly to Merrion's surprise, his host came down to dinner in a more companionable mood than he had ever seen him. He seemed to have undergone a complete transformation. All trace of weariness had left him; the curiously haggard expression which Merrion had noticed during the afternoon had entirely disappeared. His eyes sparkled, and the smallest things seemed to cause him amusement.

Dinner was consequently a very gay meal. It was excellently cooked, and most deftly served by Thorburn, who once more struck Merrion as the ideal butler. The conversation touched upon a thousand subjects, without either referring to the incidents of the afternoon. It was not until they were seated over a bottle of priceless port—of which, Merrion noticed, Hollesley partook very sparingly—that the latter referred to their visit to the Hall.

"It was just like Mavis to rush you off like that and take you for a run in that new speed-boat of hers," he remarked. "She's like a child with a new toy, and you were somebody fresh to show it to. She'll soon get tired of it, though. I don't think much of these fast motor boats myself. They are no use in anything of a breeze, and one would soon get bored with tearing up and down the river. And that's about all they're good for, really."

"Oh, I don't know," replied Merrion carelessly. "I should think one might get some very good fun, even on the river. Miss Owerton told me that one could get right up to Elderminster at high water. I expect that there are a good many motor boats kept between here and there, aren't there?"

"Not many, so far as I know. Mavis is about the only motor boat enthusiast that I know of in these parts. But then I don't know much about the river above the quay. I prefer going out to sea in my own little craft—you probably saw her as you passed, if you can see anything going at that pace. Mind you, I consider the marine motor an excellent thing in its proper place. I've got an auxiliary motor in my boat, and find it very handy in a calm. But I prefer sailing any day. You must come down some time in the summer, and we'll have a cruise together."

"I'd like nothing better. I don't know this coast at all well, and I should like to improve my acquaintance of it. If it is all like this, it must be very fascinating. High Eldersham strikes me as being one of the queerest places I have ever seen."

Hollesley laughed heartily. "You're like all town dwellers, Merrion," he said. "As soon as you come upon a remote and unspoiled piece of country, you immediately describe it as queer. The villagers of High Eldersham would find London just as queer, if they ever went there, which fortunately for them, they don't. Gippingford is about the limit of their travels. But I'd like to know, as a matter of curiosity, what you find queer about this place."

"It's difficult to define exactly. I admit that I'm a town dweller, but I can claim to know the English countryside fairly well, for all that. High Eldersham is somehow different from anywhere else I know. One gets the impression that it is a survival from the middle ages."

"So, in a sense, it is," replied Hollesley. "After all, that's only natural. No main road passes through it, and the nearest railway station, and that a very unimportant one, at which only two or three trains stop, is six miles away. There is no inducement for people from the outside world to come here. High Eldersham is a little community by itself. The inhabitants intermarry between themselves, and it is very rarely indeed that any fresh blood is introduced. I don't suppose there has been any change in the place since it ceased to be a comparatively flourishing little port, and that is well over a hundred years ago."

"Perhaps queer was the wrong adjective," remarked Merrion. "By gad, Hollesley, this is a wonderful port of yours. I didn't mean to cast any aspersions upon your native village. Interesting, is really what I meant. It ought to be a happy hunting-ground for those johnnies who amuse themselves hunting up folklore and writing books about it. The place must be full of old customs and superstitions and survivals like that."

"I dare say it is," replied Hollesley indifferently. "Personally, I'm not particularly interested in that kind of thing. Old Owerton is the man to tell you all about that, he's a regular mine of information upon those subjects. But I don't fancy that any stranger who came poking round here would learn very much. An oyster isn't in it for closeness compared with these village folk. You've no idea how good they are at playing stupid if you're trying to find out anything they don't want to tell you. What do you say to knocking the balls about for a bit? There's a very decent fire in the billiard room."

It was well past midnight when they went to bed, but Merrion, in spite of the luxurious comfort of his room, was unable to sleep. He had succeeded almost beyond his expectations in making the acquaintance of the Owertons and in the opportunity to sound his host. But the result had not been very satisfactory. He was pretty certain that the motor boat which he heard the previous night had not been Mavis Owerton's speed-boat. The sound of the engine had been entirely different. Besides, he would not entertain for a moment the idea that Mavis could possibly have anything to do with the strange rites which he had witnessed from a distance. What could there be in common between Mavis, as he pictured her, bright-eyed, leaning forward over the wheel of the speed-boat as though to inspire that lively craft with every ounce of her own resistless energy, and the sinister ceremonies of a forgotten cult? Nothing, nothing at all.

And yet he had gleaned a few scraps of information that he dare not disregard. Motor boats were scarce upon the river, and Mavis was a well-known motor-boating enthusiast. Her father, according to Hollesley, was an authority upon ancient customs and superstitions. Was it possible that the clue which he sought was to be found at the Hall? He thrust the notion from him, but it returned again and again with maddening persistence. At last he fell into a troubled sleep, in which he dreamed that he was sitting once more in the speed-boat beside Mavis, who was urging the craft to her utmost speed. Behind them was a rushing storm-cloud, from which they were endeavouring to escape, and in the centre of the cloud was Hollesley, pursuing them, stretching out a hand to grasp Mavis by the shoulder.

When he met his host at breakfast next morning, Merrion saw at once that his cheerfulness of the previous evening had evaporated, to be replaced by a sullen moodiness. He ate nothing, and replied curtly to Merrion's advances. It was not until Merrion had finished his breakfast that his host addressed him directly, and even then the former detected an undercurrent of hostility in his voice.

"I expect that you will want to be getting on your way," he said. "I've told Thorburn to pack your things and put them in the car. You've a longish run before you if you want to get to Hunstanton in decent time."

This was a pretty obvious dismissal, but Merrion determined to show no symptoms of offence. "That's very good of you," he replied. "I was going to ask you if you would mind if I cleared off early. I was anxious to arrive by lunch time, and play a round or two this afternoon. It's been very jolly to see you again."

Within half an hour he drove away, his host appearing visibly relieved at his departure. He took the road leading northwards, but, at the end of a few miles, turned into a side road, stopped the car and lighted his pipe. His destination was not Hunstanton, but Gippingford. His present business lay in the neighbourhood of High Eldersham, and it was necessary to devise some plan for remaining in the vicinity without attracting attention or being recognised. It was not an easy task, and as he studied the ordnance survey of the district his brows contracted in a perplexed frown. There was no village or small town anywhere within a reasonable distance where a stranger could put up without attracting undesirable attention.

His mind wandered from the point, and returned to his recent experiences. Hollesley was a curious chap, queer, like everybody else at High Eldersham, except, of course, Mavis. He was down one moment and up the next, his moods changing with startling rapidity. Nobody could have been more pleasant or more alert than he had been the previous evening, and then, a few hours later, he had dismissed his guest with scarcely veiled abruptness. Could anything have occurred to produce this sudden change, or was it merely that the man was temperamental?

He was obviously worried about something, Merrion decided. And perhaps it was not very difficult to guess the cause of his worry. Mavis was at the bottom of it, no doubt.

Hollesley was in love with her, and must have a pretty shrewd suspicion that his love was not returned. He had clearly resented her behaviour on the previous afternoon. Perhaps, upon mature consideration, he had decided that it would be good policy to hurry Merrion out of the way, in order to leave the field clear for himself. This might account for his lack of hospitality.

Merrion returned to the study of his map and, after a while, obtained the glimmering of an idea. But, before it could be put into practice, a good deal of preparatory work would have to be done. During his run on the speed-boat the previous day he had obtained a glimpse of the mouth of the river, but a considerably more extensive reconnaissance would now be necessary. His map told him that from the spot where he was at present a series of winding lanes ran towards the coast, where they appeared to lose themselves among the sand-dunes, about a couple of miles north of the river mouth.

It was a fine, bright morning, and Merrion reflected that a brisk walk would do him good, and quite possibly stimulate his ideas. The total distance to the mouth of the river, following the lanes and then striking across the dunes, was not very much more than five miles. The car could look after itself until his return; nobody would be likely to interfere with it. As he set out he looked at his watch. The time was twenty minutes past eleven.

His way took him through a tract of low-lying pasture land, studded here and there with grazing cattle. In the distance were one or two scattered farm houses, round which were signs of human activity. But he reached the dunes without meeting anybody, or his presence being observed.

On the seaward side of the dunes was a low cliff, and at the bottom of this a narrow strip of sand. The tide was coming in, but Merrion could see that even at high water there would be room for him to walk on the sand at the foot of the cliff. He set out in a southerly direction, and after a wearying trudge across the loose sands, arrived within view of the mouth of the river. He then left the sands and climbed the cliff in search of some spot from which he could survey his surroundings.

He found it in a dune rather higher than the rest, which commanded an excellent view both out to sea and for a short distance up the river. Just inside the entrance the river widened into a shallow lagoon, round the shores of which were two or three abandoned cottages, with the skeletons of open boats drawn up in front of them, which had apparently once been a small colony of fishermen. There seemed to be nobody about, however, and Merrion guessed that the inhabitants of these cottages had deserted them long ago. He satisfied himself that the lagoon formed an excellent harbour, and that a small craft could lie there in peace and quiet.

This done, he sat down and lighted his pipe. He was in no hurry, he told himself, there was no reason why he should not take a rest before walking back to the car. But, in his heart, he knew that this was merely an excuse. It was a beautiful day, such a day as might tempt Mavis to an exhilarating run on the smooth sea in that speed-boat of hers. The chance was worth waiting for, anyhow. It would be very good to catch sight of her, even if it were only a fleeting glimpse.

He sat there motionless, his eyes fixed upon the bend of the river round which she must appear. And, as he watched, a sail glided slowly round the point, approaching silently until a small yacht came into view. Merrion recognised her at once. It was the little five-tonner that he had seen moored in the river off Elder House.

At the sight of her Merrion shifted his position and took cover behind some tall grass. Since this was Hollesley's boat, he was probably on board her, and it would not do for him to see Merrion sitting on the dunes when he was supposed to be on his way to Hunstanton. Until he was past, it would be better to keep out of sight. It was ridiculous, of course, but there was no point in betraying to Hollesley that he had any interest in the river.

Merrion watched the advancing boat with some impatience. There was very little wind, and though she had all sails set, her progress was slow. As she came nearer, Merrion made out that there were two men on board, one of whom he recognised as Hollesley. The other he could not place, though his form seemed vaguely familiar.

The yacht came on until she reached the centre of the lagoon. Merrion watched her, expecting her to pass through the entrance. But, to his astonishment, the two men left the cockpit and came forward. Hollesley lowered the sails, while the other man busied himself with the anchor. Within a few moments she had come to rest.

Hollesley's next actions filled the watcher with curiosity. He pulled up the dinghy which had been towing astern, and with his companion's help lowered into it something bulky and apparently fairly heavy. Then both men took their places in the dinghy, and started to row ashore. Merrion saw with annoyance that their course would bring them to land at the very foot of the dune on which he was hidden.

There was no alternative between discovery and flight. He crawled away cautiously, taking advantage of what cover he could find. The undulating surface of the dunes and the long coarse grass which covered them made his task a fairly easy one. He made his way to a clump of low scrub a couple of hundred yards away, and behind this he stopped and waited.

Very soon Hollesley and his companion, whom Merrion, to his astonishment, recognised as Thorburn, appeared on the crest of the dune that he had just vacated, carrying a couple of wooden boxes between them. These they laid down and opened. Out of one of them Hollesley produced a tripod, which he erected with considerable care. From the other he took a long cylindrical metal instrument, which he fixed on the top of the tripod. These preparations completed, he unslung a pair of field-glasses from his shoulder and, putting them to his eyes, gazed fixedly out to sea.

Merrion, from his place of concealment, looked on with open mouth. "Well, I'm damned!" he muttered. "If that isn't a portable Barr and Stroud range-finder, I'm a Dutchman. But what, in the name of all that's mysterious, has friend Hollesley stuck it up there for?"

Chapter XIV

The only solution of the problem which occurred to Merrion was that Hollesley was keeping his hand in at range finding in case some future war should call him to the colours again. But this, on the face of it, seemed a trifle far-fetched. Besides, why choose for the purpose such a particularly lonely stretch of coast, where the only objects to seaward were a few distant buoys, marking the banks lying off-shore? There must be more in it than that, Merrion reflected. Was it possibly the desire to set off on these peculiar expeditions that had caused Hollesley to hurry him away that morning?

He was reflecting thus when he saw Hollesley hand Thorburn the field-glasses and point out to sea. Merrion, dodging cautiously behind his patch of scrub, looked in the direction indicated, and saw on the horizon a speck which his keen sight made out to be a vessel of sorts. An admirable object on which to practise range-finding, thought Merrion. But, to his astonishment, Hollesley did not put his eyes to the instrument. He and Thorburn stood watching the vessel, talking in low tones the while. Meanwhile, she came straight towards the mouth of the river, as though intending to enter it. Merrion made out, after a while, that she was a small motor ship, a bluff-bowed, barge-like vessel, with a short mast forward and a stumpy funnel right aft. From the latter came a rapid succession of puffs of bluish smoke, the exhaust of her heavy oil engine.

It was not until she had reached one of the distant buoys that Hollesley betrayed any particular interest in her. Then he put aside his field glasses, and applied himself to the range-finder. At the same time Thorburn took a smaller instrument from his pocket, and held it to his eyes. The motor ship held on her course for a minute or two, until she was between two and three miles from the shore. Then she put her helm over, and swung round until she was heading southwards, parallel to the coast. Hollesley and Thorburn, each with his instrument, followed her intently.

Suddenly Merrion, watching the vessel, saw a puff of smoke rise from her deck, and a few seconds later a dull report reached his ears. Somebody on board her had fired a gun, loaded apparently with black powder. But what at? The gulls, which had been circling about her, and were now scattering with indignant cries? There was certainly no other target in sight. Then he glanced quickly at Hollesley and Thorburn. They had laid aside their instruments and Hollesley was busily engaged in writing something in a note-book.

"Plotting her exact position when that gun was fired," muttered Merrion. "Thorburn's instrument was either a pocket sextant or a prismatic compass, I'll be bound. By comparing his bearing with the distance shown on the range-finder one could place the spot on the chart within a few yards. But why, in heaven's name, why? Do they make a practice of this sort of thing? What happens next, I wonder?"

Hollesley and his companion showed by their actions that they had lost all interest in the motor ship, which was fast vanishing into the distance. They busied themselves in dismounting the range-finder, and replacing it in its case. This done, they picked up the wooden boxes and carried them down to the dinghy. Merrion, following them at a distance, saw them row back on board the yacht. No sooner had they reached her than they weighed anchor and proceeded up the river, with the auxiliary engine running, since the ebb tide was beginning to run with some force.

As soon as they had disappeared round the bend, Merrion rose and stretched himself. "Well, that's another little riddle to add to the ones which have been set to me lately," he remarked to himself. "Unfortunately, I haven't the leisure to think about the answer. It's no business of mine if Hollesley chooses to practise position finding. It certainly has nothing to do either with witchcraft or the murder of Whitehead. But fancy taking one's butler out for an afternoon's amusement like that! Upon my word, unexpected things seem to happen in this place as a matter of course."

He continued to mutter to himself as he retraced his steps towards the spot where he had left the car. "Damn that fellow Hollesley!" he exclaimed irritably. "Why the devil can't he stay at home and amuse himself rationally, or, failing that, go up to London again for a bit? I wonder if he makes a habit of using that confounded dune as an observation post? If so, that pretty little scheme of mine will have to be abandoned. I wish I knew what his game was, then I should know what to do."

It was in no very equable temper that Merrion reached the car. He glanced at his map once more, and decided upon a route that would bring him eventually to Gippingford, while giving High Eldersham a wide berth. Following this, he approached the town over a range of low hills, from the summit of which could be seen the sea and the entrance to the river which led to Gippingford dock. The view caught his eye, and he stopped the car in order to enjoy it. A vessel was in the act of entering the river, and as she turned to make her way up to the dock, Merrion uttered an exclamation.

"There's no mistaking her," he said to himself. "That's the craft I saw from the dunes just now. I didn't know that vessels bound for Gippingford came so close in-shore as that. Well, she knows her own business best, I suppose."

He started the car again, and drove into the town, directing his course towards a different hotel from the one he had left the previous morning. He was anxious not to become too familiar a figure in Gippingford; it was possible that his presence there might become known, and that news of it might reach High Eldersham. He ate a large tea and put the car away in the garage. Then he strolled down towards the water-side, passing by the dock on his way.

The motor ship was already made fast to the quay side, and as he walked towards her he could read her name, *La Lys*. She had evidently been built for use rather than beauty, and there was no possible reason for stopping to admire her. Merrion passed on, until he reached a bench upon which a man wearing a sailor's cap was sitting, staring vacantly into space.

Merrion sat down beside him and held out his tobacco pouch. "Have a fill?" he suggested.

"Thank 'ee, guv'nor," replied the sailor. "I could do with a bit o' bacca." He filled a charred pipe, and handed back the pouch. "Nice day for a row, sir," he remarked tentatively.

"Very nice, but I'm afraid I've no time for that," replied Merrion hastily. The conversation lapsed, and silence reigned, until Merrion broke it once more. "Queer looking craft, that," he remarked, nodding in the direction of *La Lys*.

"She? She's one of them Belgian motor ships," replied the sailor. "Built like that to get about the canals, they are. Don't draw hardly any water, in a manner of speaking. She's in here reg'lar, that one is."

"Belgian, is she?" remarked Merrion carelessly. "I thought she wasn't English built, by the look of her."

"Aye, Hoboken built, I reckon. Belongs to Ghent, and comes in reg'lar, once every ten days. Makes a round trip, Ghent, here, London. Like clockwork she is, unless it's blowing real hard. And it takes a good breeze to stop her, there's no mistake."

After some further conversation Merrion got up and walked on. He could not get the incident of the morning out of his mind, and the more he pondered it the more inexplicable it seemed. But the sailor's insistence upon the regularity of the appearance of *La Lys* had given the affair a new aspect. Suppose that Hollesley had taken up his position on the dune in order to see her pass? He had arrived just before she came in sight, and had departed immediately she had passed. And then that gun. Was it possible that it had been fired as a signal? Was the use of the range-finder only a blind, to deceive anybody who might be in the vicinity? And, if a signal had been made, what did it denote?

This last question was unanswerable. But, if the signal theory were correct, it was arguable that Hollesley had gone to the dune for the express purpose of seeing this particular vessel pass, and not merely as a means of spending an unoccupied hour or two. If he went there again, it would not be until ten days hence, when *La Lys* would again be due. There was then no reason why Merrion should not proceed to put his scheme into operation. He quickened his steps, and in a few minutes reached the entrance of a yard, on the foreshore of which a number of yachts were drawn up, most of them fitting out for the coming season.

He entered the office, where he had a long and technical discussion with the manager of the yard. By the time he came out he had chartered *Alisette,* a seven-ton yawl fitted with an auxiliary motor, for the summer months, the vessel to be at his disposal in a week's time.

This done, there was nothing more to detain him in Gippingford. He went back to the hotel, took out the car, and set off on the way to London, where he had promised to meet Inspector Young.

He called on him, late the same evening, at his office in Scotland Yard, and told him of his adventures since they had last met. "I haven't got much further, as you see," he concluded. "But then, as I told you, I didn't expect to. What I am concerned with at present is to make preparations for the night of April 30th, May Eve. That used to be a famous witches festival, and if ancient tradition is followed, as it has been throughout, there is certain to be a meeting of the High Eldersham coven that evening. If I can't find some way of being present, now that I know where it is likely to be held, my luck will be dead out. You've nothing particular to report, I suppose?"

"Not very much. I left the Rose and Crown this afternoon, and came straight up here. There's been a change there, by the way. Dunsford has gone back to the Tower of London and his place has been taken by a man called Humby and his wife. I hadn't much difficulty in finding out all about them. He seems to have been head gardener at the Hall, Sir William Owerton's place, and managed to save a little money. After Whitehead's death he approached Sir William, and asked him to use his influence with the brewers to give him the tenancy of the Rose and Crown. It seems that Sir William knows the senior partner in the brewery and there was no difficulty. The matter went through, and Humby took up his job this morning."

"I see. So Dunsford has gone back to Gippingford, has he? Humby is a High Eldersham man, I suppose?"

"Oh, yes, born and bred. He told me with some pride that his ancestors up to the fourth generation were buried in the churchyard. I can't say that I verified his statement."

"It's probably true," observed Merrion thoughtfully. "So that the possibility of a stranger taking the Rose and Crown is eliminated. Curious, isn't it, how these things happen?"

"I confess that it didn't strike me in that light," replied Young. "However, it's all straight and above board this time. You can't suspect the brewers of being a party to this conspiracy against strangers, and it is only natural that Sir William should use his influence on behalf of one of his own employees."

"Quite. But still, the fact remains. Any other news from High Eldersham?"

"No, except that I had a visit last night from Doctor Padfield. He came up to have a chat, and also to tell me that he had sent Viney to bed, and told him to remain off duty for a day or two. He had already telephoned the information through to police headquarters at Gippingford, and he told me that although he knew it was not my business, he thought I should like to know. As I say, I think it was only an excuse to have a chat. The man strikes me as being lonely."

"What's the matter with Viney?" inquired Merrion sharply.

"I don't know. Nothing very serious, I fancy. He went to see Padfield on Sunday morning, complaining of pains in the head which made him feel dizzy. Padfield gave him something soothing, told him to go lie down, and said that he would look in later in the day. He did so, and found the pains better, but the dizziness still continuing. So, as I said, he told him to stay where he was for a day or two. He'll be all right then, the doctor says. I went to see him this morning before I left and he didn't look very fit. There's no question of malingering, or anything like that."

"Has he got a wife and family? Who's looking after him?"

"Oh, he's all right, you needn't worry. He isn't married, he lives in the police cottage by himself, and an old woman from the village comes in every day and looks after him.

She seems very fond of him, treats him more like a son than anything else."

"Who performs his duties while he is ill?"

"Oh, I don't know. It depends how the local force is off for men. I should imagine, since it is only likely to be a matter of a few days, that the man from the next parish would cover his beat. Of course, if he were to be laid up for long, headquarters would send a substitute."

Merrion sat silently for several seconds, staring straight in front of him. "Look here, old chap," he said at last. "You'll think that I'm beginning to imagine things, I know. But I can't help seeing something ominous in this illness of Viney's. He is out of action, I gather. Meanwhile High Eldersham, so far as the police are concerned, is left to the mercies of the constable from the next parish, who may possibly find time to visit the place once a day, or alternatively, to a complete newcomer, who would take some time even to find his way about the place. What an opportunity for high jinks, if any one felt disposed that way!"

"Oh, dash it all, man, that's a bit far-fetched!" exclaimed Young. "This indisposition of Viney's is only a coincidence, after all. And I tell you, Doctor Padfield doesn't think that it's anything serious. He'll be about again in a day or two."

"I wonder. It all seems ridiculous in this office of yours, surrounded on all sides by the most up-to-date civilisation in the world. But, even in this severely practical atmosphere, I can't forget that scene the night before last, and the doll that I saw being carried away from the Witch's Sabbath."

"The doll!" repeated Young in a tone of bewilderment. "Why, what on earth are you talking about? What's that got to do with it?"

"It wouldn't surprise me if it had been baptised with the name of Viney," replied Merrion quietly.

Chapter XV

The laugh with which the Inspector greeted this remark sounded a trifle forced and unreal. "Really, I can't help thinking that you attach too much importance to this witchcraft business," he replied. "I admit that, if we can get to the bottom of it, we may find the clue to the murder of Whitehead, and that is the principal thing, after all. But I think it is forcing things a bit to try to make it responsible for everything that happens in High Eldersham."

"Very likely," remarked Merrion indifferently. "We needn't labour the point at the moment. Now, I can do nothing further on the spot for a week. To-day is the tenth. That means to say that I shall go down to Gippingford again on April 17th. Meanwhile, I shall stay in London. Is there anything I can do for you while I am here?"

"Not unless you can help me to find out more about this Mrs. Fowler I spoke of the other day. I've learnt that she keeps her car in a lock-up at Huntingdon Mews, and I'm going to arrange for one of our men to make the acquaintance of her chauffeur."

"Huntingdon Mews, does she!" exclaimed Merrion. "More co-incidences; this time, I think, not due to witch-craft. I keep my car in a lock-up there, too. I ran it in there not a couple of hours ago. I tell you what, old chap, leave this chauffeur to me for a bit. I'll get my man, Newport, to sound him. It'll be far better than putting a detective on his track. You can trust Newport as you would yourself. He was with me all through the war, and I've had him ever since. He's an old sailor, and there are very few things he doesn't know, and none that he can't do after a fashion of his own. He'll squeeze Mrs. Fowler's chauffeur dry without the man knowing that he's said a word."

Young smiled at his friend's enthusiasm. "All right," he said. "I'll give this paragon of yours three days in which to get busy. I've seen him at your place, of course, and I confess I like the look of him."

"Right! Within three days you shall have the story. It was last Monday this mysterious princess of yours descended upon the outraged Dunsford, wasn't it? Now, if that's all you've got to tell me, I'm going home to bed."

Next morning, when Merrion sat down to breakfast, he put aside the morning paper which usually accompanied that meal, and called to Newport, who was busying himself at the sideboard.

"Come here, Newport, my lad, I want to talk to you," he said. "Sit down, and stop playing with those dishes; it fidgets me."

"Very good, sir," replied Newport resignedly, seating himself on the edge of a chair in the far corner of the room.

"That's right," said his master. "Now listen. We're going down to the sea in ships once more. What do you say to that, eh?"

"Going abroad, sir?" inquired Newport eagerly.

"No. We're going to explore the east coast in a seven-tonner of the name of *Alisette*. It's a silly name, and I rather suspect that her bottom is rotten. Still, since you and I shall be alone on board, it won't be any great loss if she sinks with us. We start from Gippingford next Monday. You haven't got too lazy to handle a boat, have you?"

Newport grinned. His extremely easy life in London had never really satisfied him, and the prospect of a yachting cruise filled him with delight. "I expect I can manage, sir," he replied. "I'd better see about getting in some stores."

"You can go down to Gippingford on Friday, and get the boat provisioned. You can see at the same time that the men at the yard fit her out properly, and don't put the bowsprit where the bumpkin should be. It's the fashion where we're going for yachtsmen to take their butlers with them as crew, so they won't be surprised to see you."

"Very good, sir, I will go down on Friday. You will join the ship on Monday, I suppose, sir?"

"I shall. But I've another job of work for you before you go. I want you to spend this morning at Huntingdon Mews, cleaning the car. You know most of the chauffeurs who live in the mews, I suppose?"

"Yes, sir, I fancy I've met most of them either there or at the Three Coachmen, just round the corner."

"Oh, so that's where you squander your substance in riotous living, is it? Well, do you know the man who drives a Rolls-Royce limousine belonging to Mrs. Fowler of Park Street?"

"I know the car, sir, and I've spoken to the chap as drives it, though I never heard his name."

"Good enough. Well, I want to know who it was that he drove to Gippingford, and then on to the Rose and Crown at High Eldersham, last Monday. You're not to ask him outright, mind. It was a lady, but you needn't think that I'm looking for romantic adventures, at least in that direction."

Breakfast over, Merrion set out for the Minories, where he bought a complete set of charts of the east coast, from the Wash to the mouth of London River. He took these home with him, spread them out upon the table, and set to work to study them with the idea of getting to know his waters before the cruise began. It was not long before he discovered something that appeared to interest him. He picked up a pencil and began to lightly trace a course on the chart before him. "Ah, now I see what that ugly looking craft was doing so close in-shore yesterday," he muttered.

The chart showed that a series of banks, lying roughly parallel to the coast, extended from a point a few miles north of the mouth of the Elder to Gippingford. The normal course for a deep-draught vessel proceeding to Gippingford would lie outside these banks. But, for a shallow-draught vessel, such as *La Lys*, there was enough water inside the banks. Further one of the banks, known as Vane Sand, lying opposite the mouth of the Elder, had twelve feet or more over it at high water, although it dried at low water.

Now, it had been high water, the very top of the flood, in fact, when Merrion had first seen *La Lys*. The course she had followed was now plain to him. Taking advantage of the calm sea and the state of the tide, she had crossed Vane Sand, and so reached the in-shore channel, when she had turned southward for Gippingford. And, judging by the chart, she must actually have been crossing the sands when the gun was fired.

"Well, that suggests a possible explanation of Hollesley's behaviour," said Merrion to himself. "It looks as though the skipper of *La Lys* and Hollesley were doing a bit of nautical survey on their own account. I think I've got it. *La Lys* took a sounding as she crossed Vane Sand, and fired a gun as she did so. Hollesley plotted her exact position at that moment, and so knew—or will know, when he hears what the sounding was—the depth of water at that spot. Perhaps he has a scheme for reviving the fortunes of High Eldersham as a port, and is investigating the depth of water there is round the entrance to the river."

It seemed a reasonable enough explanation. In any case, Merrion was not interested in Hollesley's observations, as long as he confined them to the days when *La Lys* was expected. He knew these dates now, and could keep out of the way.

That evening, he called once more on Inspector Young. "Newport has got the story all right," he announced triumphantly. "I knew he would. If you had him here in the Yard there wouldn't be so many of those distressing headlines. 'Police Baffled,' and all that. I've a very good mind to set him on the track of the man who murdered Whitehead."

"Do, if you think he'll succeed," replied Young. "I'm fed up with the case, I don't mind telling you. But let's stick to one thing at a time. Who was the lady?"

"A prominent member of society," replied Merrion. "But let me give you an illustration of Newport's methods. It seems that about eleven o'clock all the chauffeurs belonging to the cars kept in Huntingdon Mews repair to a pub close by, where they have a drink to keep their strength up. Newport, who knew Mrs. Fowler's chauffeur by sight, went with them this morning, took a newspaper out of his pocket, and began to talk about the Whitehead murder. He drew his man all right; you know what a sense of importance the remotest connection with any sensational event gives these fellows. Mrs. Fowler's chauffeur announced with great dignity that he knew the very place where the murder was committed.

"After that, as you might suppose, it didn't take Newport long to get at the facts. It seems that Mrs. Fowler is very generous with her car, and is always ready to lend it to any of her friends. On Monday morning she sent a message to her chauffeur, telling him to pick up a lady at 110 South Street, and put himself at her disposal for the day. Mrs. Fowler explained that the lady's own car had had an accident a few days previously and was still in dock. The chauffeur carried out his orders and drove the lady first to Gippingford, where she told him to park the car. Very shortly she reappeared, and told him to drive on to High Eldersham and to ask for the Rose and Crown."

"But that's an amazing yarn. 110 South Street is the address of Lord Applegarth!" exclaimed Young.

"Lord Applegarth was out of town that day, as I have ascertained," replied Merrion calmly. "But there's no doubt that the visitor to the Rose and Crown was Lady Applegarth. I warned you that she was a prominent member of society."

"But what possible business could a woman like Lady Applegarth have with Dunsford?" objected the Inspector. "The thing's absurd. You can't imagine people in her circumstances going round from pub to pub like that."

"Those were exactly the sentiments of Mrs. Fowler's chauffeur, so Newport tells me," replied Merrion. "He was profoundly shocked at her behaviour, which he attributes to a morbid taste for sensation. He is convinced that her reason for visiting the Rose and Crown was to see the spot where a murder was committed."

"I don't believe it!" declared the Inspector. "She had come to ask Dunsford to give her something. I heard enough to be sure of that. But I'm blest if I can guess what possible connection there can be between the two."

"Well, that's your little problem, thank heaven, not mine," replied Merrion unsympathetically. "If you should happen to want the assistance of Newport in unravelling it, you'll find him at my place till Friday." And with that last shaft he departed.

As it happened, he did not see the Inspector again before his departure for Gippingford on April 17th. Having arrived there, he found that, largely as the result of Newport's efforts, *Alisette* was lying anchored in the harbour, provisioned and ready for sea. On the following day he got under way and, after a pleasant sail in calm water with very little wind, reached the mouth of the Elder in the late afternoon. He entered the river, and cast anchor in the lagoon, out of the fairway.

Here *Alisette* remained throughout the nineteenth. Merrion gave as his excuse for this inactivity that there were several jobs to be done on board before the vessel could be described as absolutely ship-shape. Actually he hoped to catch sight of Mavis once more. But the day passed without her appearance, and in the evening Merrion gave orders for an early start next day.

"Everything seems in fairly good trim now, Newport," he said. "We'll clear out of this at dawn. It's high-water at 9.23 to-morrow morning, so that we shall carry the flood for three or four hours up the coast. And I warn you, here and now, that you're going to see some queer things on this cruise, and that you'd better make up your mind once for all not to ask questions."

"Very good, sir," replied Newport imperturbably, as he returned to his task of preparing dinner. Merrion unrolled his charts and studied them once more. His reason for leaving his anchorage was that the next day was the twentieth, on which day *La Lys* was again due. He had no desire for Hollesley to see a strange yacht in the lagoon. Concealment would be impossible, for from the dune Hollesley could see every part of her through his field glasses. And yet Merrion had no intention of going very far. He was determined to see whether, as *La Lys* approached the coast, the same performance would be repeated. Hence the early start, for *La Lys* could only cross Vane Sand at high water.

The sun was just rising on the following morning when *Alisette* left the mouth of the Elder. Once outside, Merrion put her head to the northward, keeping as close in-shore as he dared. Three or four miles up the coast he found a secluded little bay, well out of sight of Hollesley's observation post, and here he cast anchor.

"I'm going for a walk, Newport," he explained. "Put me ashore in the dinghy, and then come back to the yacht and keep a look out. I shall be back by noon, at the latest."

Once ashore, Merrion started to trudge back along the beach towards the mouth of the Elder. This time he had provided himself with field glasses, and it was not necessary for him to approach the dune so closely. He found a convenient spot some distance off, and settled himself down to watch.

He had not long to wait. At about a quarter to nine Hollesley and Thorburn arrived and set up the range-finder. Half an hour later *La Lys* hove in sight, crossed Vane Sand, and fired a gun as she did so. The range-finder was dismounted, and Hollesley and his assistant disappeared.

"Well, that's that!" said Merrion to himself. "We shan't be troubled with those fellows again for another ten days, thank goodness. And that will be May Eve, when things are likely to get lively in the village. There's nothing to prevent us lying quietly in the lagoon till then, if we want to."

He walked back to the bay where *Alisette* lay anchored. Newport saw him coming and picked him up in the dinghy.

"We'll have a spot of lunch first," said Merrion as he stepped on board. "Then we'll heave up the hook and go back to the lagoon for the night. Did you see anybody about while I was away?"

"No, sir," replied Newport. "A craft of sorts came in towards the coast, and then turned southwards, but she was too far off for me to see what she was. I haven't seen anything else, sir."

After lunch they set sail and weighed anchor. A gentle breeze was blowing, and Merrion, enjoying the opportunity for a sail, stood out to sea. The tide was falling rapidly, and the banks were beginning to show their heads above water.

In the distance could be seen Vane Sand, wet and glistening in the sunlight.

Having run out for a short distance, Merrion went about and put the yacht's head for the mouth of the river. He had scarcely done so when Newport, who was forward, hailed him. "There's a yacht of sorts coming out of the river, sir!" he said.

"Is there, by jove!" replied Merrion. "Come aft and take the helm while I have a look at her."

He dived into the cabin and produced a telescope, which he focused on the distant craft. He recognised her at once as Hollesley's five-tonner. "Damn the man!" he exclaimed. "What the devil is he playing at now? Put her about again, Newport. I don't want that fellow to see who we are."

Alisette stood away from the river once more, while the two men on board her watched with interest the evolutions of the five-tonner. She steered straight for Vane Sand, and just as she seemed about to run aground, let go her anchor. Two figures then got into the dinghy and landed on the sand itself.

"It's Hollesley and that blasted butler of his again!" exclaimed Merrion irritably. "What the devil are they going to do on that infernal sandbank? Have a picnic, or what?"

"Maybe they've gone to look for cockles, sir," replied Newport. "There's always plenty of them on these sands as dry out at low water. I remember once running aground on the Maplin, and getting a bucketful in less than half an hour."

"Just the sort of damn silly thing Hollesley would do," grumbled Merrion. "I believe you're right, Newport. They're both walking over the sand bending down as if they were looking for something. Take the field glasses and watch them."

Newport obeyed. "Aye, that's right, sir," he replied. "They're looking for cockles, sure enough. Doesn't look as if they'd seen any yet, though. Ah, the chap on the left has found one, sir!"

As Newport spoke Hollesley bent down and picked up something from the surface of the sand. Whatever it was, he had some trouble in lifting it, and Thorburn ran to his assistance. Merrion, watching through his telescope, uttered an exclamation of amazement.

"By jove, Newport, that's a hell of a cockle!" he shouted. "Why, man, it's as big as a decent-sized suit-case, and it's as much as one of them can do to carry it. And they're taking it back to the dinghy, too. Now what the dickens do you make of that?"

Chapter XVI

"It looks as if they were satisfied with what they've found, sir," remarked Newport. "They're pushing off again in the dinghy, by the look of it. Yes, there they go, sir."

Merrion, watching through his telescope, saw Hollesley and Thorburn row back to the yacht. They weighed anchor and, starting the engine, steered a course for the mouth of the river, into which they disappeared.

Not until the intervening land had hidden them did Merrion close his telescope and lay it carefully aside. "Can you beat it, Newport?" he asked. "Do you remember Lieutenant Hollesley in the days when we were at Dover? He commanded a M.L. when we knew him."

"Aye, sir, I remember him well," replied Newport. "There was a yarn about at the time that he tried to ram a buoy or something. That's him, isn't it, sir? With all respect, sir, the chaps what served under him used to say he was a bit batty, sir."

"Oh, they said that, did they?" observed Merrion. "Well, I shouldn't wonder if they were right. Anyhow, his actions seem to point that way. I don't mind telling you, Newport, that one of those fellows we've just seen treasure hunting on Vane Sand was Hollesley himself."

"Was he, now, sir!" exclaimed Newport. "And who was the other chap, if I may make so bold as to ask, sir?"

"A most efficient butler of the name of Thorburn," replied Merrion. "Keep her away a bit, I don't want to make the river until I'm sure those fellows are out of the way. Talking of Thorburn, it might be worth while for you to make his acquaintance. He'd be able to give you some useful tips about handling plates without making the infernal clatter you seem to find necessary. But that can wait. You don't happen to know anything more about Lieutenant Hollesley, do you?"

"I never met him again after we left the patrol, sir," said Newport. "But I did hear that they gave him some sort of shore job in Belgium after Jerry cleared out. I believe he was there for the best part of a year after the armistice, sir."

"You're a regular mine of gossip, Newport!" exclaimed Merrion. "How did you learn that, may I ask?"

"I happened to run across a chap I knew who was out there with him, sir," replied Newport complacently.

"By jove, I believe that's the clue!" muttered Merrion. "Here, I want to think this out. We'll get the mainsail off her, and then make slowly for the river under headsails and mizzen. That ought to give those fellows plenty of time to get out of the way before we reach the anchorage."

The mainsail having been duly stowed, Merrion retired to the cabin, where he made himself comfortable on one of the sofas. Newport's remark about Hollesley having spent a year in Belgium after the armistice had given him the rudiments of an idea. It was already evident that there was some agreement between him and the people on board *La Lys*. The firing of the gun as a signal, which, since Merrion had witnessed it twice under exactly similar circumstances, could not be a coincidence, was sufficient to prove this. *La Lys* was a Belgian boat. Was it not possible that at least the germ of this agreement had originated during Hollesley's stay in that country?

After what he had seen, Merrion had no longer any doubts as to the meaning of the signal or of Hollesley's observations with the range-finder. He had been quite correct in his assumption that Hollesley's actions were for the purpose of determining the exact position of *La Lys* when the gun was fired on board. But the signal had not been made to indicate the taking of a sounding. It had been made to show that something had been dropped overboard.

"It's one of the neatest dodges I ever struck!" murmured Merrion. "It looks to me as if Hollesley wasn't half so batty as some of us imagined. He wants to get something from Belgium without attracting the attention of inquisitive people at the port of arrival in this country. He makes an arrangement with the skipper of *La Lys*, which is so beautifully simple that there is not the slightest danger in it. The skipper of *La Lys* procures this something for him and sets out from Ghent, taking care to time his passage so that he arrives off this coast at high water. Then, with his light draught, he quite naturally takes a short cut to Gippingford across Vane Sand. Then, when he's right over the top of the sand, he drops the something overboard, and fires a gun to show that he has done so.

"Meanwhile, Hollesley and Thorburn have fixed the exact position where the thing was dropped. They plot the point on the chart and so, at low water, when Vane Sand is uncovered, they know within a few yards where to look for it. All they've got to do is to go out and pick it up, as we've just seen. That's all right, but I don't see that it helps me much. If it concerns anybody, it concerns the customs people. It certainly doesn't throw any light upon the practice of witchcraft at High Eldersham, or, for that matter, upon the murder of Whitehead."

He went on deck, and found that they were approaching the entrance. There was no sign of Hollesley's five-tonner, which had presumably proceeded up the river. It was between four and five o'clock, and the flood tide was running strongly. They sailed up to their usual anchorage and let go.

"A little tea, I think," remarked Merrion, when everything had been stowed. "You'd better give us a pretty substantial one, Newport. It may be some time before we get another meal. I've another expedition to make this evening."

Tea having been disposed of, Merrion called Newport aft into the cockpit. "Have you forgotten the art of rowing a dinghy without splashing or rattling the oars in the rowlocks?" he asked.

"I think not, sir," replied Newport. "I've had practice enough at it in my time."

"Well, let's see what sort of a shape you can make of it. I'd use a couple of dish cloths, if I were you."

Newport ran forward and fetched the dish cloths, which he wrapped round the rowlocks of the dinghy. Then stepping into the little boat, he rowed round the yacht. Merrion watched his performance with an approving smile.

"That'll do," he said. "Make the dinghy fast and come aboard again. You can leave the rowlocks as they are. Now look here. I want to explore the upper reaches of the river without attracting attention. High water this evening is at ten minutes to ten. It'll be dark by half-past eight, and there's no moon. If we start then, we shall carry the flood for an hour and a quarter, quite long enough for us to get as far as I want to. Then, when I've seen what I want to, we can drop down quietly on the ebb till we get back here. Is that clear?"

"Perfectly, sir," replied Newport. "Shall I—er—put a gun in the dinghy, sir?"

"A gun! What on earth for? Didn't I say that I didn't want to attract attention? Oh, I see what you mean. No, we aren't going poaching, you old reprobate. You can leave the gun behind, this time."

Everything favoured Merrion's scheme. As the sun set a bank of clouds rolled slowly up from the westward, and a light drizzle began to fall, and by half-past eight it was impossible from where *Alisette* lay to see even the outline of the dunes against the sky. At a word from Merrion, Newport extinguished the light in the cabin, and locked the door, putting the key in his pocket. Even in the unlikely event of anybody boarding the yacht in their absence, they would be unable to get below. Then, taking great care to avoid making a noise, the two men took their places in the dinghy and started off.

Newport had barely taken a few strokes when the outline of the yacht faded into the darkness. For all either of them could see, they might have been floating in the centre of the North Sea, instead of on the narrow waters of the lagoon. Merrion had provided himself with a luminous pocket compass, which he held in his hand, and with the aid of this he directed Newport in cautious whispers.

They made not a sound as they proceeded up the river, Newport, aided by some sixth sense, keeping the boat in the centre of the channel. The shores on either side of them were invisible; only now and then some tall tree growing near the bank floated past them, a vague and indefinable shadow. Newport rowed with slow and careful strokes, hardly more than sufficient to keep the boat on her course. The incoming tide was sufficient to carry her gently up the river.

Half an hour after they started, Merrion, from his seat in the stern, saw a light ahead and, as they drew abreast of it, he whispered a caution to Newport. From the position of the light, he guessed that it proceeded from one of the upper windows of Elder House. At Merrion's warning, Newport ceased rowing, and the two men peered intently ahead into the night. The moorings of Hollesley's five-tonner lay off the house, and it was possible that somebody might be on board her. In any case it would not do to bump into her. Newport saw her first, right ahead. He gave a quick stroke of his oars, and the dinghy drifted past. The two men in her held their breath, but there was no sign of life on board the yacht, and slowly she drifted astern and was lost to sight.

The next landmark on shore was the Hall, and Merrion gazed eagerly in the direction in which he judged the house to be. Perhaps the quest upon which he was engaged would not have been sufficient in itself to induce him to throw up everything and undertake a yachting cruise so early in the season. He had never admitted it, even to himself, but he had known within the last few days that the true reason for chartering *Alisette* and taking up an anchorage at the mouth of the River Elder had been the hope that he might see Mavis again. He was haunted by the vision of her, he seemed to hear, even now in the stillness of the night, the elusive sound of her voice. Of course, there was no likelihood of her being on the river now. But even the sight of a light in the tall windows of the Hall would have been as a token of her presence.

But the dinghy drifted past without Merrion's eyes being vouchsafed even this slight comfort. The trees in the park, now budding into leaf, were a screen between the house and the river. He fancied that he could make out the low squat shape of the speed-boat moored close under the bank, but even of this he could not be certain. And then, as Newport took to his oars and they rounded a bend, a few scattered lights, like some straggling constellation, heralded their approach to the village.

This was the most ticklish part of their journey. Merrion whispered to Newport to keep right over under the far bank, so close that he could feel the mud with his left-hand oar.

But it seemed to Merrion's anxious eyes that the night grew less dark as they approached the half-ruined wharf, that any one standing upon it must infallibly catch sight of them as they drifted past. A ray of light from some cottage window was reflected in the dark water; it seemed to Merrion to shine with the intensity of a powerful searchlight. Every moment he expected to hear a gruff hail from the shore, and he nearly started out of his seat as, without warning, the church clock chimed half-past nine. The lights drew abreast, and then receded. Not until they had passed out of sight round the next bend did Merrion venture to breathe freely.

By now the flood was almost spent, and there was very little current in the river. Newport rowed more strongly, and the boat pursued her way among the upper reaches. They were unknown to Merrion, and he was obliged to trust to luck, keeping as near as he could judge in the centre of the channel. Newport felt his way with the oars, heading off as soon as one or the other touched the mud. At last, when Merrion estimated that they were about a mile, or rather more, above the village, he fancied that he could see a black patch against the sky. This must be the clump of trees he sought.

It took them a long time to reach them. At this point the river split up into narrow channels, a maze in which they were lost for many minutes, trying one promising creek after another, only to find that it contained insufficient water over the soft and yielding mud to float the dinghy. At last they found the right one, and Newport ran the nose of the boat ashore, right under the branches of one of the outlying trees.

Merrion stepped ashore. "Stop here and keep a look out," he whispered. "If you see or hear anything, give a low whistle. I shan't be many yards away."

It was impenetrably dark beneath the trees, and Merrion walked forward with cautious steps and outstretched arms. When he was sure that he was well hidden, he took an electric torch from his pocket and, holding it on a level with his knees, directed its rays upon the ground. With this light to guide him, he progressed about sixty paces, until he came to a stretch of smooth and level turf, set in the centre of the coppice.

He explored this with considerable care. It seemed to be roughly circular, with a diameter of rather more than a hundred feet. In the centre was a burnt patch, upon which lay a few ashes and charred pieces of wood. Having looked very carefully at this, Merrion crossed the open space to its boundary, which was formed by the trees and a mass of rough brushwood growing among them. Making his way slowly round he came upon two tall trees growing some five yards apart, their interlaced branches forming a canopy above his head. And half-way between the two trunks stood a huge stone, which had at one time been roughly hewn. The top of the stone was hollowed like a saucer, and into this depression Merrion cast the rays of his torch. Beneath a layer of fallen leaves and pieces of bark the surface of the stone showed smooth and worn. But upon it were spots of candle grease, and between them dark stains as of dried blood.

This told Merrion all he wished to know. The stone was undoubtedly the altar behind which officiated the devil, the mysterious president of the coven. A glance at the sides of the stone confirmed this. It was carved with strange figures, the obscure symbols of an almost forgotten rite. A sudden horror seized him, the malign influence of this ill-omened grove. He hastened away from the open space, and plunged once more among the trees, making for where it seemed that the undergrowth was thickest.

Here for a while he searched until he found what he wanted, a patch of low-growing shrubs not very far from the water's edge. He reconnoitred this very carefully and then returned to the boat counting his steps and noting their direction as shown by the compass. Then, with a sigh of relief, he stepped on board.

"By gad, Newport, that's a beastly place!" he whispered. "All right, shove off. The ebb has begun to make."

Chapter XVII

The journey back to the yacht was accomplished without adventure. It was past midnight when Merrion turned in, tired with his day's work, and welcoming the gentle swell which rolled into the lagoon, causing *Alisette* to rock softly. No cradle seemed half so sleep-inducing as his bunk. Yet, after he had blown out the light, and lay in the utter darkness unrelieved by any sound save the soft splashing of the water against the little vessel's side, he found that sleep had deserted him.

It was easy enough in the daytime, when there was plenty to distract his thoughts. Then he could put aside this strange new longing which had come to him. He could relegate it impatiently to the background, as a subject unworthy of serious consideration. But, in spite of his rebuffs, it had a habit of returning, and it seemed to-night that it was determined to take its revenge by a general assault upon his brain.

Well, he would retreat from his advanced position of denial, and meet the assault upon his own ground. He would admit in his own heart that he loved Mavis. It was ridiculous, of course, he had only spoken to the girl once. Still, there it was, he loved her. And this sort of love, he discovered with some surprise, was a new experience for him. What the devil did one do in such circumstances? Ask the girl to marry one? It seemed to be the natural thing, somehow. But how, when, and where? Was he to lie in this confounded river until she came past in that speed-boat of hers, and then bawl the question at her? If so, he would want a megaphone to make himself heard above the roar of the engine.

No, it wasn't a bit of good fencing with the thing like that. It wasn't the question of asking her that worried him. That moment was a long way off yet. The root of the matter was that he felt a vague and most uncomfortable anxiety on her account. There was a subtle horror about High Eldersham that was beginning to affect even his robust nerves. It was impossible to define it. The fact that a murder had been committed, and that the murderer was still at large, influenced it not at all. Murder seemed a clean and honest business compared with the gruesome fancies that his mind persisted in dwelling upon. That mysterious grove, hidden in the shade of the impenetrable trees, had reminded him of the hideous rites that accompanied the worship of Isis or of Ashtaroth.

It was no good to tell himself that such imaginings were ridiculous in England of the twentieth century. It was equally ridiculous to believe that the practice of witchcraft still continued. Yet he had seen the latter, almost with his own eyes. Even admitting that this practice had been continued, or more probably revived, for some obscure purpose, and not for the sake of the thing itself, it had still produced effects of which the immediate cause was unexplained. Was it, after all, a chapter of accidents that had driven those venturesome strangers from the village? Was it a coincidence that Whitehead, who had fallen under the ban of the coven, had been murdered by an unknown hand? And then there was Viney, whose sudden indisposition Doctor Padfield had apparently been unable to diagnose. Had this mysterious influence laid its finger upon him, too?

It might well be so, and there was no telling who might be the next victim. Suppose Mavis, for some incomprehensible reason, were to incur the displeasure of a member of the coven, of any of those taciturn folk who lived in the village. Would one of those repulsive dolls be moulded and baptised with her name? The thought was horrible to contemplate, and yet the one circumstance that might guarantee her safety was even more horrible. She would undoubtedly be safe if her father were implicated in these mysterious ceremonies. He, surely, would not allow his daughter to come to any harm.

To Merrion it seemed as though he were passing from one absurdity to another. What possible reason could a man like Sir William Owerton, a magistrate and a scholar, have for countenancing such senseless practices, or still more for taking part in them? Yet, on the other hand, somebody had organised them, and that somebody had an extensive knowledge of the cult. Who was there in the village who could have acquired such knowledge? Only Sir William, whose studies were admittedly in the direction of folklore and ancient superstitions. And if Sir William were indeed the president of the coven, the unpleasant corollary was that Mavis was the daughter of a devil.

These and similar thoughts tormented Merrion all the night through until at last, when the first light of dawn began to fill the cabin, he rose and went on deck. The lagoon was deserted, except for a few gulls circling round on the look out for scraps. The tide was beginning to make, and a series of little ripples were encroaching upon the distant grey patch that marked the position of Vane Sand. Merrion, leaning against the mast, watched until the patch disappeared altogether. His thoughts had flown back to Hollesley and his actions of the previous day. The man was engaged in smuggling, of that there could be no reasonable doubt. But what was he smuggling? The object that he had picked up had seemed through the telescope to be about the size of a petrol can, and disproportionately heavy for its size. And why on earth should Hollesley, a man of considerable means, as his method of living showed, go to such pains to defraud the customs of an insignificant duty?

"Just to be in the fashion, I suppose," muttered Merrion. "Everybody in this infernal place seems to be engaged in some nefarious business or other. I'm dashed if I can understand it, unless they're all mad together. Good lord, I wish Mavis would clear out and go and live in London like a reasonable girl—Hallo, Newport, rising like Aphrodite to greet the dawn, what?"

A tousled head had appeared through the first hatch, to be followed by the rubicund and essentially sane countenance of Newport. "I heard you about on deck, sir, and wondered if there was anything you wanted," he said respectfully.

"I want a whole lot of things, most of which I'm afraid you can't provide," replied Merrion oracularly. "But there's one of them you might get busy about. Put a kettle on and let's have a cup of tea, there's a good chap."

Newport's head disappeared once more, and Merrion's thoughts returned to their former channel. But suddenly he started and gazed eagerly up the river. A faint purring sound had reached him from the distance, which, as he listened, resolved itself into a steady roar, rapidly approaching. For a moment he stood rigid, then, with a swift movement, leapt into the cabin and tore his field glasses from their case. Then, with nothing but his head appearing above the coaming, he stood and waited, his glasses trained upon the bend round which she must appear.

The roar grew more insistent, until it made itself heard in the forecastle, above the noise of the Primus stove. Newport, surprised at this unwonted disturbance, poked his head up once more through the hatch. Merrion turned sharply at the sound. "Get below, you fool!" he shouted. Then once more he turned his attention to the advancing boat.

It appeared, shrouded in a cloud of spray, steering straight for the entrance. It passed *Alisette* like a flash, a hundred yards distant. Merrion caught one glimpse of Mavis, and saw with a thrill of delight that she was alone. Then the speed-boat passed through the entrance. Had Mavis noticed the unfamiliar yacht lying in the usually deserted lagoon?

Merrion could not tell. The roar of the engine grew fainter in the distance, as the boat sped out to sea. For many minutes he listened eagerly wondering whether he would lose it altogether. Then, when it had almost faded away, it began slowly to swell again. She had merely been for a spin before breakfast and was coming back. Approaching the entrance he could see the spray, which the sun, now risen, converted into a sparkling shower of diamonds.

All at once, just as the boat entered the river, the note of the engine fell several tones, and the spray fell away, revealing the bright hull of the boat. She had slackened speed. Had she noticed *Alisette*, and was she coming to investigate? Merrion withdrew into the cabin, and took up his position at one of the port-holes. The speed-boat came straight towards the yacht, and Merrion realised that his heart was beating rapidly. Would she stop and come alongside? It was part of his scheme that nobody at High Eldersham should know of his presence on the river, and if Mavis recognised him, that plan would have to be abandoned. Yet, on the other hand, he longed for one word with her, whatever that word might cost.

The speed-boat slowed down to the utmost, came up to the yacht and passed her within a few feet. Merrion, looking through the port-hole, could see Mavis plainly as she cast her eyes inquiringly over *Alisette*. Next to speaking to her, this was the best he could expect. He devoured her with his eyes, sternly repressing an almost irresistible longing to rush on deck and hail her. Then he saw her put her hand on the throttle. The speed-boat sprang into life and shot away. Within a few seconds she was lost beyond the bend of the river.

As the roar of the engine died away once more in the distance Newport put his head into the cabin. "Tea's ready, sir," he announced.

Merrion had arranged with Young that the latter should keep in touch with him by addressing letters to the Gippingford post office, for which he would call periodically. It struck him, as he ate his breakfast, that it would be as well to call there, in case anything should be awaiting him. There was a nice sailing breeze, and the simplest method of reaching Gippingford would be to go there in *Alisette*. Besides, it might attract undue attention if the yacht were to lie too long in the lagoon.

He therefore got under way, and after an uneventful voyage anchored in Gippingford harbour about noon. He went straight to the post office and there found a note from the Inspector. "I've no news. I seem to have come to a dead end as far as the Dunsford clue is concerned. Something must have gone wrong there, I feel sure. However, as a last resort, I mean to pay a visit to the Tower of London. I shall be there about four o'clock on the twenty-first, and if this reaches you in time, it might be as well if you could join me."

The twenty-first. That was this very day. Well, that was easily arranged. Merrion returned to the yacht for lunch, and then, at about half-past three, landed once more and inquired his way to the Tower of London.

He found it in a quiet backwater just off the main street. He walked through the open door, and entered a room marked "Lounge." A party of four, two men and two women, were having tea there, and from their appearance Merrion guessed that they had come from a large closed car which he had seen standing outside. It struck him as curious that such well-dressed and opulent-looking people should choose the Tower of London as a stopping place. It was not easy to find, and there were several more inviting places in the main street. However, perhaps the seclusion of the Tower of London attracted them. Not seeing the Inspector, he came out again.

Merrion stood for a moment at the door, looking up the street. A familiar figure was coming towards him, and he strolled along to meet it. "You're punctual to the moment," he said. "Are you coming in to have a cup of tea? I tell you, this pub is a lot posher inside than you would give it credit for."

"So I've heard," replied Young. "I'm glad you got my letter in time, I want to have a chat with you. Why, good lord, man, what the devil's the matter?"

But his words were wasted. Merrion had passed swiftly through the door of a shop outside which they had been standing. It happened to be an ironmonger's, and Young could see him gazing earnestly at a row of tin kettles alluringly displayed upon a shelf. Then the Inspector's attention was attracted by a noise behind him. He turned to see a car pass slowly along the street and stop outside the Tower of London.

This not very extraordinary sight seemed to galvanise him into action. He stared after the car in amazement, then almost ran down the street on the opposite side. He was in time to see the driver of the car, who was its sole occupant, descend leisurely from his seat and pass into the inn. When the man had disappeared he returned to the ironmongers, in time to meet Merrion, who emerged carrying an ungainly parcel wrapped up in brown paper.

"Newport said this morning that he wanted a new kettle," he said unconcernedly. "Come on, let's take it to him."

"Damn your confounded kettle!" exclaimed Young irritably. "There's a man just gone into the Tower of London whom I'm particularly anxious to have a closer look at."

"There's a man just passed in a car who I'm particularly anxious shouldn't see me," replied Merrion. "That's why I bolted into the shop, in case he caught sight of me as he drove past. That's the car standing outside the pub now."

"What, do you mean to say you recognised the man too?" asked Young excitedly.

"Of course, I recognised him. I've seen quite a lot of him lately, one way and another. The last occasion was yesterday, when he and his employer went on an expedition to Vane Sand to look for cockles."

Young looked at his friend as though he imagined he had taken leave of his senses. "I don't know what the devil you're talking about," he said shortly. "You say you recognised the man. Do you know who he is, then?"

"My dear fellow, of course I know," replied Merrion quietly. "I knew the car as soon as I caught sight of it. It belongs to my respected friend, Hollesley, and the man driving it is his butler and general confidant, Thorburn."

Young laughed. "He's a butler, all right, and Thorburn may be his name, but it's not the one I knew him by," he said. "Do you remember the Gregson trial, about ten years ago?"

"I can't say that I do," Merrion replied. "Why?"

"Wait a minute. At that time the police were puzzled by a series of robberies, jewels and so forth, at smart functions, weddings, dances and things like that. It was a long time before they were traced to a gang, which operated on a most ingenious scheme. They posed as the employees of a man who kept an agency which supplied waiters, butlers and so forth, who could be hired temporarily. The man's name was Gregson. Sometimes he went to these functions himself, but more often he sent one of his men. Whoever went, laid their hands on something valuable, and passed it on to Gregson, who disposed of it. He did very well at the game until the police got on his track. And he very nearly got away with it too. It was by a sheer fluke that he was recognised and arrested by one of the police who was on duty at one of the functions where a string of pearls had been taken. I wasn't in charge of the case, but I remember it well. The man got seven years."

"Very properly, no doubt," remarked Merrion. "But why these reminiscences?"

"Because the man who has just gone into the Tower of London is either Gregson or his double," replied the Inspector.

Chapter XVIII

Merrion shrugged his shoulders wearily. "The man who went into the pub was Thorburn," he said. "Of that I haven't any doubt at all. But if Thorburn turns out to be the ingenious Gregson, I shan't be in the least surprised. I've come to the conclusion that every male resident of High Eldersham specialises in some sort of crime, and it would be odd if Thorburn proved an exception to the rule. But what are you going to do about it?"

"I'm not going to do anything," replied Young. "Gregson has served his time and, so far as I am concerned, he is just an ordinary citizen. But I'd like to find out what his business is at the Tower of London."

"A perfectly legitimate one, I have no doubt," said Merrion. "As you may have noticed, the place has an off-licence. Hollesley must have known Dunsford when he kept the Rose and Crown, and I shouldn't wonder if he continued to buy his wines and spirits from him, out of sentiment. But if you're going in to see, I'm not. I don't want it known in High Eldersham that I'm hanging round this part of the world. I'll go down to the harbour, and you can meet me there. We'll go off to *Alisette* and have a chat."

Young nodded and walked towards the inn. Merrion strolled quietly down towards the harbour, reaching the dock in time to see *La Lys* leaving the port to continue her voyage to London. He gazed at her regretfully. "I'd like to have a yarn with that Belgian skipper," he murmured. "Perhaps I should get a hint as to what it was he dropped overboard on Vane Sand. Perhaps I will, next time he comes in here, if I can think of a way of introducing myself without arousing his suspicions."

It was not many minutes before he was joined by Young, and the two men went on board the yacht together. "You don't look as though you had made any earth-shaking discoveries," remarked Merrion, as the two sat in the cabin. "What were the results of your shadowing of Thorburn, or Gregson, if you prefer it?"

"Precious little," replied Young. "He came out, less than five minutes after you had left me. It was Gregson, right enough, I was close enough to recognise him beyond a shadow of doubt. And I fancy you were right as to his business. He was followed by a young fellow, carrying a couple of cases of bottles, which he put in the car. When Gregson had seen them safely stowed, he got into the car and drove off."

"You're quite sure that the cases contained bottles, I suppose?" asked Merrion thoughtfully.

"Quite sure. They had no lids, and I could actually see the bottles. One of the well-known brands of whisky. Why?"

"It struck me as curious that Hollesley should send in and buy all that liquor. He drank extraordinarily little when I was with him. I wonder if he's a secret drinker? That might explain several things. But I take it that at present we are not concerned with Hollesley's habits, or, for that matter, with his butler, are we?"

"No, but we are concerned with Dunsford. When I came down here to-day I was convinced that your man, Newport, had got hold of the wrong end of the stick, somehow. It was utterly inconceivable that a woman in Lady Applegarth's position could have had any dealings with Dunsford. Still, I made a few inquiries about her—she's a very well-known woman, as you know, and it wasn't difficult to find out all about her. She belongs to one of the smartest sets in London, and her home is always full of people. She's far too busy enjoying herself to have time for any shady adventures.

"The next thing was to find out if she had what is euphemistically known as a past. I had an idea that she might have had some connection with High Eldersham, and that that would explain her having some secret in common with Dunsford. But not a bit of it. She comes of an old Devonshire family, and seems never so much as to have set foot in this part of the country. At the end of my inquiries I was pretty well convinced that she was not the woman who visited the Rose and Crown."

"Well, what has happened since to shake your conviction?" asked Merrion. "You didn't see her to-day, did you?"

"No, but I saw somebody else. You noticed a party of four having tea in the lounge, I suppose? Perhaps you didn't recognise any of them. But I did. That young fellow facing the door was the eldest son of Sir Jeremiah Witham."

"Was he, by jove!" exclaimed Merrion. "I've met old Witham often enough, but never his son. A particularly gay and joyous youth, I've always understood. More money than brains, I fancy. I shouldn't have thought he'd have chosen the Tower of London as the object of a little outing with his pals."

"Nor should I. Now, look here, Merrion, what does it all mean? Dunsford is just an ordinary countryman, perhaps a bit shrewder than the common run, but that's all. I lived with him for a week at the Rose and Crown, and I ought to know. Until he went to the Tower of London he had never slept out of High Eldersham for a single night and, since he's been there, he's been too busy to leave the place. Yet two most unlikely people, to our knowledge, have visited the Tower of London within the last fortnight. One must suppose they did so in order to communicate with Dunsford himself, since Lady Applegarth, finding he was not there, came on to the Rose and Crown. Leaving their motive aside, how in the world did Dunsford ever establish a connection with them?"

Merrion shook his head. "I can't imagine," he replied. "Dunsford's a dark horse, and will bear a bit of watching. But, if you don't mind my saying so, you're in very much the same position as I am. A lot of queer things seem to happen at High Eldersham, but none of them seem to have any but the remotest bearing on the murder of Whitehead, which is what we are trying to unravel. In the same way, whatever may be the dark secret shared between Dunsford and his fashionable friends, it doesn't help us on at all."

"I'm well aware of that. But, dash it, one must begin somewhere and, for lack of any better clue, I started with this one of Dunsford's. Somebody who was familiar with the Rose and Crown, even if they did not actually live in High Eldersham, committed the crime. That seems pretty certain. I saw Colonel Bateman before I met you, and he tells me that he has got the reports in from all over the county. Nobody seems to have seen a stranger of any kind anywhere near High Eldersham on the night of the murder, or, for that matter, anybody acting suspiciously. It is negative evidence, I know, but even negative evidence has its value. It is a matter of experience that nearly always, when a crime has been committed, the police are positively overwhelmed with stories of people having seen the criminal, or of suspicious actions on the part of half the surrounding population. In this case, there has been nothing of the sort. Not a word has come in, valuable or otherwise.

"Now, I can't help thinking that this is significant, especially taken in conjunction with this witchcraft business. It looks to me as though the High Eldersham people suspected, if they don't actually know, that somebody about the place murdered Whitehead. If they thought it was a stranger, they'd be only too ready with information. As it is, they are convinced that the man met his death in consequence of the spell cast upon him, and the example of his fate is quite enough to induce them to hold their tongues. And if they think the criminal is some local worthy, they are probably right.

"Look at it this way. I think we can assume that nobody in the village had a genuine grudge against Whitehead, except possibly Portch. If they had, we should have heard of it by now. Portch has an alibi which, at present at least, is unshakable. There is therefore no motive, in the accepted sense of the word. But, on the other hand, a member of the witch-gang—coven, don't you call it—had invoked the aid of the assembly and had a spell pronounced against him. If the presiding genius of all this mumbo-jumbo was to maintain his reputation, it was up to him to see that some misfortune befell the wretched man. If he had no motive, strictly speaking, he had at least an interest in Whitehead's death."

"Yes, I know," replied Merrion. "It seems utterly far-fetched, but those are very much the lines upon which I have been reasoning. I'm pretty sure that once we find out who plays the part of the devil at these confounded meetings, we shall be on the track of the murderer. They are not necessarily one and the same, but there's a connection between them, I'll be bound. I have already laid my plans for being on the spot on the thirtieth."

"Well, I hope to heaven you'll pick up some clue. I don't mind confessing that I'm as far off as ever. The chief at the Yard isn't best pleased, and I fancy old Colonel Bateman is beginning to regret that he called in outside assistance so hastily. At all events I'll bet that Superintendent Bass is chuckling to himself."

"Let him chuckle. He wouldn't have got even so far as we have, you may be sure of that. By the way, when you saw this Chief Constable of yours, did you happen to ask for news of Viney? I'm interested in his complaint, as you know."

"I did. The last report is that he is much better, and will be fit for duty to-morrow at the latest. Colonel Bateman told me that he had not troubled to send a substitute, as Doctor Padfield reported that Viney would only be away from duty for a few days at the most. The spell doesn't seem to have worked very efficiently this time."

Merrion smiled at the sarcasm in his friend's voice. "It's all very well for you to laugh," he said. "I'm still of the opinion that Viney's illness had something to do with this witchcraft stunt. I've seen more of it than you have, and I don't like the look of it a little bit. However, perhaps we shall find out more about that later. The point is now, are you likely to want me again within the next few days?"

"Not unless you have anything particular to report. Why?"

"Because I'm going to make myself scarce until the twenty-ninth, that is, to-morrow week. That afternoon, wind and weather permitting, you will find this craft lying where she is now, with me on board. I shan't call again for a letter till then, as I don't want to risk being seen about. Is that all right?"

Young agreed to this course, and shortly afterwards left the yacht to return to London. After his departure, Merrion's conscience smote him. He ought, he supposed, to have told him of the episode of the previous day. He comforted himself with the thought that he had, at least, dropped a hint of it.

His motives for keeping silent were distinctly complicated. In the first place, had he told the Inspector of his suspicions that Hollesley was engaged in some smuggling enterprise, it would have been the latter's duty to pass the information on to the customs authorities. This would have involved yet another series of inquiries at High Eldersham and, in Merrion's opinion, if he were to be successful in getting to the bottom of the chain of mysteries of which that village was the centre, it was essential that nothing should be done to disturb the existing sense of security. Besides, Merrion himself had a scheme for solving that particular riddle, without calling in the aid of the customs authorities.

Bound up with all this was his determination to shield Mavis, whatever it might cost. He never for a moment supposed that she was in any way involved in whatever dark doings might be perpetrated in the neighbourhood. But, until he had ascertained exactly where her father stood, it behoved him to move very cautiously. Any exposure of Sir William would inevitably react upon his daughter and, if it were to be brought about through his agency, Mavis would hardly be inclined to look upon him with friendly eyes in the future.

"It looks as though I were trying to race with the hare and hunt with the hounds," muttered Merrion to himself. "I can't help it, I must know more before I take any definite action. I'm not going to do anything that would possibly hurt that girl, whatever crimes her father may have been guilty of. I've a good mind to chuck up the whole business and let Young ferret out what he can without me. And yet, that won't do. If I'm on the spot, I may be able to tip the old boy the wink in time to enable him to clear out. Oh, lord, it's a complicated business, right enough!"

The more Merrion considered the matter, the more firmly he became convinced that the key to the whole puzzle lay in discovering the identity of the presiding devil. At present he had very little to guide him in that direction. He ran through the names of the more prominent men in High Eldersham with whom he was acquainted. His first suspicions had been that in the direction of Doctor Padfield. But, during the last assembly, the doctor had been chatting in his study with Young. That ruled him out. Hollesley was like-wise barred. He had only returned to High Eldersham two days after the meeting. Thorburn had suddenly assumed a new aspect owing to Young's recognition of him as Gregson, but it seemed difficult to fit him into the role. For one thing, he had not been long enough in the place to establish the ascendency which the devil would require. Dunsford was a possibility; his movements that night had been suspicious. On previous occasions he could easily have come over from Gippingford in order to preside. Dunsford, as Merrion had remarked to the Inspector, was undoubtedly a dark horse.

But Merrion could not get away from the disturbing thought that neither Dunsford nor any one else in High Eldersham, with one exception, possessed either the influence or the knowledge which seemed requisite. But this exception he refused to consider, until at least he had definite evidence against him. Newport's announcement that supper was ready saved him for the moment from the opportunity for further reflection.

Merrion's first action next morning was to write a note to Young. "In case you cannot meet me on the afternoon of the twenty-ninth, I think it would be as well if you were to be within call on the night of the thirtieth. I feel pretty certain that I shall discover something then, and it may be necessary for you to act at once. Perhaps you could spend the night at the Rose and Crown? Of course, I can trust you not to take any independent action which might possibly queer my pitch. If you do not meet me on the twenty-ninth, drop me a line to the post office here informing me of your plans."

Newport went ashore to post this and to purchase supplies. When he returned *Alisette* got under way and slipped out of the harbour.

During the following week Merrion endeavoured to soothe his restless mind by cruising along the coast, carefully avoiding any approach to the mouth of the Elder. It was not until noon the twenty-ninth that he arrived once more in Gippingford harbour.

His first visit was to the post office, where he found a letter from Young, dated the previous day, awaiting him. "I'm sorry, but I shan't be able to get down to Gippingford to see you on the twenty-ninth. I have been put upon a new case, which has certain points of interest. Nothing further has transpired in the other matter, and it looks as if the solution of that mystery now rested entirely with you.

"Since you would like me to be at the Rose and Crown on the night of the thirtieth, I will certainly be there. You seem pretty optimistic about finding something out and, though I confess I don't altogether share that optimism, I will help you in any way you suggest. Let me know if there is anything else that I can do."

Merrion pocketed the letter and returned to the yacht, where Newport was awaiting him. "All ready for sea?" he asked, as he stepped on board.

"Yes, sir," replied Newport. "We've got all the stores we want."

"Right. Start up the engine, and lend a hand with the hook. We're bound for that old familiar lagoon once more."

Chapter XIX

The lagoon was deserted when *Alisette* anchored in her old berth that afternoon. The day had been calm and overcast, more like autumn than early spring. The grey sea was smooth and unruffled, with a hint of mist upon the horizon.

"Well, here we are," said Merrion, as he and Newport stowed the sails and put the little vessel in order. "We've got a busy day ahead of us to-morrow. For one thing, that Belgian vessel is due, and I want to see if the cockling party is repeated after she has passed. It's high water to-morrow morning at a quarter-past seven, and if she means to come across Vane Sand she will have to do it then. I want to be well out of the way in that little bay we found last time, so we shall have to make a start as soon as it is light. And then, to-morrow evening, I propose to make another excursion up the river, to that place I explored the other day."

"Very good, sir," replied Newport. "You'd like to turn in early, I suppose?"

"I don't know," said Merrion doubtfully. "I'd like to make a few inquiries this evening on shore, but I don't want to run the risk of being recognised. Look here, Newport. They don't know you in these parts. How would it be if you did a little scouting for me? It wouldn't be the first time."

Newport grinned. "I'd be very glad to find out anything you want to know, sir," he replied.

"All right, then. It's after four now, and the pubs in this part of the world open at six. Take the dinghy and row up to High Eldersham. You'll have the tide with you, so it won't be much of a pull. Keep your eyes open as you pass Mr. Hollesley's place and see if there's anybody about. A little farther on you'll see a speed-boat moored, or, if she isn't there, let me know when you come back. When you get to the wharf, tie up the dinghy and go ashore. Walk straight up through the village, and about a mile from the wharf you'll come to a pub called the Rose and Crown. You've heard something about that place already."

"Yes, sir, the place I was talking about to Mrs. Fowler's chauffeur the other day, where the landlord was murdered."

"That's right. Go in there and find out what you can of the local gossip. I want to know if Mr. Hollesley is at home, and also Sir William Owerton and his daughter. You might find out as well whether the village policeman, whose name is Viney, has recovered from his illness. Keep your ears open for any remark about Dunsford, the man who keeps the Tower of London in Gippingford and who was at the Rose and Crown a short time ago.

"I think those are the main points, but any other local gossip will be useful. You'll have to have some story ready to account for your presence. Better juggle with the truth a bit. Say you come off a yacht lying at the mouth of the river, and that you are getting under way at daylight. That's true enough, and it will account for the dinghy, if anybody happens to notice it. But don't say that the owner's on board. You and another chap are taking the boat up to Lowestoft, where he means to join her. Now then, off you go while the tide's still running up. I shan't wait up for you; so you can stay at the pub till closing time if you think it's worth it."

Newport set off and reached the Rose and Crown without attracting any particular attention. The few people whom he met on his way through the village glanced at him incuriously, without so much as wishing him good-evening. It was just after six as he entered the inn, where he ordered a pint of beer and sat himself down in front of the fire. The landlord, who was apparently of a taciturn disposition, served him and resumed the occupations which his arrival had interrupted. Judging by the clatter of knives and forks which came from the kitchen, he and his family were having tea.

It was some little time before customers began to arrive, singly and in pairs. Newport, a shrewd judge of such things, amused himself by guessing their occupations. They were labourers for the most part, heavy of face and slow of speech. Listening to them, Newport caught the names of Portch, Hosier and Hammond. But their conversation was not of any interest to him. It dealt with things rather than people, of the prospects of the hay crop, of the phenomenally early potatoes in somebody's garden. Newport, whose knowledge of the soil was not his strong point, found himself wondering from time to time what in the world they were talking about.

But, as the evening wore on, men of a different stamp dropped in, forming automatically a group apart from the labourers. Newport detected a chauffeur, a man who might have been a farm bailiff, and a third who from his remarks seemed to be the proprietor of the village shop. A chance remark thrown in his direction enabled him to get into conversation with the latter, and very soon he had joined the group, his mug standing on the same table as theirs.

He made no attempt to lead the conversation. His rôle was that of a stranger who had come up to the Rose and Crown to pass the evening, and was prepared to enjoy his beer in comfort. Sitting there, he looked the part of the not over-intelligent yacht-hand to perfection, his hands stuck in the fold of his blue jersey. Any slight feeling of restraint in the presence of a stranger which the group may have had soon wore off, and they were soon talking at ease among themselves, without paying any particular attention to him.

In the course of a couple of hours he picked up several pieces of information. Sir William Owerton was at home, he and his daughter had been round the park that very afternoon, giving orders about lopping the branches of certain of the trees which threatened to grow out of shape. Newport gathered that Sir William was well liked by his employees, but they thought he would be better employed getting about the place a bit more, instead of staying shut up in the house all day. As for Miss Mavis, well, you never knew what she would be doing next. More like a boy than a girl she was, what with her boats and horses and such. Perhaps it was as well, since Master Lewis was away in India.

To Newport's disappointment, he learnt very little of Mr. Hollesley, in whom, since he knew him, he was most interested. The only piece of information he picked up about the residents of Elder House was that Mrs. Hollesley had seemed a little bit better lately, and that Mr. Laurence had decided to take the opportunity of going up to London for a few days. The car was to be ready for him the following morning, directly after breakfast, as he wished to reach London soon after mid-day. He was not expected back for two or three days at least.

Nobody mentioned Dunsford, and it struck Newport as rather curious that there was no reference to the murder. He had imagined that such an event would provide an almost unlimited topic for discussion locally, especially since the criminal had not yet been discovered. Viney, however, was mentioned, though only casually. It appeared that he had returned to duty for a few days, but that he had been compelled to return to bed a couple of days previously. Doctor

Padfield, who was attending him, did not appear to be alarmed at this relapse. He had been overheard to express the opinion that Viney would soon get over his temporary indisposition.

The landlord happened to be serving a round of drinks to the group at the moment when this remark was made. Abandoning his taciturnity, he muttered something about being willing to bet that Viney would never get any better as long as he stayed at High Eldersham. At his words a sudden silence fell upon those within hearing, and furtive glances were cast in the direction of Newport, whose face was buried in his tankard, as though he had no thoughts beyond the foaming beer which it contained. The landlord became confused, and went on to say that the air in these parts never did seem to agree with some folk. But, at a frown from one of the company, he returned behind his counter still muttering.

The group broke up and melted away, its members dispersing to their various homes. The remaining customers drained their beer reluctantly and slouched out of the bar. Newport was the last to leave, as the hands of the clock pointed to five minutes to ten. He made his way down to the village, which seemed deserted. Most of the windows were already black, only in one or two could he see the reflection of a dim light. High Eldersham was in the habit of going to bed early, he thought.

Although the sky was still overcast, the night was not absolutely dark. The moon had not yet set, and the grey diffused glow was sufficient to enable Newport to pick his way across the not over-secure timbers of the quay to the dinghy. The tide was running out strongly, as he noted with satisfaction. He would be carried back to the yacht with very little expenditure of energy on his part. He cast off and began to row in a leisurely fashion downstream.

A few strokes brought him abreast of the church, the churchyard being separated from the river by a low wall. He was drifting rapidly past it, when a faint sound attracted his attention. Instantly he stopped rowing and gazed intently towards the churchyard. There was no doubt about it. A chain of furtive figures were emerging stealthily from the shadow of a group of ancient yews.

Newport was not easily frightened; in fact, in the Dover Patrol he had borne the reputation of being absolutely devoid of fear. But, like most sailors, he was superstitious at heart, and this unexpected apparition sent a cold and most unpleasant thrill down his spine. His first impulse was to take to his oars and row for dear life from the scene of this supernatural happening. But his inborn sense of discipline overcame his terror. Mr. Merrion had told him to keep an eye upon anything that might happen on shore. At any price he must obey orders.

In spite of his resolution he was literally sweating with fear as he rowed noiselessly under the bank and landed at the foot of the low wall. He crouched there for several seconds before he could summon courage to peep over. And, when he had done so, he ducked down again immediately, his tongue thrust between his teeth to prevent them from chattering. For his horrified eyes had made out a dozen ghostly figures with shrouded heads advancing into the centre of the churchyard.

With a great effort Newport pulled himself together. He told himself that these figures were as human as himself, that there was nothing supernatural about the matter. And, when at last he peered over the wall again, his last doubts were set at rest. The cloaked and hooded figures, however unreal they seemed, were obviously flesh and blood within their voluminous garments.

He counted them as they advanced slowly towards him. There were thirteen of them, the last smaller than the rest.

Something about this figure's movements, some suggestion of outline beneath the shapeless cloak, made him imagine that she was a young girl. The rest seemed to be women, though it was difficult to distinguish details in the still and silent gloom which filled the space under the shadow of the church. As they passed more deeply into it, the shadowy figures seemed to become swallowed up in their surroundings, they seemed to disappear, as though endowed with the power of becoming invisible at will. It was only when they moved that Newport could distinguish them from the background against which they stood.

They huddled together in a knot, pressing close to the wall of the church. And as Newport watched, wondering whether the whole thing was a hallucination, whether if he leapt over the wall and walked towards them those unsubstantial figures would not change before his eyes into nothing more tangible than a shadow upon the stonework of the wall, a point of light flashed out, casting them suddenly into relief. Their outlines were now visible. Newport could see raised arms, holding what he took at first to be staves. Then each arm was lowered in turn, and the staves, presented to the point of light, took fire one after the other, and burnt with a yellow and flickering flame. And then he understood that the staves were in reality tall altar candles.

Holding these lighted candles in front of them, the silent procession moved once more out into the open. The flickering light shone upon their dark cloaks, making them seem huge and unearthly. But it could not penetrate the deep shadow of their hoods, giving the appearance of a horrible emptiness where their faces should have been. Behind them their shadows danced erratically among the tombstones, enormous and grotesque, taking on shapes that could surely never be cast by any human form.

Not far from the wall of the church the procession halted, and formed itself into a ring. The smaller figure, which Newport took to be the girl, took her place in the centre, standing upon a mound which raised her slightly above the level of the rest. The candles cast a baffling and uncertain light upon this mound. It took Newport some little time to discover that it was a heap of bare earth above a newly-made grave.

For a while they all stood motionless, while the faint air from the river breathed on the candle flames, making them gutter and smoke. A rapid sequence of light and shade played over the figure of the girl, who stood very still, as though turned into stone. Only the candle which she held rigidly before her vibrated rapidly, as though the hand that held it trembled with some powerful emotion.

Then, one by one, the figures about her handed her their candles, until she held them all in both hands as a bundle, which she slowly raised above her head. She herself was left in comparative darkness, but the massed candles shone like a beacon upon the ring of figures surrounding her. From the depths of the hoods facing him Newport could see the reflection of excited eyes, could imagine the outlines of surrounding features. Then, as he watched fascinated, the ring began to revolve about the girl as a centre, slowly at first, but with ever-increasing rapidity, until it spun feverishly in a satanic dance.

The dance ceased abruptly, as though by word of command, although no sound but that of swiftly-moving feet had reached Newport's ears. The girl descended from the mound of earth, and took her place in the ring which opened to make place for her. With a simultaneous movement the figures leant forward, and each planted its candle in the earth above the grave. Then once more they joined hands, and danced furiously in a circle about them. As before the dance ceased without warning, and the figures took back their candles. They held them aloft for an instant, then suddenly inverted them and plunged the lighted ends into the earth. A sudden darkness swooped upon the scene, which Newport's eyes were unable to pierce for several seconds. When at last he could distinguish the figures, they were trooping away once more towards the yew trees from which they had emerged.

Newport waited where he was for several minutes. But nothing further happened, and it became clear that the strange ceremony was at an end. With a feeling of profound relief he re-entered the dinghy and rowed rapidly down the river until he reached the yacht. As he made the dinghy fast, he heard the sound of Merrion's voice from the cabin. "Hallo, is that you, Newport? Come in and tell me your news."

Merrion was in bed, reading by the light of the lamp. He looked up as Newport entered the cabin. "Why, man, what's up?" he exclaimed. "You look as if you'd seen a ghost!"

"A ghost, sir!" replied Newport. "I've seen a baker's dozen of them. It's my belief that they're all possessed up at High Eldersham."

Merrion leapt out of bed and sat himself on the edge of the bunk. "Sit down and tell me what you've seen," he commanded curtly.

Newport obeyed him, and gave him an unvarnished account of his adventure. As he finished, Merrion slapped his thigh rapturously. "By jove, that's capital!" he exclaimed. "Now I know that there'll be something really worth seeing to-morrow night!"

Chapter XX

However mystified Newport might be by what he had seen, the significance of the ceremony was clear enough to Merrion. It tallied almost exactly with certain passages which he had read in the old books dealing with witchcraft, and merely served to strengthen his conviction that somebody thoroughly versed in the cult was directing its revival at High Eldersham. This being the case, it was a practical certainty that an assembly of the coven would take place on the night of April 30th, May Eve being a date of the first importance in the witch's calendar.

Meanwhile, the whole day was before him. If *La Lys* kept to her schedule, she was due to cross Vane Sand on the morning tide, and he was curious to see whether the performance which he had already witnessed twice would take place for the third time. He had at first been rather puzzled by Newport's report that Hollesley had ordered his car to be ready for a journey to London directly after breakfast. But, as he considered it, he saw that the projected journey exactly fitted in with his own scheme. Hollesley would have plenty of time before he started to observe the position where the mysterious object was dropped overboard. There was no reason why he should trouble to retrieve it during the following low-water. It would be perfectly safe where it was; nobody else would explore Vane Sand and, the surface being hard, it would not sink in more than an inch or two. He could, in fact, collect it at his leisure.

The dawn broke mistily and without a breath of wind. The crew of *Alisette* started the engine, weighed anchor, and proceeded to the little bay where they had anchored ten days before. Merrion felt some anxiety for the success of his scheme. If the mist held, *La Lys* would scarcely venture among the sands, and, even if she did, it would be impossible for Hollesley to observe her movements from the dune. However, as the sun rose, a very gentle air sprang up, and the mist thinned perceptibly. As he landed and walked along the beach towards the dune, he noticed that visibility had so far improved that he could see the distant buoys. There was nothing now to prevent *La Lys* approaching the sands, if she wished to.

Merrion reached his former place of concealment, and was very soon rewarded by the appearance of Hollesley and Thorburn, carrying the range-finder. A little later the ungainly form of *La Lys* appeared in the distance, steering for Vane Sand. The gun was fired, Hollesley and Thorburn packed up their instruments and went away, *La Lys* disappeared to the southward. The usual programme had been carried out without a hitch.

As he walked back towards the yacht, Merrion congratulated himself upon the way in which things had turned out. Hollesley's journey to London would eliminate him as a possible disturber of his plans. He would depart, knowing that the object, whatever it was, had been dropped and imagining that he would find it upon his return.

When he was on board *Alisette* once more, he explained the outlines of his plan to Newport. "Everything has happened as it did ten days ago," he said. "That Belgian craft has dropped something on Vane Sand. But, since Mr. Hollesley will not be able to go cockling there at low-water, I'm going to do so for him. It will be low-water at one o'clock, and Vane Sand should begin to uncover a little before noon. At eleven I shall take the dinghy and row down there. It's not more than three miles from here, and as the ebb runs south-wards inside the banks, it won't be much of a pull.

"If I find what I'm looking for, I shall either bring it back here, or take it to the lagoon in the dinghy and land it there. I can't say which I shall do till I see what it is. In any case, you remain here until sunset. Then, if you haven't seen anything of me, bring the yacht into the lagoon. You can easily manage her by yourself under power. By that time I shall almost certainly be waiting for you. If I'm not, it will be because I have been up to see Inspector Young, who will be at the Rose and Crown to-night. I shan't be much later than sunset, anyhow, as we shall have to make a start up the river as soon as it's dark."

Having given these instructions, Merrion settled himself with his pipe in the cockpit to wait. He kept a keen eye on the weather, watching the horizon, which was still anything but clear. About ten o'clock the light air which had risen with the sun died down again, and the mist began to close in once more. Merrion watched it with a sense of inward satisfaction. "Couldn't be better!" he said to Newport who, as usual, had found some job on deck to keep him busy. "If this holds, there won't be any risk of anybody seeing me from the shore, and butting into my business. I don't want any inquisitive eyes watching me."

"It'll be all right if it doesn't come on too thick, sir," replied Newport doubtfully. "It wouldn't do for you to lose your bearings on them sands."

"Oh, that'll be all right!" said Merrion cheerfully. "If it comes on too bad, I can always take to the dinghy. I shall have my compass with me, and if I row on a westerly course, I must hit the shore somewhere. Don't you worry about me. Of course, if it comes on as thick as all that, don't take any risks with the yacht. Just stay where you are. If I don't find you in the lagoon, I shall know where you are. In that case, come in when the fog lifts, but not before sunset. Now then, it's time I was off."

He stepped into the dinghy and cast off. The mist was certainly fairly thick, but had not attained the opacity of a true fog. Merrion had taken the precaution of obtaining the bearing of Vane Sand from the yacht while the weather was still fairly clear, and he rowed steadily in this direction. The mist grew even more dense as he advanced. All at once there came faintly to his ears a long wailing moan, ending in a hysterical shriek.

The sound, unexpected amid the pervading stillness, startled him for the moment. Then he realised what it was. "That's the fog signal at Elderness lighthouse tuning up," he muttered. "It must be pretty thick out at sea. Well, neither Newport nor I can come to any harm where we are. I can't be far off this jolly old sandbank by now."

A few minutes later the keel of the dinghy grated on the sand. Merrion stepped out of her, and hauled her well up. When he had done so, he looked at his watch. It was now ten minutes to twelve, and it would be at least two hours before the sea rose again to its present level.

"Of course, if I had Hollesley's observations, I could walk straight to where *La Lys* jettisoned this thing, whatever it is," said Merrion to himself. "As it is, I shall have to hunt over the sandbank until I find it. There's one thing, I've got a couple of hours to work in. If I don't find it in that time, I never shall. But it's no good just looking about at random."

Holding his compass in his hand, he began to walk on a bearing which he judged would take him right across the stretch of sand laid bare by the sea. He continued on this course until he came to the water's edge on the opposite side, and then took a few paces to one side, and walked back on the reverse bearing. Vane Sand was more extensive than it had appeared from the shore, and he soon realised that his task was not so easy as he had imagined, especially since he could only see a very few yards on either side of him. The sand itself, in contrast with the surrounding sea, seemed the home of weird noises, compounded of the ceaseless lapping of the ripples on the edge of it, the eerie cries of unseen gulls, and the intermittent wail of the distant lighthouse. It was an uncanny feeling, alone on this lost corner of the earth, which belonged neither to the realm of the sea or of the land.

"Almost as uncanny as poor old Newport's experience last night," muttered Merrion. "By gad, I'll bet he got the shock of his life when he saw those figures flitting about the church-yard! Jolly plucky of him to stick it, I think. Now, where the devil is this mysterious thing? Time must be getting on."

He found it, a few minutes later. It lay right in his track, a square, solid-looking object, with one corner slightly buried in the sand. He stood over it for a minute, surveying it curiously. It was an iron box, slightly larger than an ordinary petrol can, with the lid secured by bolts and nuts, screwed up tight. Merrion bent down and lifted it from the ground. "By jove, it's heavy!" he exclaimed. "I think I'll leave it here till I find the shortest way to the dinghy."

The fog was too thick for him to see the edge of the sand-bank, but he set off in the direction in which he imagined the dinghy to lie, scuffling his feet so as to leave a track which he could follow back to the box. He had not gone many paces before he stopped short and listened. A new sound had reached his ears, and, as he stood motionless, trying to make out the direction from which it came, his face assumed an expression of amazement. He could not be mistaken. It was the roar of Mavis's speed-boat, throttled down to about half its maximum speed.

"Good lord, what on earth is that girl doing out on a day like this!" he muttered. "She can't possibly see a yard ahead of her. As sure as fate she'll run aground or something. Luckily, there aren't any rocks for her to hit, so she can't come to very much harm. But what a day to choose for a run!"

He stood listening for some little time, but his ears told him nothing further. The roar of the engine seemed now to approach, now to recede, according to the varying tricks of the fog. But at last it grew definitely fainter, and it became obvious to Merrion that the boat was going away from him. He continued on his way until he reached the edge of the sea.

It was now past one o'clock, and the tide was beginning to rise, encroaching upon the surface of the sandbank. Merrion had not struck the exact spot where he had left the dinghy, but he knew that he was not far out, for he could see the traces of his own footsteps on the sand. He followed these for some little distance, expecting every moment to see the outline of the dinghy looming up through the fog. And then, all at once, he caught sight of something that sent a cold thrill right through him. With a sharp exclamation he ran forward. In the sand was a long furrow made by the keel of the dinghy as he had hauled it up. But the dinghy itself was no longer there.

The event was so inexplicable that Merrion stared stupidly at the furrow for some seconds, unable to realise what had happened. There was no question of the dinghy having floated away. The marks where it had rested were still several feet from the water. Yet there seemed no other explanation. The sand was certainly disturbed round the spot where the boat had lain, but that might well have been caused by Merrion himself when he hauled her up. And then an idea struck him. This might not be the mark of his dinghy at all.

Some one else had run a boat on to the sand, by accident probably in the fog and, having found out where he was, had pushed off again.

In that case the dinghy must be further on. He walked along the edge of the water for several yards and then came upon an exactly similar furrow. This second furrow puzzled him more than the first. And then he noticed that there were traces of footsteps, certainly not his own, leading backwards and forwards between the two.

It was plain to him then what had happened. Somebody had landed on Vane Sand after his arrival and, walking round beside the water, had found his dinghy. He had then gone back to his own boat, pushed off and rowed round to the dinghy, which he had pulled off the sand and towed away. The reason for his doing so was not apparent. Nor did it much matter. The immediate issue was what Merrion should do next.

He realised suddenly that he was in a desperate position. Very shortly the sandbank would be covered; the tide was already rising fast. The nearest point of the shore was two miles away; a distance not perhaps beyond his powers of swimming. But, if he were to try to swim it, how could he hope to keep in the right direction in this fog? He could not carry his compass, the water would very soon put it out of action. He would probably end by swimming round in circles until he was exhausted.

Merrion's first action was to shout as loudly as he could. It was a pretty hopeless expedient; the chances of his being heard were infinitesimal. Yet it was just possible that the man who had taken his dinghy had done so under the impression that it had been washed ashore on the sandbank, and had no idea that any one had landed. If so, he might still be within earshot.

Again and again Merrion shouted, but there was no reply save the screaming of the gulls. The fog seemed to shut him in like a surrounding wall, stifling his voice and re-echoing it. He retreated step by step before the advancing tide, until at last nothing remained of the sandbank but a small circle, narrowing rapidly. It was time to act.

He cast a rapid glance at the compass, to get his initial direction, and then took off his boots and coat. Having done this he waded into the water towards where he judged the nearest point of the shore to be and, with a stout heart, started to swim, with a long and easy stroke.

Merrion was an accomplished swimmer and, had he been able to see the opposite shore, he would probably have had no difficulty in reaching it. But the fog, although as he plunged into the water he fancied that it was lifting a trifle, was still far too dense for him to be able to retain any sense of direction. Besides, although he knew that the flood tide set roughly northwards along the coast, he had no experience of the strength of the current, or how much to allow for drift. He could only swim blindly, trusting to providence that he would eventually reach the shore.

It was no use over-exerting himself, and so wearing himself out before he had covered the distance. He plodded along easily, varying his stroke from time to time, and husbanding his strength as best he could. He had been swimming for about twenty minutes, when suddenly his foot struck the bottom. With a heart-felt sigh of relief he stood up and thrust forward through the water. He had reached the land sooner than he expected, the tide must have drifted him in-shore. But it was curious that the beach did not shallow more rapidly. He had walked forward several paces by now and the water seemed if anything to be growing deeper. He changed his direction slightly, but the same thing happened. Then he realised what had happened. He had swum in a circle and once more reached Vane Sand, now covered with three or four feet of water.

Probably for the first time in his life Merrion felt the touch of the cold hand of despair. He was already feeling the strain and was nothing like so fresh as he had been. Although the circle of visibility had perceptibly widened, it was not yet clear enough for him to see the shore. He no longer had his compass, and he had entirely lost his sense of direction. If he were to start again, he had no idea which way to set his face.

Yet he must start. He could not stay where he was, even had he wished to. Already the tide, sweeping over the bank, threatened to carry him off his feet. Breathing a fervent but inarticulate prayer, he launched out once more.

Very soon he lost all sense of time and space. He seemed to be swimming for eternity in an enclosed space of which the wall receded before him and closed in again behind. In spite of himself, his stroke grew more desperate, yet, at every effort he made, his strength grew less. More than once he made up his mind to allow himself to sink, to end this hopeless struggle which could have but one end. But every time his determination triumphed and he forced his weary limbs into mechanical action.

At last he heard a roaring in his ears. This was the end, he thought. He had just enough strength left to remain upright, treading water. The roaring increased in volume until it filled the whole universe, and then suddenly died away. And then he realised that it was not in his head, but that it proceeded from the water close by.

He tried to shout, but only a hoarse gurgling escaped him. With a last desperate effort he forced his voice into something resembling a hail. A clear call answered him, and he heard the splash of oars. A dark shadow appeared through the mist, rapidly drawing nearer. Would it reach him in time? He felt himself sinking lower in the water, tasted the bitter sea as it closed over his mouth. Then something struck his shoulder and a hand grasped the collar of his shirt.

"You're all right now," said a well-remembered voice. "I'll hold you up till you can climb into the boat."

He rested for a moment, supported by the steady hand. Then, with a mighty effort, half-lifting himself, half-dragged by his rescuer, he scrambled over the gunwale and fell in a heap at Mavis's feet.

Chapter XXI

He lay there for several moments, too thankful for his escape to be capable of any other thought. The engine of the speed-boat sprang into life again, and he felt the sensation of swift motion. Then he slowly gathered himself together, and seated himself by Mavis's side.

She was gazing straight ahead of her, her keen eyes striving to pierce the wreathing coils of mist. But she shot a swift glance at him, and it seemed to Merrion that the colour mounted to her face. "Why, it's Mr. Merrion!" she exclaimed. She resumed her former attitude of undeviating attention to the boat's progress, and when she spoke again it was in a tone of studied carelessness, as though she wished to obliterate the concern her first words had expressed.

"Well, I didn't expect to meet you here, Mr. Merrion. How do you come to be bathing in the middle of the North Sea?"

"That's rather a long story, Miss Owerton," replied Merrion. "I landed on Vane Sand at low-water and my dinghy drifted away. It's the most fortunate thing that ever happened to me that you were cruising about in the vicinity. I was very nearly gone when you picked me up."

"You were," agreed Mavis. "I wondered what it could be when I heard you shout. It was lucky I had stopped my engine, or I should never have heard you. But if you started from Vane Sand, you must have been swimming away from shore. You were well out to sea when I picked you up."

"It's very likely. I had lost all sense of direction in the fog. I can't understand how you have any idea where we are."

"I? Oh, I know this coast fairly well. I have been out all the morning, rather enjoying the sense of being lost in the fog. I thought just now that I couldn't be far from the Outer Vane buoy. There's a bell on it and I stopped my engine to listen for it. I heard it, quite close, just after I'd picked you up. And now I'm running on a course for the entrance of the river."

"Isn't it a bit risky, cruising about outside in a fog like this?" asked Merrion, with a note of reproof in his voice.

"Risky? Perhaps, but that's half the fun of it," she replied seriously. "Besides, I felt that I had to get away by myself for a bit. But aren't you perishing with cold in those wet things, Mr. Merrion?"

"Oh, no, I'm all right. I dare say you won't mind landing me as soon as we get inside the river. I can run about and get myself dry."

"I shall do nothing of the sort!" exclaimed Mavis. "You're coming up to the Hall with me, where you can have something hot to drink. I dare say we can rig you up in some of father's clothes. You can't very well wander about High Eldersham in a shirt and a pair of trousers."

Merrion paused before he replied. He was lost in admiration of this girl who, however surprised she might be at meeting him under such circumstances, had studiously refrained from asking questions. He would gladly follow her to the end of the earth, could they have made that journey alone together. But to appear at the Hall now would be to announce his presence in High Eldersham, and that might spell the ruin of his plans. On the other hand, though he was quite prepared to juggle with the truth where others were concerned, he could not bring himself to lie to this girl. The only thing to do was to admit her into his confidence. Surely her discretion had proved her worthy of it.

"Look here, Miss Owerton," he began awkwardly. "I've been sailing under false colours, I'm afraid. You thought I was in High Eldersham the other day as a friend of Hollesley's. Well, I'm not."

At the mention of Hollesley's name a frown passed across her face. "I'm not altogether sorry to hear that," she replied. "But I didn't ask you for any explanations, Mr. Merrion."

"I know you didn't, and that's why I want to make them. I'm hanging about the place in connection with the murder of that poor fellow Whitehead at the Rose and Crown."

"Really? Are you a detective, Mr. Merrion? How thrilling! I've always wanted to meet one in real life. But I never expected to fish one so scantily clothed out of the middle of the North Sea."

"I'm afraid you'll be disappointed, but I'm not really a detective. I happen to be a friend of Inspector Young, who is in charge of the case, and he asked me to help him. I'd give you my card if I had one, but I'm afraid I left them all in my coat pocket on Vane Sand. But I assure you that I'm a comparatively respectable member of society."

"How dull!" exclaimed Mavis. "You quite raised my hopes for a moment. But I don't really see that it matters what you are. You've got to be warmed and clothed before you can resume your occupation, whatever it may be."

"It's awfully good of you, Miss Owerton. But, you see, I don't want people to know that I'm in the neighbourhood."

"Oh, I see what you're driving at. Well, you can set your mind at rest. Nobody need know of your visit to the Hall except myself and old Christy, and he won't say a word to anybody if I ask him not to. Father's away for the day, and won't be back till dinner time. You will be perfectly safe, and you can slip away whenever you want to. Hallo, here we are!"

The fog appeared to be less dense in-shore and, as Mavis spoke, Merrion saw the dim outline of the dunes looming up ahead. Mavis turned the wheel a trifle and the boat sped towards the gap that marked the mouth of the river.

"Not a bad shot," remarked Mavis complacently. "What do you think of my skill as a navigator, Mr. Merrion?"

"Marvellous!" replied Merrion, with heart-felt ad-mira-tion. "You couldn't have judged your course better."

They entered the river, and within a few minutes Mavis brought the boat up to her moorings at the bottom of the park. "Now then, come along," she said as they landed. "There's nobody about, and we can get into the house by the side door."

After a brisk walk through the park, they gained the house unobserved. Without a word Mavis led Merrion upstairs, and opened a door. "I think the bathroom is the best place for you," she whispered. "I'll see Christy, and tell him enough to keep him quiet. He'll bring you some clothes and a hot whisky. And when you're ready, you had better come down to the library and we'll have tea. That is, of course, if you can spare the time."

She disappeared before Merrion could reply. In a few min-utes the old servant, whom he had seen on his previous visit to the Hall, appeared, solicitous for his welfare, but display-ing a commendable lack of curiosity. Merrion plunged into a hot bath and, as he sat there, letting the grateful warmth percolate through his chilled body, he considered how this unexpected adventure would affect his plans.

He must somehow contrive to reach the grove after dark, that was evident. He dare not miss this opportunity of witnessing the assembly, since it might be a long time before the next was held. The recovery of the iron box could wait. Although he was very curious to know what it might contain, it could have no connection with the object of his quest, and any investigations in that direction were merely in the nature of a side-show. The same applied to the mystery of the disappearance of his dinghy. It might have been removed under a misapprehension, though Merrion could not resist the suspicion that the action had been deliberate. Still, although but for an amazing stroke of fortune, it would have cost him his life, he could afford to defer his inquiries until to-morrow, all the more since nobody could guess that he had been rescued.

The only trouble for the moment was that for the rest of the evening he would have to rely upon himself. The only way in which he could get in touch with Newport would be to walk along the shore to the bay where *Alisette* was anchored. Even then, he could only reach her by swimming, since the dinghy was lost, and Merrion had had enough of swimming for one day. Besides, there was scarcely time for that and, even if he reached *Alisette,* Newport would be of very little assistance to him, since they still would not have a dinghy. Better leave Newport to his own devices. Sooner or later he would bring the yacht into the lagoon and he could join her somehow after the assembly had ended.

There remained Inspector Young, who some time during the afternoon would arrive at the Rose and Crown. But Merrion was determined that at all costs Young must be kept in ignorance, until he had discovered the identity of the mysterious president of the coven. If it should prove to be Sir William, he would keep the secret to himself. Whatever the consequence might be, Mavis should not suffer. He had no idea what course he would take. It was no use making plans in advance. He could only watch circumstances as they developed, and take what action seemed best. One thing was certain, that everything had sunk into insignificance compared with the preservation of Mavis's happiness.

Merrion, looking strangely unlike his usual dapper self in his borrowed clothes, was conducted by the imperturbable Christy to the library. Mavis was not in the room, but Christy assured him that she would join him shortly. He amused himself by walking round the room, scanning the titles of the books which almost filled it. At last he came to what he had dreaded to find, a whole case full of books devoted to witchcraft and demonology, ancient and modern.

He turned away guiltily and came back to the fireplace, where he stood staring gloomily into the heart of the smouldering logs. The entry of Mavis aroused him from his reverie. She had changed her dress and was now arrayed in shimmering silk, looking in Merrion's eyes, lovelier than ever.

"Sit down, Mr. Merrion," she said. "Christy is just bringing tea. Really, the clothes he found you are not at all a bad fit."

"I think they're wonderful," agreed Merrion. "Savile Row couldn't have managed better. I hope that you will allow me to keep them for to-night. I will call and return them to-morrow without fail."

"To-morrow?" she repeated, raising her eyelids slightly. "Then it won't matter if you're seen to-morrow? I can't undertake to smuggle you in and out of the house indefinitely, you know."

"I do not think that it will matter if my presence becomes known to-morrow," replied Merrion gravely. "In fact, I shall probably find reason to call on Sir William in the course of the day."

For an instant she looked puzzled and then her brow cleared. "Oh, yes, he's a magistrate, of course. It is something to do with poor Whitehead's death, I suppose. By the way, Mr. Merrion, how do you propose to get back to Gippingford, for I suppose that is where you are staying?"

Merrion grinned in spite of himself. "Well, as a matter of fact, I'm not," he replied. "I'm living on board *Alisette*, that seven-tonner yawl you were so interested in the other day at the mouth of the river. I've chartered her for three months. And she's lying a few miles up the coast at this very moment."

"But how thrilling!" exclaimed Mavis. Then, in a tone of reproof. "Do you mean to say that you were on board that day when I was inquisitive enough to come and look at her?"

"I was," confessed Merrion. "But, you know, I wasn't anxious for anybody to know it."

"And, quite naturally, you couldn't trust a woman's tongue. You thought I might tell Laurence Hollesley, I suppose?"

There was a bitterness in her tone that startled Merrion. "Him, and others," he replied lamely.

Christy had brought in tea by this time, and the two were sitting together over the fire. Mavis sat silently for several minutes, staring straight in front of her. And then suddenly she spoke in a low voice. "Would it surprise you if I told you that I was afraid of Laurence, Mr. Merrion?"

Merrion almost leapt from his chair. "Afraid!" he exclaimed. "Why, what's he been saying—?"

"Oh, I'm not afraid on my account," she replied hastily. "But we had a bit of a scene this morning. That's really why I went out in the speed-boat. I wanted to get away, somewhere I should be alone. I'll tell you the whole story. It seems that Laurence started in his car for London about half-past nine. Father had business in Gippingford, and he started out in our car about the same time. Laurence saw him and turned in here, knowing that I should be alone.

"Well, to make a long story short, he asked me, for the third time this year, I think, if I would marry him. I told him I wouldn't, and said that he might just as well make up his mind that I meant what I said and stop worrying me. He was in one of those queer moods of his when he hardly seems to know what he's doing or saying. He flew into a rage and said that he was tired of this foolish resistance on my part. It didn't really make any difference whether I said yes or no, for he had power to obtain what he wanted. He could force me into marrying him any time he wanted, and if I wouldn't do it willingly, I should have to do it unwillingly. Both I and father were entirely in his power, and he would have no difficulty in making us do what he wanted. I never heard anybody go on in such a way in my life. Before I could get a word in, he burst out of the house, jumped into his car and drove away. But I confess he left me with a very uncomfortable feeling. I simply can't imagine what he meant when he talked of our being in his power."

"It is popularly supposed, among those who know him, that Hollesley is a trifle mad," replied Merrion. "I shouldn't let rantings like that worry you, Miss Owerton. Confound his impudence! I wish I'd been here to have a word with him. I don't mind telling you, in the strictest confidence, that I fancy I know something about friend Hollesley that would make him sing very small if I were to disclose it."

"As I say, I'm not worried for myself," said Mavis. "It's on father's account, really. He's as innocent as a lamb, poor old dear, and any unscrupulous person could easily get a hold over him. I'm perfectly certain that it can't be anything serious."

Merrion made no reply. A look of sternness, utterly foreign to him, came upon his face as he pondered Mavis's words. What could be the clue to Hollesley's power over Sir William? Did he know of the assemblies in the grove, and of their president? What dark mystery underlay the sinister practices which took place at High Eldersham? Most important of all, how was he to save Mavis from the horror of her father's exposure and disgrace? He turned towards her abruptly. "Look here, Miss Owerton, will you trust me till to-morrow?" he said. "Something is going to happen to-night,

I can't even hint to you what it is, that will probably place me in possession of facts that I have been seeking for weeks. When I have learnt them, I may be able to tell you what is behind Hollesley's threats. In any case, I promise to come and see you and Sir William as early as I can to-morrow."

"I will trust you," replied Mavis simply. "I won't even ask you to give me some hint of what your mysterious words may mean. But, in return, will you trust me enough to let me help you, if there is anything I can do?"

"I will, and that gladly. As it happens, you can help me. As I told you, I lost my dinghy this afternoon. Will you lend me yours until midnight?"

"Of course I will, I hoped you would ask something more difficult," she replied with a smile.

For some while longer they sat talking, deliberately choosing indifferent subjects. Then as the clock struck seven, Mavis rose. "If you do not want father to see you, it is time you were going," she said. "He will be back very soon now. I will come down to the river with you, in case you lose your way in the fog."

Side by side they walked down through the park. The fog had descended thicker than ever, and without Mavis's guidance Merrion would inevitably have taken the wrong path. She led him to where the dinghy was tied up, then suddenly, as he was about to step into it, she laid a hand upon his arm. "You're not going to do anything—dangerous, are you?" she asked softly.

He swung round and faced her. There was a note of solicitude in her voice which made the blood run madly through his veins. Obeying a sudden impulse he caught her in his arms. She lay there for an instant, then gently disengaged herself.

Breathing one last word, "Mavis!" he stepped into the dinghy and picked up the oars. The girl's figure faded from his eyes into the surrounding mist.

Chapter XXII

The fog was all in Merrion's favour. There was no need for him to wait until darkness fell before proceeding to the grove. This was the more convenient, since it was now high water, and there would be no difficulty in landing on the island, an operation which might have been attended with some inconvenience when the tide was out. He started to row steadily up stream, taking care not to make a noise, but satisfied that, if he took due precautions, nobody could see him from the bank.

He reached the island soon after eight, and landed at the same spot as before. His thoughts were so full of Mavis and of his parting from her that it was not until then that an obvious difficulty presented itself to him. What was he to do with the dinghy? His original scheme had been that Newport should take it back to the yacht. He could not leave it drawn up on the shore of the island; that would be to betray his presence to the first comer. The only alternative was to push it out into the stream, which was running strongly down the river. In all probability it would be carried out to sea, to be picked up, perhaps days later, by some fisherman and hailed as treasure trove.

Well, there was no help for it. It had seen its best days, anyhow, and he could easily buy Mavis a new one in

Gippingford. That would be the second dinghy he had lost that day. With a pang of regret he pushed the little boat away from the bank, and watched it until it passed out of his sight downstream. Then he turned to explore the island once more.

The fog was not so thick that he could not make out his whereabouts. He had retained in his mind a knowledge of the topography of the island, and his first action was to proceed to the narrow causeway that joined it to the mainland. Sheltering behind the trees, he peered out cautiously. There was nobody in sight, and however intently he listened, he could hear no sound that might indicate the presence of anybody near him. Having satisfied himself of this, he proceeded to explore the island foot by foot, until he was certain that nobody was hidden upon it.

Then he made for the little patch of undergrowth which he had noticed on his first visit, and settled himself as comfortably as he could in the centre of it, in such a position that he could look out across the grove in the direction of the altar. He could feel a faint air upon his cheek and it seemed to him that the fog was thinning once more. This did not concern him. Darkness was falling rapidly and that would serve to screen him. Automatically he felt in his pockets for a pipe, before he remembered that he had left it with his coat on Vane Sand. Perhaps it was just as well. Nobody was likely to come along yet, but he could not take too many precautions. His thoughts would provide him with plenty of occupation meanwhile.

He lay there, weaving dreams of Mavis, lost to all sense of time and environment. Then, suddenly, he came back to himself with a start. The distant sound of a human voice had come to him very faintly through the still night.

Merrion's nerves braced themselves to the coming ordeal. He had no means of telling the time, but he judged that it must be somewhere between ten and eleven. The fog had cleared considerably, but a mist still hung in the branches of the trees above his head, dimly visible as a silver curtain faintly radiant from the moon, not yet at its full. But, on the ground beneath, it was still very dark and in the centre of Merrion's hiding-place the gloom was impenetrable.

Again he heard the voice, this time much closer. He made out that two men were approaching, and had reached the causeway. They spoke in low tones and Merrion could not hear what they said. They came on steadily and, as they did so, Merrion saw a shaft of light strike upon the surrounding tree trunks.

This was awkward. These men, whoever they were, were obviously equipped with electric torches. He crouched still lower in the undergrowth, like a hare in its forme, motionless, scarcely daring to breathe. The light flashed uncertainly as the men advanced. He could hear the twigs cracking beneath their feet. They came out into the grove itself, and Merrion could see two cloaked and hooded figures, each with a torch in its hand.

They passed within ten yards of him, their torches illuminating the brushwood just above his prone figure. The least impulse of inquisitiveness, and he must infallibly be discovered. But obviously they regarded their duty as merely perfunctory. They walked on to the edge of the island, where they separated, each taking a different direction. Merrion realised that they were making a tour of the bank, and hugged himself for his foresight in sending the dinghy adrift.

The light grew fainter until it finally disappeared, and the footsteps grew fainter in the distance. Merrion guessed that these men were the sentries whom he had seen on the occasion of the last assembly. They would now take up their position on the far side of the causeway, to guard the island from the approach of any unauthorised persons. He was now safe from discovery, and could await in security the events that were to follow.

Half an hour elapsed before Merrion heard anything further. Then there was a sound of rapid footsteps, and a shadowy form, of which he could not see the outline, entered the open space in the centre of the grove. Others followed at intervals, until the turf was covered by a strange, silent multitude. They uttered no word, but Merrion could hear their quick breathing, the rustle of their garments as they swayed rhythmically upon their feet, occasionally an hysterical sob, quickly repressed. They stood there waiting, their eyes within the depths of their hoods staring intently towards the altar, hidden under the shadow of the trees.

Then Merrion became conscious of slow and majestic footsteps advancing through the gloom. They approached the grove, but ceased before they reached the open space. And, as they did so, a queer wailing cry broke from the assembled worshippers. Merrion, staring intently from his hiding-place, could see nothing. But he guessed that the devil, the mysterious president of the ceremonies, had taken up his position in the deep gloom behind the altar.

There was a moment's silence, as the shadowy figures bowed down to the earth. Then a feeble, flickering light appeared out of the shadow. In its dim radiance Merrion could see that it proceeded from a wick set in a bowl of oil upon the altar. One by one the figures approached, each drawing a tall candle from the folds of its cloak. With a deep reverence each held the end of its candle to the flame, then returned to its place, bearing the lighted candle.

The scene, thus illuminated, was awe-inspiring in its solemnity. The candle shone upon these figures, rigid as statues, round which played gigantic and distorted shadows as the bright flames flickered in the night air. The grove itself was filled with a dim, uncertain light, but the altar, upon which the lamp had been extinguished when the last candle was lighted, could only faintly be discerned, a dark and menacing mass. And, behind it, under the overhanging branches of the trees, all was in utter and profound gloom.

All at once a strange, hollow voice, inhuman in its ghostly intonation, rang out from the heart of the shadow. Merrion could not catch the words, but he recognised it as a command. As it ceased, three figures advanced, two of them supporting the third between them. The centre figure was small and slight, as that of a young girl. Merrion felt a thrill of anticipation. This was undoubtedly the figure that Newport had seen on the previous night, standing on the newly-made grave. This girl was a neophyte, about to be admitted to the coven. The ceremony which Newport had witnessed had been one of preparation. Now the rite of initiation was to take place.

The three figures advanced until they stood before the altar, the girl in the centre swaying as though she would have fallen had she not been supported. Again the inhuman voice rang out, muffled and indistinct, but obviously questioning. The worshippers replied in a strange wailing chant. "We present her to thee, Master." Then another question, and the chanted reply, "She comes of her own free will, Master!" A third question, and again the reply, "Body and soul, to work thy will, Master!"

One of the supporting figures bent down and whispered something in the girl's ear. She shuddered violently, as though awaking from a trance, and stretched out one trembling arm above the altar. Her supporters drew back the fold of the cloak which covered it, so that the flickering light of the candles fell on the bare white flesh. Then something moved in the gloom, and Merrion, with a thrill of horror, saw a gigantic hairy arm, terminating in a cloven hoof and holding a bowl, stretched out of the darkness. It laid the bowl on the altar, and drew back, to appear again holding a shining knife. With a swift movement it descended, severing one of the smaller veins in the girl's arm.

Once more she shuddered violently, but made no sound. It seemed to Merrion that she was insensible to pain. The bright blood spurted into the bowl, a few crimson drops splashing upon the stone itself. More and more slowly it came, until at last the ghostly arm shot out once more and applied some kind of salve to the bleeding arm. Then, as the figures on either side of her withdrew their support, the girl swayed for an instant and, with a shrill strangled cry, fell senseless at the foot of the altar.

The arm appeared once more, holding a vase in the shape of the naked and distorted body of a woman, from which it poured some clear and sparkling liquid in the bowl. The contents bubbled up for an instant in a pink froth, and then subsided. Then the figures which had supported the girl picked up the bowl and carried it round the assembly, holding it to the lips of each in turn. Then, when all had drunk, they drained the dregs themselves and replaced the bowl on the altar.

The draught seemed to mount like fire into the brains of the worshippers. Clasping one another at random, they broke into a mad formless dance, whirling in intricate confusion through the whole width of the glade, holding their candles above their heads. This wild pandemonium lasted for several minutes, and then ceased, at a word of command from the figure behind the altar, as suddenly as it had begun. The spectral figures resumed their attitudes of rigid expectancy.

Once more the hollow voice began to speak, this time in tones so low that Merrion could not at first make out the purport of the words. But very soon the voice became broken with passion, and grew louder. It seemed to Merrion that it was invoking some curse on all those who interfered with the actions of the assembly. It broke into a kind of diabolical litany, to the sentences of which the worshippers replied with muttered responses. It ended with a name which came clearly to Merrion's ears, that of Viney.

As the voice ceased, one of the figures advanced towards the altar and drew something from beneath its cloak. The light of the candle carried by the figure fell on the object, and Merrion recognised it as a roughly moulded doll, with a needle plunged into its head. The doll was laid upon the altar, upon which the lamp had been relighted. The unseen president muttered a few words over it, and then taking a needle held it in the flame until it grew red. This he plunged into the heart of the doll. A drop of molten wax oozed like blood from the stab and fell upon the cold stone.

Merrion felt a cold shudder as he watched this symbolic deed. The needle plunged into the head had typified the pains that Viney had already complained of. This second needle, plunged into the heart, must be his death warrant. So absorbed was Merrion by what he saw, so deeply had the sense of mystery entered his mind, that he did not pause to consider how the symptoms were transmitted from the effigy to the individual. He felt that he was in the presence of something devilish and inexplicable, that here before his eyes he saw the operation of a power beyond man's understanding. Every sense told him that he was surrounded by horror; the impression of satanic power was too strong to be combated.

The figure which had produced the doll received it back from the ghastly limb to which he had delivered it. That it had been a man, Merrion was sure from his gait. But any further recognition was impossible beneath the garments that veiled him as a shroud. Merrion began to grow anxious. The proceedings had already lasted a considerable time, and as yet he had seen nothing of the figure hidden in the darkness behind the altar but that awful arm. Would he remain hidden throughout the ceremony, and then disappear as furtively as he had come? If so, Merrion's vigil would have been wasted, and he would be no nearer the solution of the mystery than before.

A sudden summons from the hollow, unearthly voice recalled his attention to the scene before him. Twelve figures detached themselves from the rest and approached the altar. As they reached it, they drew from under their cloaks half-burnt candles, which they laid upon the stone. The hidden president received them and began to break them in pieces.

This action puzzled Merrion, until its significance dawned upon him. These were no doubt the candles which had been plunged into the grave earth the previous night, and thus devoted to some sinister purpose. He watched, fascinated, as the broken pieces were collected and placed in a metal bowl. This in turn was deposited on two stones, so that it rested above the flame of the lamp. The wick burnt luridly, emitting a pungent, acrid smoke, which drifted slowly across the clearing. The watching figures joined hands and silently arranged themselves in a circle, planting their candles upright in the ground in the centre. Then the ring began to revolve, slowly and with a strange swaying motion, the feet of the dancers seeming to glide over the smooth turf. But slowly the speed increased, the supine forms of the dancers grew more animated, they swayed backwards and forwards from the hips in growing excitement. And the pungent smoke of the lamp flitted in thin wisps across their faces.

Once more the gigantic hairy arms were extended from the darkness behind the altar, but now they terminated in human hands. These plunged into the bowl, kneading the softening wax, until they withdrew it as a plastic lump. Then the swiftly working fingers moulded the shapeless mass into the rough semblance of a human figure, round the neck of which they wound something that resembled a wisp of hair. The voice rang out, hoarse and passionate, as though its owner were drunk with some satanic ecstasy. At this inarticulate cry the ring dissolved instantly, and the over-wrought worshippers, reeling and giddy, staggered back to their original positions.

The hands held the figure aloft, as though to display it to the assembly. The voice rang out, vibrant with demoniac fury: "This is the image of one henceforward in my power!" Then with a swift movement, the extended arms were lowered, and the doll was laid upon the altar. The right hand vanished, to reappear once more holding the knife, with the sharp point of which it pricked the left wrist. Two drops of blood fell slowly, one after the other upon the head of the doll. And as they did so, the hollow voice spoke once more.

"I baptise thee Mavis Owerton!"

Chapter XXIII

At the sound of that name a low murmur rose, as though in assent, from the assembled worshippers. But Merrion scarcely heard it. A wave of horror swept through him, so potent that he felt as though chilled with a sudden frost. This was succeeded by an access of fierce rage, so that, before he could restrain himself, he half rose from his crouching position. His eyes were fixed upon the hands holding the doll. At the first sign that they were about to plunge a needle into its grotesque form, he would have rushed out and torn the vile thing away, regardless of what might happen to himself.

But nothing of the sort happened. After its revolting baptism, the doll was laid aside behind the altar, and once more the bowl took its place. The hands, once more covered by the cloven hoofs, poured some deep-red liquid into it from the vase, and then one of the worshippers advanced and received it kneeling. This figure then rose and, carrying it aloft, presented it in turn to each member of the assembly, who put their lips to it and drank.

This seemed to be the final scene. As each drank, the candle it held was inverted and extinguished by being plunged into the turf. The candles thus went out, one by one, until none of the flickering lights remained. But a faint ghostly radiance still illuminated the scene. The mist seemed to have vanished almost completely, and the moon, though now low in the heavens, lit up the centre of the grove with a pearl-grey light, sufficient for Merrion to see the shadowy outlines of the worshippers as they formed themselves into a ring once more and danced in a mad and whirling circle before the altar. The ring seemed to break up with its own impetus; fragments of it broke off and vanished among the surrounding trees. At last nothing of it remained, and the grove stood empty.

But, though the assembly had thus broken up, the island was not yet deserted. In the silence about him, from the thick shade of the trees, Merrion could hear sounds that betrayed the presence of the worshippers; stealthy footsteps, furtive half-stifled cries. This, somehow, was more horrible than the actual ceremonies had been. Merrion, quivering with disgust, longed for the moment when he could escape from this accursed island. His long inaction was becoming more than he could bear. He felt the instant need of doing something, of returning to the sane world where these nightmares could have no power. And, above all, he must unveil that atrocious and invisible figure, so rightly named the devil, and render it impossible for him to harm the girl he loved.

So, for a minute or two, he waited, his ears strained for the departing footsteps which should announce that these ghastly hooded figures were leaving the island. And then a movement by the altar arrested his attention. As he stared eagerly in that direction, the moon threw a monstrous shadow across the smooth turf of the grove. And, in another instant, the form which had cast that shadow emerged from out of the darkness.

Its appearance froze the blood in Merrion's veins with terror and repulsion. There, in the uncertain light it stood, enormous and horrible. Its body and limbs were covered with the skin of some animal, making them appear swollen and grotesque. The legs terminated in enormous cloven hoofs, upon which it moved unsteadily, with a horrible rolling movement. And the head was that of some huge goat, horned and bearded, surmounting a pair of shoulders which were undoubtedly those of a man.

Merrion watched the slow progress of this figure with awful fascination. Vainly he told himself that this apparition was no more than a man, masquerading in the disguise of a grotesque beast. The horrible things which he had witnessed, the disappearance of his worshippers, wrought up to deeds he dare not guess by the potency of evil, gave to this figure the significance which the whole ceremony had been designed to convey, that of the Prince of Darkness. In Merrion's eyes the figure took on the attributes of the devil himself, malignant, all-powerful, concerned only to reap the harvest of the evil he had sown.

But Merrion had not much leisure for observation. The figure advanced only a few steps, until it stood beside the form of the newly-initiated girl, who still lay insensible where she had fallen. Deliberately it bent down, and lifted the girl in its dreadful, hairy arms. She lay there limp and lifeless, a slight tremor of her limbs the only sign that she still breathed. Then, bearing its burden, the figure slowly retired once more into the deep and impenetrable gloom behind the altar.

At that moment, had Merrion possessed a weapon, he would have used it, careless of the consequences. But he was helpless, surrounded by an overwhelming force of frantic worshippers, who would undoubtedly have rallied to the defence of their leader at the first alarm. But even this would not have restrained him, had not a more powerful consideration filled his brain. He must remain hidden, at whatever cost of diabolical practices being performed almost under his eyes, until the island was once more empty. If he were discovered, there could be no doubt as to what his fate might be. And then there would be nobody to stand between Mavis and things so horrible that he dare not contemplate them.

For many long minutes he lay there, trying to divert his senses and his thoughts from this hellish present by weaving schemes as to what action he should take as soon as he could escape from the island. There could no longer be any question of his keeping his own counsel. In face of the peril to Mavis, a peril utterly vague and intangible, but none the less desperately urgent, he must act without respect of persons. He must go straight to Inspector Young, tell him the whole incredible story, and leave it to him to act. Before morning High Eldersham could be surrounded by a cordon, and the participators in this ghastly orgy rounded up. The identity of the ringleader could be discovered by the wound on the left wrist where the knife had pricked it.

As these thoughts coursed through Merrion's brain, the shadowy figures began to stumble back into the grove, reeling as though drunk with some strong liquor. They seemed careless how they went, pushing their way through the undergrowth, brushing aside the over-hanging branches. So, suddenly, almost before Merrion became aware of his danger, the discovery came. A figure, pressing blindly forward, walked straight upon the tangle of low shrubs in which he was concealed, tripped as the twigs entangled its feet, and fell right upon him. It uttered a scarcely human cry, and a second figure, closely following it, started back in stupefied amazement at the sight of the stranger. Merrion heard a wild beast-like howl of rage as this second figure flung itself towards him, and knew that the time for concealment was past.

He leapt to his feet, the superstitious terror which had preyed upon him swept away in a desperate lust of fighting. He struck out, with the whole weight of his body behind the blow, and the figure before him fell like a stone. He had just time to recover himself when the whole pack were upon him, striking at him blindly, stretching out claw-like hands to pluck his eyes from their sockets. He felt hands upon him everywhere, hands that strove to pull him down and tear him limb from limb. And then, as he fought desperately to beat them back, the devilish figure of their president appeared from behind the altar and came swiftly towards the scene of the struggle, a broken branch in his hands.

At the sight of him a wild desire possessed Merrion. He could not hope to escape; he knew that within a few minutes his mangled and mutilated body would be buried in the soft and yielding mud that edged the river. But first, before the end came, he would do his best to kill the awful thing which menaced the girl he loved. With a supreme effort he shook himself free from his assailants, and launched himself towards the gigantic and menacing figure before him.

He never reached it. Before he could cover a couple of paces he felt his legs grasped from behind and he fell heavily, a horde of struggling creatures hurling themselves upon him as he did so. His arms were pinioned to the ground, leaving him powerless. He resigned himself to the inevitable, agonised by the longing for some less loathsome death. Better far that he should never have been rescued from the clutches of the sea! Death beneath the clean salt waves would have been a merely falling to sleep. But the horror of those bent and eager fingers, the last vile embrace of the all-devouring mud!

And then he heard an angry snarling, as of dogs beaten from their prey, and above it the strange hollow voice raised in insistent command. He became aware that their leader was beating back the pack with his branch, all but half a dozen who were pinning Merrion to the ground. Some sort of order was restored, and Merrion, in spite of his struggles, was securely bound and gagged. He lay quiet at last, trussed like a fowl, unable to move hand or foot. The hideous goat-like mask bent over him and it seemed to him that the eyes behind it flashed malignantly. Then the figure moved slowly away, driving its worshippers before it.

Merrion, lying on his back, could no longer see anything but the light slowly fading in the topmost branches of the trees, as the moon sank below the western horizon. But his acute hearing still remained, and he could detect the sound of many footsteps, slowly vanishing into the distance. The members of the coven were leaving the island, so much he could tell with certainty. But what next? What fate awaited him, lying bound and apparently forgotten? That he would not be allowed to see another sunrise he felt sure.

As he lay there he lost count of time. All he knew was that the moon had set and a profound darkness took possession of the island. This must have happened between midnight and one o'clock, he reckoned. He had long ago abandoned the attempt to free himself from his bonds. These had been tied by hands accustomed to securing hay-ropes, and were beyond his powers to cope with. There was nothing for it but to wait with what patience he could summon, and lean upon the infinitely remote chance of some occurrence which would interfere with the seemingly inevitable end.

At last he heard the sound of approaching footsteps. Whoever it was, he was welcome. The strain of lying motionless, chilled to the marrow, was beginning to tell upon Merrion's nerves. They were coming to finish him off now, no doubt. Without any particular emotion he wondered what manner of death his would be. The inquest upon Whitehead returned to his memory. Death must have been practically instantaneous, the doctor had said. Would he be fortunate enough to share Whitehead's fate? A quick thrust, then oblivion. Well, there were worse ways of leaving this world than that. The pang lay not in death, but in the thought that, once dead, he would be powerless to protect Mavis from the fiend who threatened her.

The footsteps drew nearer, and to his surprise Merrion made out that whoever was approaching was alone. He considered the matter with languid curiosity. One man could murder him without any difficulty, trussed as he was. That part of the affair would be simple. But how was he going to dispose of the body? He would never venture to leave it where it was, surely. That would be taking too great a risk. But, on the other hand, it would need considerable strength even to drag it as far as the mud at the water's edge. And then, the traces that would be left!

It was far too dark for Merrion to see anything, but he could tell that somebody had approached him and come to a standstill beside the spot where he lay. He braced himself for the blow which he felt must even then be poised above him. But instead came a sudden blinding light, dazzling him and making it impossible for him to see even the hand that held the torch. Then the light was switched off suddenly, and the footsteps retreated towards the edge of the water.

Again there was silence, for what seemed to Merrion an eternity, but may have been half an hour. Then a new sound came to his ears, the steady plash of oars, rapidly coming nearer. They ceased, and he heard a low-toned conversation, the words of which he could not catch. The man standing by the waterside had been joined by another, who had arrived in a boat; so much was clear.

The two men left the bank of the river, and advanced towards the clearing. From the sound of their footsteps Merrion guessed that they were carrying some burden between them, and he wondered dully what it could be. Something that was to play a part in his own murder, he supposed. But they laid their burden down at some little distance from him, and remained with it some time, talking to one another.

Then at last they seemed to remember his existence, and came over to where he lay. Once more the torch flashed in his eyes, and a mocking voice addressed him.

"Really, Merrion, my dear fellow! I should have thought you would have known better than to poke your nose into things that don't concern you."

So it was Hollesley after all. Merrion had suspected as much, ever since he had heard Mavis's name pronounced before the assembly. Little as he knew of the man, Merrion knew that he could expect no mercy. Hollesley would never dare to let him escape, holding the secrets that he did.

The light was switched off again, and Merrion heard Hollesley's voice speaking to his companion. "This was the fellow whose boat you found on Vane Sand and towed away, I suppose, Thorburn," he said. "How the devil he got off and found his way here passes my comprehension. We shan't ever know, and it doesn't much matter. I think the plan I mentioned to you just now will be the best. We'll take him out to sea and drop him overboard with a pig of ballast tied to his feet. It's a better fate than he deserves. I half wish I had left him to those idiots who wanted to tear him to pieces just now. After all, it would have put them more than ever in my power."

"Better take him out to sea," growled Thorburn. "He won't leave any traces then."

"Yes, you're quite right," agreed Hollesley. "We'll deal with him when we've settled the other little matter we have in hand. Did you find any difficulty?"

Thorburn laughed, a mocking unpleasant laugh. "Difficulty?" he replied. "No fear! It was as easy as shelling peas. I had meant to go up to the Hall and wake that old fool Christy with a yarn that some old woman in the village was very ill and Doctor Padfield wanted her to come and bear a hand. But, as I landed at the foot of the park there, blast me if she didn't come running to meet me. Looks to me as though she was on the look out for some one, guv'nor."

Hollesley uttered a furious oath. "She won't wait for any one else but me again!" he growled.

"Well, that's as may be," remarked Thorburn. "I went up to her, crept up behind, and then suddenly clapped the cloth over her head. I didn't hurt her, I'll swear. I don't believe she even felt the prick of the needle. And then I just picked her up and brought her along."

And then, in one overwhelming wave of sickening horror, Merrion understood that the burden which had been laid beside the altar was the unconscious form of Mavis.

Chapter XXIV

Inspector Young, on his return to London after his interview with Merrion at Gippingford on April 21st, was in a very despondent mood. As things were at present, it seemed to him that the solution of the mystery of Whitehead's murder hung upon a very slender thread. Merrion was convinced, on what the Inspector considered purely speculative grounds, that the clue to the murder would be found in a meeting to be held at High Eldersham in nine days' time. And that, apparently was the only progress to be reported.

All very well, thought Young, but suppose Merrion's theory should turn out to be a mare's nest? Suppose the assembly should never take place, or, even if it did, should yield no clue? The Inspector regretted the impulse that had led him to call Merrion to his aid. That highly-imaginative person seemed to have surrounded the crime with a smoke-screen of occult and wholly irrelevant mystery, with the result that he himself was no further advanced than when he started. It would have been far better if he had proceeded along conventional lines; summoned one of his assistants, and interrogated everybody within a ten-mile radius of the Rose and Crown. He would surely then have got hold of something more tangible from which to work.

Something of this he tried to explain to his chief at Scotland Yard. He gave an outline of all that had happened since the murder, and candidly confessed his failure. "I'm sorry to say, sir, that I can't see any further ahead than I did when I first went down there," he said. "I believe I've been working on the wrong lines, so far. But it's not too late to make a fresh start. If you think fit, sir, I'll go down there again straight away and examine everybody in the place. I could take Hodges with me to help me."

The Assistant Commissioner was a wise man, who knew exactly the capabilities of his subordinates, and never interfered with their methods except under pressure of the most urgent necessity. He had the greatest confidence in Young, and felt sure that he would not have acted as he had done unless he had considered it advisable. Something might come of it yet; he knew from experience that clues had a habit of appearing from the most unexpected places.

"It's a most extraordinary story, Young," he said, after a pause. "But, as you realise yourself, it's of more interest to anthropologists than to the police. More than one Act of Parliament prescribes heavy penalties for witchcraft, and I don't suppose that they've ever been repealed. They're probably still on the statue book, but you'd cause a bit of a sensation these days if you instituted a prosecution for witchcraft. But that's not the point at the moment. We're concerned with the murder of this man Whitehead. You're absolutely free to do as you like. If you think it advisable, go back to High Eldersham and round up the village, by all means. Have a cigarette?"

He handed Young his case, and lighted a cigarette himself. "There's just this about it," he continued reflectively. "You know as well as I do that, when a crime has been committed, it sometimes pays to induce a sense of security in the criminal. Many crimes have been brought home to their perpetrators long after the police have appeared to have forgotten all about them. In this case, in my own opinion, nothing will be lost and something may possibly be gained by waiting for a few days. Mind, I don't want to influence you in any way. You've been on the spot, and you know more about it than I do. But, if you agree, I'll find you another job which will keep your mind off this business for a few days, but will leave you free to meet your friend, Merrion, on the thirtieth."

Young agreed, readily enough, and after some further conversation he left the Assistant Commissioner's room. But it was not long before he was summoned there again, to find his chief frowning over a message he had just received.

"Hallo, Young," he said, as the Inspector entered. "I've found the very job to keep you busy for a few days. Did you ever hear of Vincent Faxfleet, a young fellow who writes books and things? There's a play of his on at the Escorial now."

"Yes, sir," replied Young promptly. "I've read one of his books. Morbid sort of stuff, I thought, with about as much indecency thrown in as he thought the censor would pass."

"I didn't know you were a literary critic. We'll have to put you on to the job of looking out for immoral literature. However, that can wait for the moment. Vincent Faxfleet was found dead this morning in his flat in Chelsea. You'll observe that everybody suffering from the artistic temperament flocks to Chelsea. Cause of death, an over-injection of heroin. Syringe found by his bedside, and with it a representative assortment of drugs of all kinds. May have committed suicide, or may have given himself an overdose by mistake. I don't know which, and I don't much care. But what I do want to know is where those drugs came from. There seems to be no question of his having had a doctor's prescription.

"Now, this drug business is always cropping up, and we shall never be able to stamp it out entirely. If people mean to get drugs, they'll get them, by hook or by crook. Personally, so long as it is confined to a few individuals, here and there, I don't see that it matters much. The best thing to do with a confirmed drug addict is to let him or her have enough of the stuff to finish them off. What we want to stop is the opportunity for fresh people acquiring the craving. They will only do so when drugs cannot be acquired more or less easily. The possession of this assortment of drugs by young Faxfleet proves that they can be so acquired. You see what I'm getting at, Young?"

"I do, sir," replied Young. "You want me to find out how Faxfleet got hold of the stuff?"

"Exactly. It won't be easy. These things are handed along from one person to another, and there's every possibility of missing a link in the chain somewhere. If you're not absolutely up-to-date, I recommend you to study the records for a bit. You'll find there pretty well all we know of the existing methods of distribution. Don't rely on that too much, for as fast as we find out one dodge, another is substituted for it. There are brains behind this business, as there should be behind any other. You might let me know from time to time how you get on."

Before the Inspector started on this new investigation, he followed his chief's advice, and consulted the records. Here he found detailed accounts of what had already been discovered of the means of distributing dangerous drugs. Armed with this information, he proceeded to Faxfleet's flat in Chelsea, where the sergeant in charge put him in possession of the details.

"We've been over the place pretty thoroughly, sir, and this is what we've found," said the sergeant proudly, pointing to a row of half a dozen glass stoppered bottles. "We found those in one of the drawers in the bedroom, tucked away behind a lot of socks and things. They're most of them more than half full, sir."

Young strolled over to the bottles and examined them carefully. Each bore a label in a neat handwriting, with the name of the drug upon it; Cocaine, Morphine Hydrochloride, Heroin, and so forth. Some contained minute tablets, others a white crystalline powder. It was, as the Assistant Commissioner had said, a representative assortment.

One thing was immediately clear to the Inspector. No man, however addicted to drugs he might be, could possibly require so many varieties for his own consumption. It was more than probable that Faxfleet had been a link in the chain of distribution, as well as a drug-taker himself. If the source from which he had obtained the contents of these bottles could be ascertained the chain would be traced back one link further towards its origin.

Young left the bedroom and passed into a large room which Faxfleet had evidently used as a study. It was still in the state of disorder in which he had left it; the large table under the window was covered with sheets of paper and odds and ends of correspondence. Young looked over these rapidly, but nothing of any particular interest caught his eye. He then turned his attention to the waste-paper basket. This was filled to overflowing with opened envelopes, fragments of manuscript in the same handwriting as the labels on the bottles, and similar rubbish. Young turned the whole lot out upon the floor. At the bottom of the basket were at least a dozen empty matchboxes, of a brand specially prepared for smokers.

The Inspector desisted from his task and looked round the room. The original grate in the fireplace had been removed, and an electric heater stood in its place. The room was electrically lighted. There were no signs of pipes, cigarettes, ash-trays, or any of the paraphernalia of the smoker. What in the world did Faxfleet want with all those match-boxes, and where were their contents? There was not so much as a match stand to be seen anywhere.

A puzzled frown crossed the Inspector's face as he started to walk round the room, examining every object he came to.

On a bookcase against one wall was a Japanese bowl, and in this he found what he was seeking. It contained a quantity of matches, which he recognised as being of the same brand as the empty match-boxes. He emptied the bowl on to a sheet of paper. There were only sufficient matches to fill three or four of the boxes, at the most.

Once more he turned his attention to the waste-paper basket, looking this time at the dates of the postmarks on the envelopes which it contained. None of them were more than two days old, and it was therefore a fair assumption that the basket had not been emptied since that time. If the empty match-boxes had been placed in it as recently as that, how had Faxfleet disposed of the remainder of the matches?

A sudden inspiration struck Young. He picked up one of the empty boxes, and examined it closely through a magnifying glass. As he did so, an exclamation of satisfaction escaped him. Adhering to the bottom of the box, and in the joints of the box itself, were a few grams of white powder. The whole thing was now clear to him. The boxes had undoubtedly served as receptacles for the drugs. The matches had been taken out of them and replaced by drugs, probably made up into packets like a chemist's powder. Then a layer of matches had been placed on the top. To any casual observer, the box would look as innocent as before. And one could hand a box of matches to any one without attracting the slightest attention, in the street or elsewhere. This no doubt was how Faxfleet had acquired the drugs.

The Inspector returned hot-foot to Scotland Yard, where his suspicions were confirmed. Upon analysis, the white powder in the bottom of the boxes proved to consist of particles of drugs of various kinds. The next step must be to trace, if possible, the source of the match-boxes.

It was obviously useless to base the investigation upon the match-boxes themselves. They were of a brand that is to be found in every place where matches are sold throughout the whole country. But there was another way of approaching the matter. Faxfleet had been a man with a rapidly-growing reputation and, since he made a good deal of money, had a wide circle of friends. Young, by diligent inquiry, discovered those with whom most of his time had been spent recently, and sought them out, male and female.

In the process of interviewing them he learnt many things about the dead man's habits. He learnt, for instance, that it was an open secret that he resorted to drugs when in search of inspiration. He learnt the details of a particularly sordid little episode, in a fit of remorse for which Faxfleet might well have decided to take his own life. He deduced sufficient from his various conversations to make it fairly certain that Faxfleet had supplied drugs to many of those to which he spoke. But this was following the chain in the wrong direction. He could glean no information whatever as to the next link towards the origin.

Nobody had ever known the dead man to carry a box of matches, much less to buy one. He did not smoke, he did not carry cigarettes about with him to offer to his friends. Those who were sufficiently familiar with his flat knew of the matches kept in the Japanese bowl, to which they were in the habit of helping themselves. So far as they knew, these were the only matches in the whole flat.

Young pointed out that if Faxfleet's visitors used the matches from the bowl, it must occasionally require replenishing. Surely he must have bought matches for that purpose? But his informants stuck to their previous statements. They supposed that his house-keeper looked after that sort of thing. Not one of them could remember a single instance of Faxfleet having bought a box of matches. It seemed pretty clear that the match-boxes were not passed openly, at any rate.

Then how were they acquired? Faxfleet seemed latterly to have had a distaste for being alone, and Young had no difficulty in tracing his movements over a considerable period. He could account for almost every hour of his time, except a period of about six hours on the day before his death. He had left his flat at half-past nine in the morning, telling his housekeeper that he had business with a theatrical manager. He had walked into his club at half-past three that afternoon. But no theatrical manager that Young could unearth had set eyes upon Faxfleet during that period.

In all probability these six hours had been employed by Faxfleet in procuring the drugs. Of course, he might have transacted other business as well, but, if that had been the case, Young felt that he would certainly have come across some acquaintance of the dead man who would have had knowledge of his actions. But, if the procuring of the drugs alone had taken six hours, it seemed to follow that they were not obtainable close at hand, that a journey of some kind had had to be undertaken. Faxfleet had possessed no car of his own. Young therefore set inquiries on foot among taxi-drivers and others who might have seen him.

Things had reached this stage by the morning of the thirtieth. Young, who had become deeply interested in his new quest, was tempted to break the promise he had made to Merrion. But he reflected that the reports of his assistants could not possibly be complete for another couple of days. Not without some inward reluctance he took an afternoon train to Gippingford. He dined there and, after dinner, hired a car to drive him out to the Rose and Crown, where he arrived shortly after ten o'clock, having been delayed on the road by fog in the valleys.

From what he could see of the village, High Eldersham wore an air of the most profound repose.

Chapter XXV

After Merrion had left the yacht at eleven o'clock on the morning of the thirtieth, bound in the dinghy for Vane Sand, Newport, left to his own devices, set to work to scrub out the forecastle. He tackled the job thoroughly, whistling to himself as he worked. He was thoroughly enjoying the cruise and, knowing his master as he did, looked forward to some interesting development in the near future.

From time to time he put his head up through the hatch and looked around him appraisingly. The mist was certainly growing thicker, developing into a genuine fog, in fact. Already the shore had faded from sight, and out to sea it looked thicker still. Newport wondered how this would affect his master's plans. He would find it difficult to row back either to the yacht or to the lagoon. But he had a compass with him, and he could always make for the shore and then follow it in whatever direction he desired. Newport satisfied himself that he need not be anxious about Mr. Merrion.

The day wore on without anything happening to disturb Newport's serenity. He heard in the distance the roar of Mavis's speed-boat, and imagined that the fog a few miles away must be less dense than where the yacht was anchored. Indeed, during the afternoon it became perceptibly thinner, and Newport regretted that he had orders to stay where he was till sunset. It would have been an admirable opportunity for regaining the lagoon.

The lift in the fog proved to be only temporary, and about five o'clock it came down thicker than ever. Newport had given up expecting his master to return to the yacht. If he had meant to return direct from Vane Sand, he would have been back long before this. He had undoubtedly rowed into the entrance of the river, not caring to run the chance of missing the yacht in the fog. There was nothing for it but to take *Alisette* round there to meet him as soon as possible after sunset.

Sunset came, and with it very little clearing of the atmosphere. It was not until eight o'clock that the moon pierced the mist sufficiently for Newport to judge it safe to weigh anchor. Had *Alisette* been his own, he would have started before this, and trusted to his sailor's instinct to enable him to nose his way somehow into the entrance of the river. But in the absence of her owner, he did not care to take the responsibility, not knowing what plans might be jeopardised if he happened to run the yacht ashore.

He edged warily down the coast, with a sounding line in his hand and the engine running dead slow. He was gazing intently ahead, trying to locate the entrance, when he saw a dark blur upon the water on his port bow. After a little, he made it out to be a boat. He could not see the movement of the oars, and imagined that it contained some fisherman, intent upon his lines.

It was not until he came abreast of it that he saw that it was empty.

"Well, that's a rum go!" exclaimed Newport softly, as he put up his helm and steered for the boat. "She can't be anchored out here in the open, surely? Best go and have a look and see what's up."

As he approached the boat he saw that she was drifting with the tide, which was now ebbing fast, and that her oars and rowlocks were neatly stowed. He stopped his engine and dropped slowly down to the boat, stretching out and grasping her painter as he did so. "Somebody's dinghy, by the look of it," he muttered, as he put the yacht on her course again. "Must have drifted away from somewhere up the river, I suppose. Nobody has fallen overboard from her, that's certain. The oars wouldn't be stowed like that if they had. Better take her in with me. Somebody will be looking for her in the morning, sure enough."

After some little searching, he found the entrance, and brought the yacht to her usual anchorage in the lagoon. Here the mist had almost cleared away, and the moon illuminated the shore clearly. Newport looked round but could see no signs of Merrion or of the yacht's dinghy. It was curious, for if Merrion were about he must have heard the sound of the yacht's engine and the splash of her anchor, which would carry a long way in the still night. The only conjecture that Newport could make was that he had got tired of waiting and gone up the river by himself.

But, reason with himself as he would, Newport could not rid himself of an uncomfortable feeling. The events of the previous evening had left their impression upon his superstitious nature, in spite of his efforts to banish them from his mind. There was something uncanny about this river and the people who lived by it. The very shadows on shore looked mysterious and menacing in the silence of the night, under the cold moon. What if the queer influences which he felt about him had laid hands on Mr. Merrion in the fog?

The unshakable conviction that something was not right fixed itself in his mind. It was now getting on for eleven o'clock, and he could not face the prospect of remaining idly on the yacht when his presence might be badly needed. He fidgeted impatiently, his ears strained for some sound that would indicate the return of his master.

The minutes passed, and the silence grew more intense, more threatening. The thought that he might be badly needed preyed upon his mind until it forced itself upon him as a certainty. Badly needed. Yes, but where? Would it be worth while to follow his master's tracks, and so endeavour to discover something of his whereabouts?

At last, more from the sheer impossibility of sitting still than because he hoped to do any good, he turned abruptly to the dinghy he had picked up, sprang into it, and cast off the painter. By the time he reached Vane Sand the tide would be low enough for him to land on it. And Vane Sand had been Mr. Merrion's objective.

Of course, his expedition was sheer folly, he knew that. His master could not possibly have left any traces which would not have been obliterated by the intervening tide. But it was something to do, at all events. The physical exertion entailed in rowing two miles to Vane Sand and back again might woo his mind from its queer sense of insecurity. He felt unaccountably anxious, and the encounter with this strange dinghy, drifting so mysteriously in the open sea, had not tended to decrease his anxiety. It was not *Alisette's* dinghy, certainly, but Newport could not rid himself of the conviction that it was somehow connected with his master's movements.

Under the powerful strokes of his oars the dinghy made rapid progress towards Vane Sand, Newport glancing over his shoulder from time to time until he made out the rounded form of the shoal just appearing above the water. In the moonlight the surface of the sand shone like silver, and Newport, having run the dinghy aground, stepped out and surveyed the lonely scene with eager eyes. There was nothing on the sand, of course. What should there be? What could he possibly have expected to find? He was about to re-enter the dinghy and row back to the shore, when something caught his eye. The receding waves were washing round something that looked like a small rock. No, it couldn't be a rock, it was of too regular a shape for that. Newport walked up to examine it. It was the iron box that Merrion had found on the previous tide.

Newport pushed his cap back and scratched his head thoughtfully. Now, what in the world could this mean? His ready logic set to work to grapple with the problem. Mr. Merrion had set off for Vane Sand in order to find what had been dropped by the Belgian vessel. This remarkable box was not a natural object of the sea-shore and, since it showed no signs of rust, could not have lain where it was for long. The natural assumption was that it was the object dropped from the vessel. Why, then, had Mr. Merrion not taken it away with him? Only two reasons suggested themselves to Newport. Either he had never landed upon Vane Sand at all, or, having landed, he had missed the box in the fog, which at that time had been very thick.

It was very fortunate that he had obeyed his unreasoning impulse, Newport thought. Although Mr. Merrion had somehow failed to find the box, he could repair his oversight. He bent down, picked up the box, and hoisted it on to his shoulder. He had not gone many paces towards the dinghy when his feet struck a small hard object, almost completely buried in the sand. The kick it received unearthed it and, with a sudden exclamation, Newport bent down and picked it up. It was Mr. Merrion's pocket compass.

So his master had landed on Vane Sand, after all. But the discovery of the compass made his actions still more inexplicable. The spot where the compass lay was not half a dozen yards from the box. If Mr. Merrion had dropped it where it lay now, he could hardly have escaped seeing the box, even had the fog been at its densest. Why, then, had he left it behind? And how was it that he had not noticed the loss of the compass, which he certainly would have required when he left the sandbank?

There was something inexplicable about all this, and Newport's anxiety returned more strongly than ever. He carried the box and the compass to the dinghy, pushed off, and rowed back to the lagoon. Surely Mr. Merrion should have returned by now; it was past midnight. But there was no sign of living soul anywhere on those deserted shores, nor had *Alisette's* dinghy returned to the yacht.

Newport put his hands to his mouth, and uttered a long drawn-out hail. The echoes of it resounded among the dunes, dying away to leave a silence undisturbed by their clamour. But no answering hail came to his ears, and once more Newport felt the urgent need of action. If only there were somebody whom he could consult, who would advise him how to act in this disturbing situation! And then he remembered that Mr. Merrion had told him that Inspector Young would be at the Rose and Crown that night.

His mind was made up on the instant. He would go to the Rose and Crown at once, and see the Inspector. Very possibly he would find his master there too, in which case he would merely be called a fool for his pains. Never mind, his relief would be so great that he would willingly put up with much worse than that. And, if Mr. Merrion were not there, the Inspector would find him in no time. Newport had an unbounded faith in the powers of the police.

Once more he took to the oars and rowed up the river, taking the box and the compass with him as evidence. In spite of the agitation of his mind, he kept his eyes open for any signs of activity upon the river bank. But everything appeared to be in its normal state of peacefulness. He passed Hollesley's five-tonner, securely riding at her moorings off Elder House.

A little further on he passed the speed-boat, also moored as usual. He was approaching the village now, and he glanced fearfully towards the churchyard. But all was quiet there too, there were no ghostly forms gliding among the graves. He reached the quay, made fast his dinghy, and climbed ashore, the box on his shoulder and the compass in his pocket.

The village, as he passed through it, was deserted. Two or three prowling cats glided stealthily out of sight at his approach, but, with this exception, the straggling street was empty. Here and there a dim light burned behind a curtained window, that was all. He walked rapidly to the Rose and Crown, shifting his burden from time to time from one shoulder to the other. At last he reached the inn, and uttered a sigh of relief as he saw a light burning in the bar.

He knocked at the door, which was immediately opened by Inspector Young himself, who stared at Newport for a second before he recognised him. "Hallo!" he exclaimed, as he remembered where he had seen the face before. "You're Mr. Merrion's man, aren't you? Come in. Have you got a message for me?"

"No, sir, I haven't," replied Newport, entering and laying his box on the table. "I came to ask you if you'd seen anything of Mr. Merrion to-day."

Something in the tone of Newport's voice caused Young to glance at him sharply. "No, I haven't," he said. "I've only been here three hours or so, and I'm waiting for him now. Why, has anything happened?"

"I don't know, sir," replied Newport. "I last saw Mr. Merrion about eleven o'clock this morning, and he hasn't turned up since, though I was to have met him this evening. I can't help feeling that something queer is in the wind, sir."

It was obvious to the Inspector that Newport was more anxious than he cared to own. "Sit down and tell me what you know," he said.

Newport obeyed him dutifully. He told him of his master's visit to Vane Sand, and of the reasons which inspired it. He then went on to repeat the instructions which he had given him before his departure, and recounted his own actions since that time. The Inspector listened with the utmost eagerness and, when he had finished, nodded approvingly.

"You were quite right to come to me," he said. "I believe I know where Mr. Merrion is, though I confess that I expected his return long before this. But I can't understand about this box. You say you have reason to believe that it was dropped overboard on Vane Sand, and that on a previous occasion you saw Mr. Hollesley and his butler recover something from the sand at low water. This morning they were observing a vessel which crossed the sand and made a signal, and Mr. Merrion went out to investigate. You went out just now and found the box. Is that right?"

"That's right, sir," replied Newport. "What I can't understand is why Mr. Merrion left the box there instead of bringing it away."

"It certainly seems curious," agreed Young. "Still, now that we have the box here, we may as well see what's inside it. The landlord and his wife have gone to bed, but there's a box of tools in the kitchen, I know. Wait here a moment while I fetch them."

He left the room, and returned with a very serviceable looking spanner. Between them, he and Newport unscrewed the nuts which secured the lid of the box, and prised it open. The greatest care had obviously been taken to make the box watertight. A rubber washer had been placed under the lid and, when this had been removed, a tin container, exactly fitting inside the iron shell, was exposed to view. They tipped this out, and found that the container had been carefully soldered up.

The Inspector disappeared again, to return this time with a tin opener. "This will do the trick," he remarked, as he began to cut a hole in the top of the container. "It won't be long now before we see what Mr. Hollesley's little game is."

Inside the container were a number of tin boxes, carefully packed in sawdust. Young drew them out one by one, and laid them in a row upon the table. There was no need to open them, for each bore a boldly-printed label. And the names on the labels were those of the very drugs which had been found in Faxfleet's room.

The Inspector gazed at them with a light of understanding in his eyes. "Well, I'm damned!" he exclaimed softly.

Chapter XXVI

For many seconds Inspector Young continued to stare at these sinister tins, as though fascinated. But his thoughts were working swiftly, in spite of his seeming abstraction. He had discovered a part at least of the secret of this mysterious village. But how did this amazing discovery, important enough in itself, bear on the murder of Whitehead?

It was plain enough that Hollesley, with the assistance of Thorburn, alias Gregson, the ex-convict, had been engaged in a scheme for smuggling drugs into the country. But, as his investigations during the last few days had shown him, there were many links in the chain of distribution between the smuggler and the consumer. He had found, most unexpectedly, the beginning of the chain. Was it possible that Whitehead had formed one of the links? In that case, had he been murdered because he had in some way become a danger to the organisation?

This was possible, certainly, but as yet Young realised that he had nothing with which to substantiate his theory. The immediate question concerned the steps that he should take. And on this point his mind was swiftly made up. He would obtain a warrant for the arrest of Hollesley and Thorburn, and take them into custody. The evidence against them which could be supplied by Merrion and Newport would in itself be sufficient to obtain their conviction. But it could be made even more conclusive. He could secure the arrest of the master of the vessel which had dropped the box and, by the exercise of a little tact, it would probably not be difficult to extract the whole story from him. Merrion, no doubt, would be able to give him the information necessary for this second step.

But what could have become of Merrion all this time? He had expected his appearance, long before this. However, Merrion must wait. He would undoubtedly turn up in the morning. And by that time he must have Hollesley and Thorburn under lock and key. He dared run no risks of allowing them an opportunity to escape.

He turned abruptly to Newport. "You'd better come with me," he said. "I'm going to apply for a warrant to arrest Hollesley and Thorburn. We'll go and call up Constable Viney, and then go on to the Hall and see Sir William Owerton. He's a magistrate, and by applying to him I shall save time."

"I don't think it is much good going for the policeman, sir," ventured Newport. "When I was up here last night I heard that he was ill. It was one of the things Mr. Merrion wanted to know."

Young's face darkened. "Well, if that's the case, you'll have to take his place," he said. "I don't anticipate any trouble, but I may want some one to help me. We'll go straight along to the Hall in that case."

"And Mr. Merrion, sir?" ventured Newport.

"Since he hasn't come up here, I expect that he's gone back to the yacht long ago," replied Young. "I'll get you to go and find him later. Come along."

They walked swiftly to the Hall, taking a short cut which avoided the village. The place was wrapped in darkness, and they had some difficulty in making anybody hear. But at last the door was unbarred, and Christy appeared, in his shirt sleeves and apparently not more than half-awake. He blinked at the intruders, and seemed disposed to shut the door in their faces.

"I am Detective-Inspector Young of Scotland Yard," said the Inspector. "Here's my card. I must see Sir William Owerton at once upon a matter of the most urgent importance."

Christy still seemed doubtful, but a glance at the card which the Inspector produced reassured him. "You'd better come in, sir," he said. "This way, if you please. If you'll wait in the library for a few minutes, I'll call Miss Mavis. I don't like to disturb Sir William myself, sir."

Young nodded, and he and Newport followed the old servant to the library. Here Christy left them. They could hear his shuffling step slowly ascending the stairs. And then, a few moments later, they heard him return, apparently in the most desperate haste. He burst into the room without ceremony, a picture of frightened bewilderment. "Miss Mavis isn't there!" he exclaimed feebly.

"Not there! What do you mean?" replied Young with a frown. "In that case you must wake Sir William yourself. I must see him at once."

But this insistence was lost upon Christy. "I can't make it out," he rambled. "Miss Mavis isn't in her room, and her bed hasn't been slept in. I daren't tell Sir William, I don't know what he'll say—"

Young realised that it would be impossible to get the man to the point until the matter of his mistress's absence was settled. He interrupted him sharply. "When did you last see Miss Mavis?" he asked.

"After dinner, sir, in this very room. She and Sir William dined together, and I served them with coffee in here afterwards. I didn't come in again, sir, till I went to bed at ten o'clock. But Miss Mavis seemed restless, sir, ever since the gentleman left this afternoon."

"What gentleman?" demanded Young.

Christy hesitated. "Well, sir, I didn't ought to tell you about it. Miss Mavis told me to say nothing to anybody, even Sir William. But, seeing as she's not here, and you're from the police, perhaps there wouldn't be any harm in my telling you, sir. She brought Mr. Merrion here about half-past three this afternoon, sir. He was soaking wet, and looked as if he had fallen into the water. Miss Mavis asked me to find some of the master's old clothes for him to put on. I've got Mr. Merrion's shirt and trousers drying in my pantry at this very moment, sir."

The Inspector and Newport exchanged a rapid glance. "What time did Mr. Merrion leave?" inquired the former.

"About seven o'clock, sir. Miss Mavis saw him out, and then returned just as Sir William came back from Gippingford. And, as I say, sir, Miss Mavis didn't seem herself all the evening."

For a moment Young made no reply. He was completely puzzled by this new complication. Was it possible that Merrion had applied to this girl for assistance in the task which he had set himself for that night, and that she had slipped out of the house to meet him somewhere? It seemed the only way of accounting for her disappearance. However, the necessity for the immediate arrest of Hollesley and Thorburn was upper-most in his mind.

"I don't think you need worry about Miss Owerton," he said soothingly. "Mr. Merrion is a friend of mine, and if, as seems likely, she has gone to meet him, it is for some good purpose, you may be sure. Now then, go and call Sir William, quickly, please. There is no need to inform him of his daughter's absence."

Christy tottered off, and Young turned to Newport. "Well, what do you make of this?" he asked.

Newport shook his head helplessly. "I don't know what to make of it, and that's a fact, sir," he replied. "But I'd give a good deal to know where Mr. Merrion is, sir. There's something about this place I don't like."

"There are several things about it that I don't like at all," agreed Young. "I wish I had had a couple of men sent down here to-night. It's devilish awkward there being only two of us. Hush, here comes Sir William."

The door opened and Sir William appeared, attired in dressing-gown and bedroom slippers. He glanced sharply at Young. "You want to see me, Inspector?" he asked. "We met at the inquest upon poor Whitehead, I remember. I take it that something very urgent accounts for your visit at this time of night?"

"It does, sir," replied Young gravely. "I would not have troubled you unless it had been absolutely necessary. I have to apply for a warrant for the arrest of Mr. Hollesley, of Elder House, and of Thorburn, alias Gregson, his butler."

Sir William went suddenly white, and grasped the edge of the table for support. He stood thus for a moment, and then let himself slip into a chair. "The arrest of Laurence Hollesley!" he managed to stammer at last. "But that's ridiculous! Mr. Hollesley is a personal friend of mine. What charge do you bring against him, may I ask?"

"The very serious charge of being engaged in trafficking in dangerous drugs, sir," replied the Inspector steadily.

Sir William, huddled up in his chair, gazed for a moment uncomprehendingly before him. Young's words seemed to have deprived him of the power of speech. His hands drummed idly on the table before him. Then, after a long pause, during which he seemed entirely unconscious of the presence of his visitors, he spoke, in a queer croaking voice.

"But it's impossible! I can't grant a warrant on your word alone, Inspector. Laurence Hollesley is a man of considerable standing. He cannot be arrested upon such an absurd charge. Besides, he is in London at the moment. I saw him this morning, and he was on his way there then."

Young did not seem in the least disconcerted by Sir William's attitude. "Mr. Hollesley went to London this morning, you say, sir," he replied. "Can you give me his address there?"

"He usually stays at the Coronation Hotel, I believe," replied the magistrate, who seemed to be collecting his wits. "If you care to arrest him there, it is of course no business of mine. You will be able to procure a warrant for the purpose elsewhere, I have no doubt."

"Would it be possible for you to verify the fact that Mr. Hollesley intended to stay at the Coronation Hotel to-night, sir?" persisted the Inspector.

Under the unwavering scrutiny of Young's eyes Sir William began to falter. "I—I really can't say," he replied, with a feeble attempt at bluster. "It is surely your business to find that out for yourself. Perhaps my daughter may know. I will ask her in the morning."

"I should request you to do so at once, but for the fact that I believe Miss Owerton is not in the house at present," said the Inspector quietly.

For the second time during the interview Sir William became deathly white. He sprang from his chair, and stood confronting Young, searching his face as though to discern the meaning of his words. "Not in the house! Mavis not here!" he exclaimed. "What are you talking about?"

"I understand from the manservant who admitted us that Miss Owerton is not in her room, and that her bed has not been slept in," replied Young, his eyes fixed upon the magistrate.

Sir William's mouth worked feverishly, but his throat seemed too choked to allow him to utter a word. "Good God," he gasped hoarsely at last. "Hollesley would never dare—he's not in London, he's—"

Young took a hasty step forward, but he was too late to do more than lower Sir William's unconscious form gently to the floor. "The shock has been too much for him," he said over his shoulder. "See if you can find that servant, Newport. He's not far off, I expect."

Newport opened the door of the library, to find Christy waiting in the passage. The old man threatened to crumple up into hysterics at the sight of his master prone upon the floor, but Young managed to soothe him by the promise that he would go straight to Doctor Padfield and ask him to come immediately to the Hall. With a parting injunction to Christy not to leave his master for an instant, Young departed, taking Newport with him.

"I'm beginning to see daylight now," he remarked as the two hastened towards the village. "But I wish to heaven I had a few men here. Some of this gang will escape if we don't take care."

"Well, I'm glad you understand it, sir," replied Newport. "It looks to me all tangled up like a new main sheet."

They roused Doctor Padfield, who glanced queerly at Young as he let them in. "Glad to see you again, Inspector," he said. "Although it's a queer time to pay a visit. What's wrong?"

"Sir William Owerton has had a collapse of some kind, up at the Hall," replied Young tersely. "He fell down suddenly unconscious. It was only a few minutes ago; I have come straight here to ask you to go up and see him."

"Oh, I'll go all right," said Doctor Padfield cheerfully. "It sounds as though he had had some sort of a shock, doesn't it?"

"Very likely," replied the Inspector grimly. "Now, there's one other thing I want to ask you, doctor. May I use your telephone, now I'm here?"

"Oh, yes, certainly. It'll take me a minute or two to collect the things I want before I start for the Hall."

With some difficulty Young roused the slumbering operator, and demanded to be put through to the police station at Gippingford. Having been connected to the sergeant on duty, he gave his name and proceeded to issue his instructions.

"I want you to send half a dozen men, or as many as you can spare, to High Eldersham at once," he said.

"Let them come out in a car, and meet me at the Rose and Crown. Yes, it's very urgent. Within an hour, you say? Yes, that'll do."

He rang off, and found Doctor Padfield at his elbow. "Finished?" inquired the latter curtly.

"Yes, I needn't trouble you any more," replied Young.

"Very well, then, I'll get off and see Sir William."

The three men left the house together. Doctor Padfield, carrying his bag, disappeared in the direction of the garage, from whence came the sound of his car being started. Young and Newport walked down the road until they were out of earshot, and then the Inspector turned to his companion.

"Pity Sir William didn't hold up a little longer, till he'd finished his sentence," he remarked. "However, it's clear enough that Hollesley's supposed visit to London was a blind, and that he's in the neighbourhood somewhere. The old chap seemed to think that he had something to do with his daughter's disappearance. Well, if Hollesley is about, he is probably at Elder House, in which case we will round him and Thorburn up as soon as the reinforcements arrive from Gippingford. Meanwhile, as we've an hour to spare, we may as well spend it in trying to find Mr. Merrion and that girl. They can't be far away."

"Mr. Merrion told me that he meant to row up the river to-night, sir," said Newport. "He was going to visit a clump of trees on a sort of island."

"Yes, I know," replied Young. "But he ought to have been back long ago. Why, it's after three o'clock! He's probably asleep on board the yacht by this time. I think you'd better go and see."

"Very good, sir," said Newport cheerfully. "I've got a dinghy tied up against the wharf."

"All right," replied the Inspector. "I'll walk down as far as that with you."

The moon had set by now, but a pale glimmer still lingered in the sky, giving enough light for them to see where they were going. Everything was very still, the village showed no sign of life. They reached the wharf, and Newport was bending down to feel for the dinghy's painter, when he suddenly paused and straightened himself. He laid his hand on the Inspector's arm, and drew him into the deep shadow of some buildings near by.

"Hold on a minute, sir!" he whispered. "There's a boat coming down the river!"

Chapter XXVII

There was no doubt about it; a boat was being rowed towards them. The Inspector and Newport, straining their eyes through the darkness that overlay the grey ribbon of the river, made out at last an indistinct blur from which proceeded the regular plash of oars skilfully plied. The blur approached, growing more distinct until it resolved itself into the outline of a small boat, propelled by one man.

"We had better get round the corner," whispered Young. "He's probably going to land at the wharf, and we don't want him to see us."

"I don't think so, sir," replied Newport, whose experienced eyes were accustomed to night watches. "He's keeping too far in the middle of the stream for that. I'm pretty sure that he bound down the river, sir."

Newport was right. The boat did not approach the shore, but kept steadily on its course. Suddenly, when it was abreast of the wharf, Newport clutched the Inspector's arm. "That's that fellow Thorburn, sir, or I'm a Dutchman!" he whispered excitedly. "And, what's more, he's got a bundle of some kind lying in the stern sheets."

"Thorburn!" exclaimed the Inspector, taking a step forward. "Are you sure? I can't recognise him at that distance."

Newport laid a restraining hand upon his arm. "It's Thorburn, right enough, sir," he replied confidently. "If you'd like to have a chat with him, it won't take us long to overhaul him."

"I'll chat with him all right when I lay my hands on him," replied Young. "Come along, where's that dinghy of yours?"

"Half a mo', sir," said Newport confidently. "Let him get round that bend first. We'll catch him sharp enough when we want to."

Young waited, with what patience he could summon, as the outline of the boat slowly faded into obscurity. Then, when at last it vanished altogether, Newport slid out of the shadow and, moving stealthily as a cat, climbed down the shaky ladder into the dinghy. The Inspector followed him, and Newport cast off and rowed swiftly but noiselessly away from the wharf. "We'll be on top of him in five minutes, sir," he whispered cheerfully. "This boat's a lot lighter than his, and I reckon I can row stronger than he'll ever manage."

The Inspector nodded, and leaned forward in his seat in the stern of the dinghy, staring intently ahead. Newport kept under the bank, where the flood tide ran less strongly, and where the boat was hidden in the deeper shadows. His muscles worked rhythmically and seemingly without effort, driving the dinghy swiftly through the water. As they rounded the bend Young exclaimed sharply under his breath. The other boat was not more than a hundred yards ahead of them.

It was clear enough that Thorburn had not yet seen them. He was toiling steadily at his oars, with no thought of pursuit. Newport overhauled him steadily, still keeping in the darkness beneath the bank, and rowing without a sound, until the two boats were abreast, though still a considerable distance apart. And then, all at once, Thorburn detected their presence.

Young could see him clearly, could almost fancy that he recognised him. He wasted no time in trying to discover the identity of his pursuers, but strained feverishly at his oars in a wild endeavour to escape. He forged ahead, but at a word from the Inspector, Newport abandoned his cautious tactics and shot out towards him with no attempt at further concealment. For a minute or two the boats maintained their relative positions, and then slowly the distance between them began to decrease.

And then a curious thing happened. Thorburn, after a few frantic strokes, suddenly laid down his oars and stood up. Then with a swift movement, he bent down towards the bundle which lay in the stern of his boat. He seized it, and with a tremendous effort lifted it in his arms and flung it into the river. Then he sank back on to the thwart, and applied himself once more to his oars with the energy of desperation.

The Inspector uttered a shout of amazement. Swiftly as the incident had taken place, he had recognised in the bundle the outline of a human form. There was no doubt about it; it lay in the river a few yards ahead of them, the top of the head just visible, hands and feet beating the water feebly.

"Good God, he's thrown somebody overboard!" exclaimed Young. "Pull your right oar a bit, man. Steady now!"

The boat drew alongside the struggling figure, and the Inspector and Newport, leaning out, grasped it as it was on the point of sinking. The reason for its feeble struggling was then evident. It was a man, gagged with a muffler which completely hid his face, and with his hands and legs securely bound. It was with the utmost difficulty that Young and Newport managed to lift him into the boat.

The Inspector produced his torch and flashed it on to the figure. "Who the devil's this, I wonder?" he muttered, as he wrestled with the muffler and the bonds. "He's got somebody else's clothes on, by the look of it. Why, heavens above, it's Merrion!"

He had managed to remove the muffler, exposing Merrion's face. Another second, and he had torn the gag from his mouth, while Newport cut through the straps with his clasp-knife. Merrion shook himself, seated himself on the thwart, and seized the oars. Without a word he swung the boat's head round, and began to pull madly up the river.

"Here, what are you doing?" exclaimed Young. "The other way, man! Thorburn's heading down river."

"To hell with Thorburn!" replied Merrion, without for an instant relaxing his efforts. "Mavis is in that devil Hollesley's hands on that infernal island. It's just possible we may get there in time. Here, Newport, take one of these oars, we can pull together."

Newport took his place unquestioningly by Merrion's side, and under their united efforts the boat flew up-stream. Only once in their desperate race did Merrion speak. "This is Mavis's dinghy. How did you come to find it?" he inquired tersely.

"I found it drifting about off the mouth of the river, sir," replied Newport.

"Then there's a Providence watching over us, even in this hell-stricken spot. Pull for your life!"

Newport needed no urging. The little boat, heavily laden though she was, flew through the water like a racing skiff. They left the wharf behind, and very soon the dark mass of the trees loomed up against the horizon. Without wasting time seeking a landing place, Merrion drove the dinghy towards the nearest point of the island. Her impetus carried her over the strip of mud, and the three men leapt out on to comparatively firm land.

"Run round to the causeway, Newport, and stop anybody who tries to come that way!" panted Merrion. "Come on, Young, follow me as close as you can."

The two men, aided by the light of Young's torch, crashed through the undergrowth, heedless of the twigs and brambles that tried to bar their progress. They came out at length into the clear space of the grove, and started to race across it. And then the rays of Young's torch fell upon the altar, and he stopped with a gasp of horror, checking Merrion as he did so.

The spectacle revealed by the powerful beam of the torch was certainly surprising enough. The massive stone gleamed whitely, the grotesque and horrible figures carved upon it standing out with hideous clarity. At the foot of the stone lay the outstretched figure of a girl, clad in a thin evening frock, which the dew had soaked through and through until it clung closely about her, revealing every line of her lovely figure. One bare arm was stretched across the turf, and from a wound in the forearm the blood still welled slowly, running in a crimson stream over the white skin.

Young recognised her at a glance as the girl whom he had seen at the inquest. The whole course of events was still incomprehensible to him, and he felt as though he had reached the crisis of some nightmare from which he must at any moment awake into a world of sanity. The girl was not dead, so much was evident. She seemed to be in the throes of awakening from unconsciousness or from some strange sleep. Her head moved slowly from side to side, her unseeing eyes fixed in puzzled bewilderment upon the shadowy and leafless branches above her head. Her fingers twitched spasmodically, feeling at the blades of grass which surrounded her.

But it was when Young's eyes rose to the shadows above the altar that he refused to believe the reality of his vision. The rays of his torch scarcely penetrated the brooding darkness; they merely relieved it with a faint glimmer. And into that dim and uncertain radiance came forward a monstrous shape, the shoulders of a man surmounted by the gigantic head of a goat, with long hairy arms bearing before it a bowl brimming with some nameless liquid.

As the figure appeared, Merrion shook himself free from the Inspector's restraining grasp, and hurled himself towards it. But the figure scarcely seemed to see him. It threw back its head, set the bowl to its lips, and drank its contents at a draught. The hasty movement caused some of the liquid to overflow and run in a thread of crimson down the beard of the goat and on to the white surface of the stone. Then, the bowl drained, the figure hurled it at the advancing form of Merrion and disappeared into the black shadow of the trees.

Merrion, blinded by fury, failed to avoid the hurtling bowl, which glanced off the side of his head, causing him to stagger momentarily. Young dashed forward to his aid, but he recovered himself and dashed into the shadows among which his assailant had disappeared. The Inspector stopped, and fell on his knees beside the prostrate girl. He satisfied himself that the wound on her arm was not serious, and that she was rapidly regaining consciousness. He stripped off his overcoat and laid it over her, then dashed on after Merrion, whose progress he could follow by the crashing of the undergrowth.

Young found his torch of very little use among the tangled brushwood and the trunks of the trees. He had to judge of the progress of the chase by its sound alone. The island was strange to him, and he very soon lost his sense of direction. It seemed to him that he was running in circles through an interminable jungle of briars and low-growing branches, which entangled his legs and lashed him sharply across the face. All at once he heard a shout, and recognised Newport's voice. "Here he is, sir! No, he's dodged in again among the trees."

From close at hand came Merrion's answer. "All right, Newport, stay where you are. Shout if you see him again."

The chase continued, a blind pursuit in the darkness that shrouded the island. Once Young stumbled and fell, and, on casting the rays of the torch on the object which had tripped him up, saw that it was the skin of an enormous goat, still flecked with moist crimson spots. The disguise had been discarded, then. He went on a couple of paces, and found himself suddenly on the bank of the river.

To his astonishment it seemed surprisingly light out here in the open, after the gloom which had reigned beneath the trees. The further bank of the river was visible; even details near at hand were beginning to appear. And then he realised, with a thrill of relief, that the first faint light of dawn was beginning to break.

A sudden and uncanny quiet had settled down upon the island. No sound of movement came from its depths; it was as though pursuers and pursued were crouching exhausted, each listening intently for the slightest sign from the other. Until all at once Young heard a faint rustling among the bushes, close at hand. He stood perfectly still, and in a few seconds a man whom he recognised as Hollesley, with his clothes torn to shreds and a wild, hunted look in his eyes, emerged cautiously on to the bank.

As he looked round he caught sight of the Inspector. But, instead of retreating once more under the shelter of the trees, he began to run swiftly along the edge of the water round the island. Young, shouting to Merrion to head him off, gave chase. But he could gain nothing on his quarry, and after a few yards a sudden uneasiness seized hold of him. The dinghy in which they had landed could not be far away. If Hollesley should reach it first, he could leave the island in it, and perhaps make his escape down the river.

Still shouting, Young pressed on. There lay the dinghy, not fifty yards ahead. Hollesley caught sight of it and uttered a cry of defiance. He was in the very act of pushing it off the mud when a figure rose from beside it and delivered a blow which made him stagger backwards. In an instant Merrion and Hollesley were locked in a savage struggle.

Before Young could reach them, Hollesley hurled his opponent from him, and Merrion, missing his footing, staggered backwards into the mud. Quick as lightning Hollesley turned to meet his new assailant, and, as Young hurled himself at him, he had time to see the diabolical fury of his expression. Every muscle of his face was twitching; his eyes, which seemed to be starting out of his head, glared with a baleful malignity. So much Young saw before their bodies met.

The Inspector's object had been to pinion Hollesley's arms, but the man was too quick for him. With an incredibly rapid movement he drew the sacrificial knife from somewhere within his shirt, and aimed a savage blow at Young's face. Fortunately the impetus of the latter's rush carried him within Hollesley's guard before the blow fell. And before the blow could be repeated, he had sprung back out of harm's way.

The two men stood watching one another, breathing heavily, Hollesley's arm ready for a blow. But the end was at hand. Merrion, up to his waist in the soft oozing mud, had nevertheless managed to grasp the painter of the dinghy. He coiled it rapidly in his hand, and flung the end of the rope against Hollesley's legs. It twined round them, and as it did so Merrion threw all his weight into one sharp pull. Hollesley staggered and slashed at the rope with his knife, cutting it as easily as a thread. But it was too late. The inspector seized his opportunity and flung himself upon him. Gripping his right arm with both hands, he gave a vicious twist, and the knife fell harmlessly at Hollesley's feet. Another instant and the two came crashing down together.

The fall seemed to stun Hollesley momentarily, and he lay still. Before he had pulled himself together Merrion had contrived to clamber out of the mud. He picked up the knife and cut the painter off short. It was the work of an instant to bind Hollesley's hands and feet securely.

Young picked himself up and stood regarding the outstretched form of his captive. "Well, that's one of them, anyhow!" he exclaimed, in a tone of satisfaction.

But Merrion did not hear him. He had already disappeared among the bushes, and Young could hear him as he ran rapidly towards the clearing.

"Good heavens, I forgot the girl!" exclaimed the Inspector. "What the devil are we going to do with her, I wonder?"

Chapter XXVIII

But Inspector Young had other matters to think of, more important at the moment than the disposal of Mavis Owerton. It was evident that a pretty close understanding existed between her and Merrion, and he could be counted upon to look after her for the present. There remained Hollesley, and the necessity for getting him to some place of security. After that, there was Thorburn, or Gregson, to be thought of.

Hollesley appeared to have recovered from the shock of his fall. But he made no attempt to move. He lay very still, regarding the Inspector with a curious mocking smile, as though defying him.

Young bent over him. "Are you going to behave yourself?" he asked sternly. "You'll have to come with me to Gipping-ford, where I shall charge you with trafficking in dangerous drugs. And, if you take my advice, you'll come quietly."

Hollesley's only reply was to burst into peal after peal of hysterical laughter, which echoed and re-echoed from bank to bank of the river, startling the silence of the dawn. It was obvious that in his present state he was not responsible for his actions. And it occurred to Young that he was probably a victim of those very drugs in which he dealt.

The Inspector shouted to Newport, who left his post by the causeway and joined him. "Keep your eye on Mr. Hollesley until I come back," he said. "I am going up to the Rose and Crown to fetch the men from Gippingford. They ought to be there by this time."

"Very good, sir," replied Newport impassively. Now that he was satisfied of his master's safety, he was prepared to obey orders without question. The Inspector left him and made his way to the clearing, where he found Merrion and Mavis engaged in earnest conversation, his arm around her shoulders.

They sprang apart, rather self-consciously, at his appearance. But Young seemed oblivious of the movement. "I hope you are none the worse for your experiences, Miss Owerton," he said politely. "Perhaps you can tell me how it was that we found you here?"

"Oh, I'm all right now," replied Mavis bravely. "A little bit muzzy in the head, that's all. But I can't tell you how I came here, I'm afraid. I didn't even know where I was till Des—Mr. Merrion—told me."

Her face flushed scarlet as she corrected herself. Her loveliness seemed to Young as a ray of light in the dark cloud of evil that brooded over the island. Even his own heavy greatcoat, in which she stood tightly buttoned up, seemed unable to hide her natural grace and dignity.

"I'll tell you all I know," she continued in a low voice. "Mr. Merrion came to the Hall yesterday afternoon and borrowed my dinghy. He didn't tell me what he wanted it for, but I was rather anxious about him. You see, I had found him under rather unusual circumstances a few hours before." She broke off and glanced inquiringly at Merrion.

"Miss Owerton saved my life yesterday afternoon," said the latter gravely. "However, I'll tell you all about that later."

"Mr. Merrion told me that he wanted the dinghy till midnight," continued Mavis. "I felt I couldn't rest until I knew he had come back safely. So at about a quarter to twelve, after everybody had gone to bed, I slipped out of the side door, taking the key with me, and went down to the river. The dinghy wasn't there, and I was wondering whether I should wait, when something was flung over my head, and I felt my arms seized from behind. Of course, I kicked and struggled, but it was no good. Whoever held me was much stronger than I was. Then I felt a sharp prick on my arm, and everything gradually faded away. I don't remember anything more until I woke up here and heard the sound of people shouting and running about. And then Mr. Merrion came and picked me up, and told me he had come to find me."

The Inspector gave an audible sigh of relief. At least this girl had been spared the horrors of the night. But there was still a blow awaiting her, and he hesitated to break it to her so soon after her recent experiences. But, as it happened, Merrion interposed before he could say anything.

"It was Thorburn who carried her off and brought her here. I know that, for I heard him say so himself. It seems to me, Young, that your next job is to lay hands on him. Apart from his attack on Miss Owerton, I've got a little bone to pick with him. He tried to drown me yesterday afternoon, and he was on the point of making a proper job of it when you and Newport descended out of the blue just now. What about it?"

"I don't think you need worry your head about Thorburn," replied the Inspector complacently. "Within half an hour I shall have a cordon round High Eldersham that nobody can possibly break through."

"He won't be such a fool as to try to get away by land!" exclaimed Merrion. "He'll be on board that yacht of Hollesley's by this time, heading out to sea somewhere. The swine will give us the slip yet! He's got over an hour's start, as it is."

"Only an hour?" remarked Mavis eagerly. "Then there oughtn't to be any difficulty about catching him."

The Inspector looked at her with a puzzled expression on his face. "I'm afraid I don't quite follow, Miss Owerton," he began.

"Why, the speed-boat, of course! He couldn't possibly get away from her. But we ought to start at once."

"Well done, Mavis!" exclaimed Merrion. "I'll row you back to the Hall, and then take the boat out. I dare say that you can spare me a man from this cordon of yours to go with me, can't you, Young?"

So it was arranged. But before the Inspector took his departure from the island, he drew Merrion aside, and told him of his interview with Sir William. "I'm afraid the old chap got a terrible shock when he heard of his daughter's disappearance," he said. "He fell down in some sort of fit, and I don't know how she'll find him. I sent Doctor Padfield to him at once, but you'd better prepare her for the worst."

Merrion nodded, rather gloomily. How far Sir William Owerton was involved in the horrible practices which he had witnessed it was impossible to tell. Mavis, at all events, must be kept in ignorance, if it were humanly possible. Perhaps it would be best if her father never recovered consciousness. Great though her grief might be, the revelation of the truth might prove even more agonising.

He went to bring the dinghy round to the landing-place, while Young set out across the causeway to walk overland to the Rose and Crown, leaving Newport to keep guard over his prisoner. The Inspector felt distinctly elated. He had captured the principal in what would probably prove to be one of the most extensive drug-smuggling enterprises of recent years. His lieutenant could hardly escape being overtaken by the speed-boat. And once these two were in his hands, it should prove a comparatively easy task to discover the remaining links in the chain and round them up before they had any inkling of their danger.

He reached the Rose and Crown, to find a car containing half a dozen constables, in charge of a sergeant, awaiting him. To the sergeant he gave a rough outline of the case, and with his help he detailed the tasks which the party were to perform.

One man, who professed familiarity with boats, was despatched to the Hall, with orders to join Merrion. A second was sent to bring Hollesley up to the car. The remainder were posted in various exits from the village, with orders to allow no one to pass. Then, accompanied by the sergeant, Young proceeded to Elder House.

They had some difficulty in arousing the servants, but at last were admitted by an elderly housemaid, who exhibited the utmost indignation at their intrusion. Young contrived to pacify her, but his questions did not succeed in eliciting any useful information. Mr. Hollesley had gone up to London on the previous morning. He had given Mr. Thorburn two days' holiday, and the butler had left the house shortly after his master's departure. He had not returned, of that the housemaid was convinced.

Satisfied that she was speaking the truth, Young took his departure, leaving the sergeant to watch Elder House. After all he had not expected that Thorburn would venture to return; his visit had been merely a precautionary step. He went on to the Hall, and, as he hurried through the park, caught sight of Merrion in conversation with the constable whom he had sent to join him.

"Hallo!" he exclaimed as he drew up to them. "Haven't you started yet?"

"No, we haven't," replied Merrion with a wry smile. "Nor, I'm afraid, are we likely to. The speed-boat has disappeared."

"Damn! I never thought of that," exclaimed Young. "Thorburn's made off in it, of course. Well, it can't be helped. He's bound to land somewhere, sooner or later, and I'll have his description sent out to every police station in England by that time. Where's Miss Owerton?"

"Gone in to look after her father. I asked her to send Christy out with news. Ah, here he is."

The old servant appeared, and came hurriedly, stumbling in his haste, towards the group. "Sir William has recovered consciousness, sir," he said breathlessly. "He is asking to see Inspector Young."

"Ah, I'm glad of that!" exclaimed the Inspector. "I'll come at once. Is Doctor Padfield with him?"

"No, sir. He came very shortly after you left, and went away again almost at once. I am expecting his return at any moment."

Young followed Christy to the house, and was shown up to Sir William's room. He was lying in bed, looking very weak and frail, with Mavis seated on a chair beside him. But at the Inspector's entry she rose and glided silently from the room, leaving the two men alone.

Sir William fixed his eyes upon his visitor. "What has become of Laurence Hollesley?" he asked eagerly.

"He is in custody, sir," replied Young. "I shall take him to Gippingford and charge him with the crime of which I spoke to you."

"And with nothing else?"

Young could hardly fail to perceive the note of anxiety in the feeble voice. "I think that charge will be sufficient, unless it transpires that he has committed some more serious crime," he replied guardedly.

The old man closed his eyes for a moment, and then opened them suddenly. "I did not know that Laurence was smuggling drugs," he said. "Of that at least I am innocent. I would not have lent him my assistance for that. And yet, I do not know what I could have done. I had placed myself in his power."

"How did that happen, Sir William?" asked Young.

"I will tell you. You probably imagine that I am a rich man, because I live in a house like this. As a matter of fact, I am practically a pauper. The effort to keep up appearances, to live in the style in which my grandfathers did, has ruined me. My income has been diminishing for years, and the war threatened me with ruin. I had made up my mind to the inevitable, when Laurence came back after the armistice. He made me an offer, to lend me a sum of money the interest on which would enable me to live here for the rest of my life. In return I gave him a mortgage on the place, and promised to put no obstacle in the way of his marrying Mavis.

"A year or so later he came to me again. He told me that he had devised a scheme which would prove extraordinarily profitable to him, and also to me, if I consented to help him. But this scheme would necessitate his obtaining such an influence locally that no one would dare to run counter to his wishes. The scheme was of a secret nature, and the betrayal of it would be disastrous. He had decided that such an influence could only be obtained by arousing a superstitious fear among the villagers, and to this end he proposed to revive the practice of the witch-cult, of which the tradition still lingers in these parts.

"Of course I was horrified, and refused to have anything to do with such a thing. But he gave me to understand clearly enough that unless I helped him he would foreclose the mortgage. I had not the money with which to pay him off; much of it had already been spent in necessary repairs. Foreclosure on his part would have meant ruin for me and for my daughter, and that I was determined to avoid at any cost.

"I need not occupy your time with an account of my struggle with my conscience. It is enough to say that eventually I agreed to instruct him in the ancient ceremonies. Secret formula played a great part in these, and I was able to supply him with the essential facts concerning them. Doctor Padfield was admitted to the secret, and he was able to make up the modern equivalents of the traditional potions, in which drugs played the principal part. The procedure was simple. In order to manifest his power, Hollesley proclaimed himself able to injure miraculously any person who fell under the displeasure of the members of the coven. The ceremony of making a mommet and piercing it with a needle was gone through. Hollesley then consulted Doctor Padfield, and means were found of administering some deleterious substance to the individual in question, members of his family, or cattle. To do so was easy to Doctor Padfield, who was necessarily in attendance upon the inhabitants of the village, and who was in the habit of dispensing his own medicines."

"You cannot fail to be aware, Sir William, that Whitehead was murdered after one of these dolls was made to represent him," remarked Young sternly.

"I am aware of it," replied Sir William. "As soon as I heard of his death, I taxed Hollesley with the responsibility for it. I told him that things had gone too far, and that I should be compelled to tell you everything. Hollesley assured me that his death had nothing whatever to do with his having offended a member of the coven, but that it was due to purely fortuitous circumstances, connected with his life before he came to the Rose and Crown. He assured me that he had no part, direct or indirect in the murder, and that any precipitate action on my part would ruin us all. I am, even now, convinced that he was speaking the truth."

"That may be so," said Young shortly. "Now, Sir William, unless you have anything else to tell me, I must proceed with my duties."

He left the house and rejoined Merrion, who looked at him anxiously. "Well?" he inquired. "What next?"

"We must get to Gippingford as quickly as we can. There's nothing more to be done here at present. And, if you don't mind, I'd like you to come with me. I shall want your evidence as to the dropping of that box."

"Oh, Newport's told you about that, has he?" Merrion strove to speak lightly, but it was evident that he was consumed with anxiety. He walked beside the Inspector for a few paces in silence, then, without warning, blurted out what was in his thoughts.

"I say, old chap, are you going to tell off any of your fellows to keep an eye on Sir William?"

"No, I am not," replied the Inspector. "So far as I know at present, there are no grounds for any charge against him."

"Thank heaven for that!" exclaimed Merrion fervently.

Chapter XXIX

On the way to Gippingford in the police car Merrion and the Inspector told one another of their experiences during the last few days, and discussed the steps to be taken next.

"Of course, the first thing is to circulate a description of this man Thorburn or Gregson," remarked Young. "Apart from his attempts upon your life and his abduction of Miss Owerton, he seems to be as deeply implicated in this drug business as Hollesley himself. I fancy that we shall learn more about the whole business from him than from his master."

"Very likely," agreed Merrion. "But, when you do get hold of him, I would rather that you confined your charge to trafficking in illicit drugs. Both Mavis and I are anxious to keep out of the picture as much as possible, as I expect you can understand."

"Well, if neither of you lodge an official complaint, I dare say that it can be managed," replied Young. "But I shouldn't be surprised if Thorburn makes a clean breast of everything as soon as he's arrested."

"You seem pretty confident that he will be arrested," remarked Merrion doubtfully.

"Naturally. As I said before, he's bound to land somewhere. I doubt that there's enough petrol on board the

speed-boat to carry him across the North Sea and, even if
there is, we shall notify the police on the other side."

"Hasn't it occurred to you that he may not land at all, at
least not yet? Look here, I've been thinking what I should
do in his place. The skipper of that Belgian craft, *La Lys*, is
obviously in the secret. Now, *La Lys*, having dropped the
box on Vane Sand, proceeds to Gippingford, where she stays
just long enough to unload what cargo she has for that port.
On the last occasion, I noticed that she left the day after
her arrival, and went on to London. Yesterday she must
have arrived in Gippingford fairly early, about nine or ten.
I expect that she would be ready to leave this morning at
dawn; in fact, I should not wonder if she were on her way
to London now."

"Well, that doesn't matter. I shall telephone London and
have her boarded at Gravesend. But I don't see what all this
has got to do with Thorburn."

"Don't you? Remember that Thorburn probably knows
her movements as well or better than I do. He escapes
from you and Newport by the simple process of chucking
me into the river, knowing that you will stop to pick me
up, and that I shall insist upon going back to the island to
rescue Mavis from the clutches of that brute Hollesley. He
thus ensures himself plenty of time to reach the speed-boat
and get clear away out of the river. He would know that it
would be risking certain arrest to attempt to land. But he
does not know that there is any charge against him but that
of attempted murder. He does not know that the box has
been recovered from Vane Sand, and that its contents have
been discovered. Even though he considers the possibility of
this having happened, he does not know that we have any
reason to connect the box with *La Lys*.

"This being so, one pretty obvious line of escape is open
to him. He imagines *La Lys* to be as free from suspicion as

any other of the hundreds of coasters which frequent the Port of London. All he has to do is to run down the coast in the speed-boat and wait for her to come out of Gippingford. He then boards her, scuttles the speed-boat and lies low. There is nothing to prevent him remaining concealed on board her while she stays in London. Then, when she arrives in Ghent once more, he could easily slip ashore, with his appearance so altered that he would run no risk of being arrested from his description. Anyway, I'd try it in his place."

"By jove, there's something in that! We'd better push on to Gravesend and wait for *La Lys* there."

"There's no particular hurry. It is seventy-two nautical miles from Gippingford to Gravesend. From what I have seen of *La Lys*, I am pretty sure that she won't make more than eight knots, especially as she'll have the ebb against her most of the way. Even if she left Gippingford as early as five, she can't get to Gravesend before two, and possibly an hour or so later. We shall be in Gippingford by half-past seven. It is just over sixty miles from Gippingford to Tilbury, which is on this side of London River, opposite Gravesend. If you order a police boat to wait there at two o'clock, that will be in plenty of time. Say two and a half hours to reach Tilbury in a car. That means leaving Gippingford at half-past eleven. You will have four hours in Gippingford, in which you can do a lot. Personally, I'm going to get some breakfast somewhere. Anyhow, even if *La Lys* gets to Gravesend earlier than two, you can order her to be detained till you arrive."

When the car reached Gippingford, Merrion went in search of breakfast, while the Inspector conveyed his charge to the police station. Hollesley appeared to be in a state of collapse, and Doctor Barrett, on being summoned, ordered his immediate removal to hospital. "The man's suffering from the after-effect of drugs," he said. "You'll get nothing out of him for several days, even if you do then. He'll probably be a nervous wreck when he gets over this attack. Judging by the state he's in, he must have been a drug addict for years."

Hollesley having been disposed of, Young proceeded to the telephone, and held a long conversation with Scotland Yard. He arranged for Thorburn's description to be circulated, and for a police launch to await him at Tilbury jetty. He also requested that a man should be sent from the Yard to meet him there, with full particulars of Thorburn's previous arrest and conviction under the alias of Gregson. This done, he sought out Colonel Bateman, to whom he outlined the whole story.

"Well, it's the most amazing thing I ever heard!" exclaimed the Chief Constable, when he had finished. "I always felt that there was something queer about High Eldersham, but I never imagined that it was anything like this. An organised scheme of drug smuggling, covered by the practice of witchcraft. It's incredible and, frankly, I don't know what we're going to do about it."

"If I might suggest, sir, I think the two might be kept entirely separate," replied Young. "My charge against Hollesley and Thorburn is solely one of trafficking in drugs, and is not concerned in any way with the practice of witchcraft."

"Yes. But what about the murder of that poor chap, Whitehead?" objected Colonel Bateman.

"I believe that I am at last on the track of that, sir. If I am correct, I think that it will be found that that, too, had no connection with the curious conspiracy existing at High Eldersham. Of course, that conspiracy was illegal, but I fancy that it would be very difficult to obtain evidence which would lead to conviction of any of the persons concerned. The only course would be to proceed against Doctor Padfield for causing grievous bodily harm by the improper administration of drugs, and I think that it is very doubtful if we should be able to prove our case."

"So that your advice is that we should ignore the question of witchcraft altogether?"

"It is, sir. I don't think that any harm will come of it. The practice is bound to cease with Hollesley's arrest, for it is very unlikely that any one else will take his place. You will doubtless instruct the police to watch the place very carefully in future."

"I think you're right, Inspector. To raise the question would involve a tremendous scandal, in which my old friend, Owerton, would be involved, without producing any results which would compensate for it. Unless future developments render it absolutely necessary, I think it will be best for us to keep our mouths shut on that particular subject. What is your next move to be?"

"I propose to pay a visit to the Tower of London, sir. And I should like the assistance of some of your men."

"Take who you like. I'll tell Superintendent Bass to put the whole force at your disposal. Now, you want to get to work, I expect. You haven't too much time if you're going to start for Tilbury at half-past eleven."

Young, congratulating himself upon the result of his interview with the Chief Constable, went to the rendezvous which he had appointed with Merrion, and told him what had happened. "I don't think that there will be any need for either Sir William's or his daughter's name to appear to all," he said. "Of course, you'll have to give evidence as to the finding of the box and your watching Hollesley and Thorburn on the dune, but that's all. Now then, if you would like to assist at an interesting little function, come along."

They called once more at the police station, where Young gave certain instructions, and then walked slowly to the Tower of London. Since the place was not yet open for the sale of liquor, there were no customers about, and the lounge was empty save for a boy busily engaged in polishing the tables. From him they learnt that Mr. Dunsford and his son were in, but that Mrs. Dunsford was out shopping.

"Very well, then, I'll see Mr. Dunsford," remarked Young. "Just run along and tell him that an old friend would like a word with him, will you?"

As soon as the boy had left the room, Young turned to Merrion. "As soon as you see me talking to Dunsford, slip out and find his son. You'll find him in the bar probably. Tell him that his father wants him in here."

"All right," replied Merrion. "What's the game?"

"You'll see in a minute or two. I want all the members of the family under my eye for a bit. The house is surrounded by now, and if Mrs. Dunsford comes back she'll be brought in here, too. Ah, here's Dunsford, I think."

The door opened and Dunsford came in. He did not look overjoyed at recognising the Inspector, but when he spoke it was heartily enough. "Well, I never! I didn't expect to see you, Mr. Young. What can I do for you?"

"I was wondering whether you could let me have a box of matches, Mr. Dunsford," replied the Inspector quietly.

"A box of matches! Why, certainly," said Dunsford, going to a cupboard and unlocking it. "Here you are."

Young glanced at the box and shook his head. "No, not that kind," he said. "I want the kind that you supply to Lady Applegarth."

Dunsford's eyes flashed, but his face assumed an expression of deliberate stupidity. "I don't know who you mean, Mr. Young," he replied. "But this is the only kind I keep in here. If you want any other sort, I'll have to go and get them."

"Oh, don't trouble," said Young, with a glance at Merrion, who slipped quietly out of the room. He met the boy in the passage, and sent him with a message to young Dunsford, who appeared shortly and entered the lounge to join his father.

A moment later Young opened the door and beckoned to a constable who seemed to be interested in the pavement outside. "Keep an eye on these two for me, will you?" he said, and then, turning to Merrion: "Come along, and we'll see if we can find those matches for ourselves."

Merrion followed him as he opened various doors in turn until he found the Dunsfords' private sitting-room. On a table in one corner stood a safe, a clumsy old-fashioned concern. Young produced a bunch of keys, and opened it without much difficulty. Inside it lay a dozen boxes of matches.

"Ah, those are the kind I want!" exclaimed Young. "Take them out and have a look at them."

Merrion took out one of the boxes and opened it. "Do you usually take all these precautions before you steal a box of matches?" he remarked. "They look ordinary enough to me. Hallo, they're not half-full! They're packed with paper or something. Looks to me like very short measure."

He shook out the matches as he spoke, and drew a paper packet from the bottom of the box. "Hallo, what's this?" he said as he opened it, disclosing half an ounce or so of white powder.

"Cocaine, I should say," replied Young negligently. "Can't say for certain till it's been analysed."

Merrion gave a low whistle. "So that's the game, is it!" he exclaimed. "But how did you know the stuff was here?"

"In the safe?" replied Young. "I didn't. I only tried it first because it was the sort of fool place that a man like Dunsford would keep it in."

"Oh, shut up!" exclaimed Merrion irritably. "How did you know it was in this pub, I mean?"

"Perfectly simple, my dear Watson," replied Young. "My well-known powers of deduction led me infallibly to the spot. In the first place, I discovered within the last few days that the stuff was being distributed in match-boxes. In the second, I knew that all sorts of unlikely people, of whom Lady Applegarth is an example, came to visit Dunsford for some mysterious purpose. In the third, I gathered from the conversation I overheard that Dunsford could not supply what was demanded while he was at the Rose and Crown. Then, when I learnt that Hollesley and Thorburn were engaged in drug-smuggling, I remembered that we had seen him come here on the day after a consignment had arrived. It was a pretty easy guess that Dunsford was in the plot, and formed the first link in the chain of distribution. Got it? Now, if you'll stay here for a minute and watch these boxes, I'll arrange for Dunsford to be taken round to the station."

Very shortly afterwards the Inspector and Merrion were seated once more in the car, speeding towards Tilbury. The former was in high spirits at the success of his raid on the Tower of London. "I have a feeling that my luck is going to hold, and that we shall get hold of Thorburn all right," he said. "It's wonderful how a business like this straightens itself out, once you get hold of the right end of the stick. The only thing I can't quite understand is that witchcraft business. How on earth did Hollesley get all those folk at High Eldersham to believe in that mumbo-jumbo of his?"

"You would have understood it clearly enough if you had seen it as closely as I did," replied Merrion soberly. "It was so impressively staged that an uneducated person could hardly fail to be convinced that there was something mysterious behind it all. Besides, it didn't really matter whether they believed in it or not. The psychology of the thing seems fairly simple to me. The members of the coven derived a definite advantage from the ceremonies. Any one against whom they had a grudge suffered accordingly. But things were a good deal deeper than that. The real attraction was the drugs mixed in the bowl which was handed round, and the sensations they produced. It's all pretty horrible, but there isn't the slightest doubt that the meetings ended in an orgy of promiscuous lust, no doubt excited by some form of aphrodisiac. If you study some of the old records, you'll find these things described in detail. Hollesley's whole idea, of course, was to turn the village into a more or less criminal society, no member of which would dare to give him away. I shouldn't wonder if every one in the place knew about the drug smuggling. And it's quite likely they all know who murdered Whitehead."

"No, I wouldn't go as far as that," commented Young, with an enigmatic smile.

Chapter XXX

It was twenty minutes to two when the car arrived at Tilbury. A plain-clothes man from Scotland Yard was waiting there, and came forward to greet the Inspector.

"I've brought the information you asked for," he said, as he handed Young an official envelope. "There's a police launch waiting at the steps, and I've communicated with the Port of London Authority people at Gravesend. *La Lys* has not passed here yet. She'll be bound to stop when she does in order to pick up a river pilot."

"That sounds all right," replied Young. "You'll recognise her as she comes up the river, won't you, Merrion?"

"I shall recognise her, all right," said Merrion with a smile. "I've seen her too often to be easily mistaken."

"Very well, then. Let's walk out on to the pier. We shall be able to see her coming from there."

It was a bright spring morning, comfortably warm in the sun. Merrion and the Inspector, having seen where the police launch was lying, strolled out to the pier, whence a view could be obtained down river. Young drew the official envelope from his pocket and opened it. It contained a couple of sheets, closely typed. The Inspector ran through the contents eagerly and suddenly uttered an exclamation of satisfaction.

Merrion glanced at him inquiringly. "What's up now?" he asked.

"You'll see as soon as we get aboard *La Lys,*" replied Young. "It's about time she was in sight, if your calculations are correct. While you were having breakfast, I telephoned to the dock at Gippingford. She left there soon after five."

"You needn't be so scornful about that breakfast of mine. I think you'll admit that I earned it. And, what's more, we don't look like getting any lunch to-day. I wish this confounded craft would hurry up."

The minutes went by and still there was no sign of *La Lys.* Merrion stood, leaning against the rails of the pier, his eyes fixed upon Coalhouse Point, round which she must come into sight. The confidence which he had felt earlier in the morning began to desert him. Suppose he had brought Young on a false errand, after all? He still felt pretty sure that his forecast of Thorburn's actions had been correct, that he would have seen his only chance of escape in reaching *La Lys.* But what if he had persuaded her skipper to abandon his usual route and double back across the North Sea, where he could be landed at some deserted spot and get clear away? And then, as he was about to confess his misgivings, a familiar squat form came slowly round the point.

"There she is!" he exclaimed. "Come along, let's put out and meet her."

"There's no hurry," replied the Inspector quietly. "Wait till she stops to pick up her pilot. We don't want to alarm the people on board of her unnecessarily by the sight of a police launch."

To Merrion's impatience the progress of *La Lys* up Gravesend Reach seemed maddeningly slow. But at last she drew nearly abreast of them, and a pilot boat put off from the Gravesend shore to board her.

"Come along!" said the Inspector shortly.

They ran down the steps into the police launch, which immediately cast off and shot out into the river. The man at the helm, experienced in such work, dodged in and out of the crowded shipping, until the launch reached the side of *La Lys*. The pilot boat was still alongside, and the men in the launch tumbled out of her, across the deck of the pilot boat and so on board the Belgian motor-ship.

The skipper of *La Lys* and the river pilot were obviously engaged in argument. "It's no use, captain," the latter was saying. "Orders is orders, and I've got to obey them. My instructions are that you're to anchor here till a message comes from the shore. Ah, this is it, I expect."

Inspector Young came forward and touched the skipper on the shoulder. "I have a warrant to search this ship, captain," he said. "I have to warn you that a very serious charge will probably be laid against you, and that anything you may say will be used in evidence against you. You are suspected of having on board a man of the name of Thorburn or Gregson, for whose arrest I have a warrant. Are you prepared to produce him?"

The skipper, who evidently understood English perfectly, went deathly white. "A charge against me!" he stammered. "It is impossible. And this man—how do you say his name? I know nothing about him!"

Young shrugged his shoulders. "All right," he said. "We'll deal with your case later. You aren't making things any easier for yourself, you know. Will you proceed to search the ship, please, sergeant?"

The sergeant of the river police, an expert in such matters, gave the necessary orders, and the search began. Meanwhile the pilot took charge. He rang the engine-room telegraph, and the propeller began to churn slowly. He swung *La Lys* out of the fairway, and in a few minutes her anchor dropped with a dull splash into the muddy water of the river.

Merrion and the Inspector watched the river police at their work. They began at the forward end of the vessel, and worked steadily through her, leaving not a cubic foot of space unexplored. The forecastle, the holds, the officers' quarters, were all examined in turn, until nothing remained but the engine-room. And into this they descended without ceremony.

"I don't believe that the blighter's on board, after all!" whispered Merrion nervously.

"Doesn't look like it, does it?" replied the Inspector. "There's one thing, if he is, you can bet these fellows will find him. Come along, and let's see how they are getting on down there."

They descended the hatch into the engine-room, which, on the first appearance of the police, had been vacated by every one except the chief engineer. He apparently did not understand English, for he shook his head violently at every question the sergeant put to him. But it seemed to Young that his broad Flemish face showed symptoms of great perturbation, and to this the Inspector drew Merrion's attention.

"That chap knows something, I'll be bound," he whispered. "Of course, it may be that he knows about the drug-smuggling, and thinks that that's what we're after. Keep your eye on him, though."

The police went systematically through the engine-room, opening lockers and lifting floor-plates. At last nothing remained but a low iron door, right in the stern of the ship. The sergeant tried it, it was locked. "What's in there?" he asked.

"I don't think our friend here understands you," remarked Merrion. "At all events, he's not going to let on, if he does. I expect you'll find that that door leads into the shaft tunnel."

"Well, he's got to open it, anyhow," growled the sergeant. "Here, mossoo, where's the key? Key, savvy? Open, toute suite, pronto! Come on, hand it over."

There was no mistaking the sergeant's meaning. A hunted look came over the chief engineer's face, and he glanced at the hatchway, as though meditating a flight to the deck. But the hatch was blocked by one of the constables, and at last, reluctantly, he put his hand in his pocket and produced a key.

The sergeant took it from him, inserted it in the lock, and flung open the door. Within, all was darkness, except for the polished propeller shaft, which reflected dully such light as managed to enter. But, as their eyes grew accustomed to the gloom, Merrion and the Inspector discerned the outlines of a short and narrow tunnel, moist and spattered with grease. And at the end of it crouched a figure, so smeared with dirt as to be unrecognisable, holding an iron bar in its hand.

The sergeant drew out his torch and directed its rays into the tunnel. "Is that your man, sir?" he asked in a business-like tone.

Young bent down and peered through the doorway. "Yes, that's the chap," he replied. "You'd better come out of that, Gregson, I want you."

The figure made no reply, but the arm holding the iron bar stiffened. Crouched there, at the end of the dark tunnel, with the white gleam of his teeth showing between his grinning lips, he reminded Merrion of a rat at bay.

Young turned to the sergeant. "It's going to be a job to get him out of that," he said. "The only way to get into that tunnel is to crawl in, one at a time, and he'll knock us all on the head while we're doing it."

"Oh, I'll fetch him out, sir, sharp enough," replied the sergeant reassuringly. "Run up on deck, a couple of you and rig the fire hose. When you've done that, bring the nozzle down here."

Two of his men obeyed him, and in a couple of minutes the sergeant was standing opposite the doorway, with the nozzle in his hand. "All ready?" he inquired. "Right. Now then, you in there, for the last time, are you coming out?"

He waited for a few seconds, but no reply came from the depths of the tunnel. "Open the valve!" ordered the sergeant sharply.

A powerful jet of water leapt from the nozzle and broke at the end of the tunnel, filling the whole of the interior with spray. "He won't stand this long," remarked the sergeant calmly. "Watch out for him and mind that bar."

The sergeant's prediction was justified. Gregson stood it for the inside of a minute, and then dashed out of the tunnel, brandishing his bar, a shadowy figure in a cloud of flying water. He aimed a blow at the sergeant, who dodged it and directed the full force of the stream upon him, knocking him flat upon the steel floor. Before he could recover himself, two men had flung themselves upon him, and in a few seconds he was securely hand-cuffed.

"Well, that's that," observed the sergeant. "Turn off that water, one of you. What are you going to charge him with, sir?"

"The wilful murder of Samuel Whitehead, by stabbing him with a knife at the Rose and Crown in High Eldersham on the evening of March 31st last," replied the Inspector.

It was not until Thorburn, or Gregson, as Young preferred to call him, was safely lodged in the police station that Merrion had a chance of a word alone with him. And then he could no longer restrain his curiosity. "How the devil did you find out that this butler chap murdered Whitehead?" he asked abruptly.

"Well, I can't honestly say that I have found it out," replied Young with a smile. "I'm banking on a certainty, that's all. Look here!"

He drew from his pocket the official communication which he had received upon his arrival at Tilbury, opened it and underlined a few words with his pencil. "That's an account of Gregson's previous exploit," he said. "I told you something about it, you remember."

Merrion took the paper and read the words which Young had underlined. "The name of the constable who carried out the arrest was Samuel Whitehead. He was shortly afterwards raised to the rank of sergeant."

"Oh, yes, it's obvious enough, I know," remarked Young, as Merrion handed him back the paper. "The unerring sleuth would have run that fact to earth within five minutes of the murder. But I confess that I had High Eldersham and its customs on my brain to such an extent that I never thought of looking further. It wasn't until Sir William hinted to me last night that the motive of the murder was to be found in some incident of Whitehead's past that this line of inquiry suggested itself to me. Call me a fool, if you like."

"No, I won't do that," replied Merrion slowly. "If you hadn't gone about the investigation in the way you did, Hollesley would still be at large, and I shouldn't have met Mavis. But, look here! You've only established the motive, you haven't got any evidence that Gregson actually committed the murder."

"No, I haven't," agreed Young. "But I fancy I shall have when Hollesley is well enough to talk."

The Inspector's anticipations proved to be correct. The conspirators, upon being interrogated, displayed a most unedifying haste to throw the blame upon other shoulders. The skipper of *La Lys* confessed to having smuggled drugs from Belgium for years, for which service he had been handsomely paid by Hollesley. Dunsford declared that he had been in the habit of receiving match-boxes from Hollesley, through Thorburn, which he distributed only to people who mentioned a particular word, known to Hollesley and himself alone. He maintained stoutly that he had no idea what these boxes contained, a statement which the magistrates declined to believe. Finally, Hollesley himself, confronted with the weight of evidence against him, made a statement revealing the whole organisation of the scheme.

After this, Young found very little difficulty in extracting from him what he knew about the murder of Whitehead. Thorburn had confessed his guilt to him an hour after the murder had been committed, knowing that he dare not betray him, and demanded his protection. It appeared that Hollesley, requiring an assistant, had advertised for a butler. Thorburn had replied, among many others, and Hollesley had chosen him as soon as he hinted that he had a somewhat disreputable past. About the same time Whitehead came to the Rose and Crown, and Thorburn recognised him. The recognition was not mutual, for Thorburn took very good care to keep away from the inn, but he nevertheless determined to revenge himself on the man but for whom he would have escaped arrest.

He saw his opportunity when, at one of the meetings of the coven, Ned Portch declared his grievance against Whitehead, and demanded that the curse should be put upon him. He took to watching the Rose and Crown, until, on the evening of March 31st, he found conditions favourable. He crept in just before ten o'clock and stabbed Whitehead as he was dozing in his chair, with the sacrificial knife used at the ceremonies.

Thorburn, or Gregson, as his real name proved to be, stoutly protested his innocence at first. But when he learned that Hollesley was in custody and had told the whole story, his nerve failed him and he confessed. He was sentenced to death and duly executed. Hollesley, a broken man, his nerves shattered by drugs which he had taken, was sentenced to a long term of imprisonment, which he seemed likely to pass in the prison infirmary.

Much to the relief of everybody concerned, Doctor Padfield disappeared and was never heard of again. "He must have overheard me telephoning that night, and gathered from the conversation that his only chance of escape was to clear out before the police arrived from Gippingford. That's why he only stayed five minutes or so at the Hall. I'm very glad he made himself scarce, for if we had found him at home we should have been bound to take proceedings, and then the whole unsavoury story would have come to light." Such was Inspector Young's pronouncement.

Merrion and Mavis were married very quietly in London, Inspector Young being best man at the wedding. But Sir William never recovered from the shock which he received on May Eve, and died within a few months. Mr. and Mrs. Merrion have succeeded him at the Hall, where, though Merrion is a foreigner, they are exceedingly popular among the villagers.

But Merrion acquired property in High Eldersham, even before he was married. He bought the island which had been the scene of so many strange ceremonies, and, on the night after the purchase was completed, he and Newport went there, armed with sledge hammers, and broke the altar into little pieces, which they threw into the river.

"Reminds me of that chap in the Old Testament, sir," remarked Newport, as he mopped his brow after his labours. "What was his name, sir?"

"Gideon. 'Throw down the altar of Baal that thy father hath, and cut down the grove that is by it.' Yes, I think we'll make a job of it, and have these trees down too. Things haven't changed much since those days, have they?"

Select Bibliography:

Miles Burton and Golden Age Detective Fiction

J. Barzun and W.H. Taylor, *A Catalogue of Crime* (1971)

H.R.F. Keating, *Murder Must Appetize* (1975)

J. Barzun and W.H. Taylor, *A Book of Prefaces to Fifty Classics of Crime Fiction, 1900–1950* (1976)

Charles Shibuk, "John Rhode", in *Dictionary of Literary Biography, volume 77: British Mystery Writers 1920–39* (1989)

John Cooper and B.A. Pike, *Detective Fiction: The Collector's Guide* (2nd edn, 1994)

John Cooper and B.A. Pike, *Artists in Crime: An Illustrated Survey of Crime Fiction First Edition Dustwrappers, 1920–1970* (1995)

Melvyn Barnes, "John Rhode", in *St. James Guide to Crime and Mystery Writers* (1996)

Curtis Evans, *Masters of the "Humdrum" Mystery: Cecil John Charles Street, Freeman Wills Crofts, Alfred Walter Stewart and the British Detective Novel, 1920–61* (2012)

Martin Edwards, *The Golden Age of Murder* (2015)

To receive a free catalog of Poisoned Pen Press titles, please provide your name, address, and email address in one of the following ways:

Phone: 1-800-421-3976
Facsimile: 1-480-949-1707
Email: info@poisonedpenpress.com
Website: www.poisonedpenpress.com

Poisoned Pen Press
6962 E. First Ave. Ste 103
Scottsdale, AZ 85251

CPSIA information can be obtained at www.ICGtesting.com
Printed in the USA
BVOW05s0035270416

445746BV00001B/1/P